JUNE FOSTER

Out of Control

Woodlyn, Book 2

By June Foster

Copyright © 2018 by June Foster

Forget Me Not Romances, a division of Winged Publications.

All rights reserved as permitted under the U.S. Copyright Act of 1976. No part of the publication may be reproduced, distributed or transmitted in any form or by any means, or stored in a database or retrieval system, without prior permission of the publisher.

This book is a work of fiction. Names, characters, places, and incidents are the product of the author's imagination and are used fictitiously. Any resemblance to actual events, locales, or persons, living or dead, is coincidental.

All rights reserved.

ISBN-13: 979-8-8691-3942-9

Let us throw off everything that hinders and the sin that so easily entangles, and let us run with perseverance the race marked out for us. Hebrews12:1

Chapter One

Tim clenched his teeth and pushed through the double doors out the front of the church for a quick breath of cool, rain-filled evening air. The fresh Pacific breeze on his face did nothing to calm him. He stomped down the stairs glaring at the ground. Each foot clunked on the sidewalk toward the parking lot. Then he tumbled forward, his body bumping against another. He flailed and reached out to stop both of them from plummeting backward.

"Oh," the feminine voice murmured against his ears even as her purse clamored to the ground spilling its contents onto the concrete. Another bag bounced against her side but remained secure on her shoulder.

He steadied them both and pulled away.

The teenage girl infuriated him almost as much as Johnny Thompson. "Sorry, but why can't you kids show up on time?" Young people lacked responsibility these days, one thing his father had drummed into his head.

The startled teen stared up at him.

"I'm Pastor Tim. You're a bit late for the girls'

fundraiser meeting."

The young girl peered at him with crystal blue eyes as she bent down to collect her belongings. "I'm sorry, I had to—"

"Teens. Always have an excuse," he mumbled.

Johnny tested Tim's patience—his outbursts in class, his pranks. He'd never trust the kid after tonight.

The girl stuffed a brush, makeup case, lipstick, and a pen into her bag before he had a chance to help. She stood and hiked the strap over her shoulder.

One remaining item she'd missed lay next to an azalea bush near the pavement. Conviction hit him with more force than the September rain falling on them. He bent to pick it up and handed her the small black Bible.

Without looking at him, she stuffed it in her pocket.

He didn't have to take his problems out on another kid. She had nothing to do with Johnny lying to him when he said he needed the key to Tim's office to borrow his concordance. He should've known it was a scheme.

Since Johnny had taken more than fifteen minutes coming back to the classroom, Tim figured he'd better check on the kid, but the door was locked. Only when Tim found the spare key in the main office could he get in. Johnny and his girlfriend were leaning against the wall kissing. The nerve of the boy. Tim would speak to the teen and his wayward girlfriend about making out on church property.

Tim's frustration ebbing, his breathing returned to normal.

The late arrival was probably upset with him, for which he didn't blame her. The teen's long blond hair, held back in a clip, flowed down her back. She must be new to the senior high group. "So what high school do you attend?"

"I don't—"

"Well, you're welcome anyway." She could be home schooled—or maybe a dropout. "I'm sorry I bumped into you. Probably didn't make you feel very welcome. Let me show you where the girls are waiting. With the help of a volunteer, Ms. Ratner, they're organizing a fundraiser for our annual camp held during spring break."

He started up the sidewalk but paused to allow her to catch up. Rain covered the walkway. With one final breath, the volcano inside Tim ceased its uncontrollable churning.

The girl paced next to him and lifted her eyes, this time amusement flitting across her lips.

Was she going to be one of those rebellious teens who didn't respect authority?

"So you're the youth pastor. I haven't attended Woodlyn Fellowship for long." She blinked a drop of rain from her eye.

"Well, newcomers are always welcome, but I recommend you arrive on time. We generally have a lot of material to cover during our meetings." They climbed the steps he'd just tramped down.

"Good advice, Pastor Tim, but now might be a good time to introduce myself." She gave him a sneer. "I've been out of my teens for over six years, but I'm flattered you think I look that young. I'm a hairstylist at Larry's Hair Design near downtown Woodlyn." She stuck out her hand. "Roxanne Ratner."

*****

Roxanne chuckled as Tim propped the door open with his shoulder, his jaw nearly hitting the floor. The handsome pastor with dark brown eyes and spiked hair could probably put a size thirteen shoe in his mouth.

"You... you're Ms. Ratner? The guest volunteer?" He allowed the door to close after them, drops of rain dampening the tile inside the foyer.

With a sly smile, she smirked. "I don't look young enough to be mistaken for a teen, but thank you." The darkened glass windows and locked door gave the impression the church office was closed. "I'm twenty-six, Pastor. And you're welcome to call me Roxanne."

"My profound apologies. I don't have any excuse for my rudeness other than trying to cool off after a problem with one of the boys earlier in my high school group. Thank you so much for coming. Let me show you to the Sunday school room."

With lips pressed together, the good-looking guy walked with a rigid gait down a long hallway opposite the church offices and slowed at the corner room.

The day the pleasant church secretary cajoled Roxanne into heading the event, she'd jumped at the opportunity to work with the high school girls. But now she'd have to deal with the intense youth pastor. If his manners were always this bad, maybe it wouldn't be as easy as she thought.

Roxanne touched her fingers to the silver cross around her neck. Though she'd only asked Jesus into her life six months ago, she was anxious to serve others. A makeover fundraiser was perfect. Maybe she'd even drum up some business and expand her clientele.

Rapping his fingers on the closed door, Tim paused

then opened it. "This way, ma'am. Girls, I'd like you to meet Ms. Ratner. She's from Larry's Hair Design and attends our church."

Ten teenage girls sitting around a large round table stared up at her. Some smiled, a few gawked, and one folded her arms over her chest with a scowl.

"You can call me Roxanne, girls." She turned around to Tim again, and he nodded at her.

"Sit here." He held a chair out between a dark-haired girl and a blonde. "Don't forget, you're planning an event where women of this church and anyone else from the community can make appointments for all the stuff you're going to do."

The dark-haired girl raised her hand. "Like facials and make-up."

"Right, Mandy." Tim laughed. "Ms. Ratner, I know our efficient secretary, Nancy, briefed you on this so I'll just be in my office if anyone needs me." He backed toward the door, tripping over his feet and hitting his backside on the wall.

With a snicker she hoped wasn't audible, Roxanne watched the fumbling pastor.

He backed all the way out the door and pulled it shut after stepping into the hall.

Her gaze remained on the door a moment then she turned to the girls. The name badges on each caught her attention. "I'm happy for this chance to work with you."

A petite redhead, who's nametag said *Betty,* smiled at Roxanne. "We're anxious to work on the project. It's just that Pastor Tim makes us nervous sometimes. He gets mad at us for no reason."

"I understand he's fairly new. Maybe it'll take awhile for him to get comfortable."

"Yeah, right." A girl across the table folded her hands over her chest. Tiffany. The scowling teen glared at Roxanne a few more seconds. "He loses it for no reason. Johnny..."

Her upheld hand silenced the girl. Tim had mentioned a problem with one of the boys, but Roxanne didn't want to get involved. "We need to work on our fundraiser, and not talk about Pastor Garrett when he's not around."

She opened her bag full of Kathy May products and set everything on the table. "We'll ask the ladies of the church to sign up for appointments before the morning of the event. I sell a line of makeup but plan to donate all proceeds to the church."

Around the circle, eager faces beamed.

"Your job will be to demonstrate the available products—makeup, facial toners, anti-aging creams, and nail polish. One of you will take orders. I'd like you to decide what you're interested in doing."

Tiffany uncrossed her arms and leaned forward. "I do my mom's toenails all the time. Sign me up for nails."

"Good, Tiffany. I'm making a list of the job each of you will do, and we'll talk about advertising and setting up the schedule." Though she'd been a bit nervous before she arrived, the time flew. She glimpsed her watch. They only had fifteen minutes left.

"Before we wrap up tonight, I want to invite you girls to come to my salon for a free haircut and style, but you'll need to make an appointment." Roxanne passed out her card to each.

Mandy smiled. "We really appreciate you doing this for us. You're a lot easier to get along with than Pastor

Tim."

"Just give him time." Roxanne placed a jar of face cream and a bottle of toner in her bag.

"No, Roxanne." Tiffany wrapped her arms over her chest again. "He's so unfair. He takes the fun out of the meetings. The boys are just kidding around. Johnny didn't mean anything earlier..."

The rest of the items went back in her Kathy May carrier. "Girls, I'm sure that being a youth pastor comes with a lot of responsibilities. I'd encourage you to give Pastor Garrett a break."

"Maybe he should give us a break." Tiffany scowled. "One day we might all walk out and not come back." She tromped to the door and flung it open.

Roxanne shook her head and followed the girls to the entrance of the room. She'd seen Tim in action...

Mandy caught up to Roxanne. "Pastor Tim is a good Bible teacher, and we learn a lot, but when some of the boys challenge him, he freaks out. They know how to get to him, and some of them do it on purpose. But nobody tells their parents because mostly we're the ones who start it."

"Yeah, they know how to push his buttons." Betty tossed her red hair and laughed.

Mandy shouldered her backpack. "I'll have to admit, some of the girls give him a hard time, too. We just want to see him get riled up."

For some reason she believed the teens. How did the man keep his job if he acted like that? The question plagued her, but another matter preyed on her even more. How could a youth pastor called by God lose control of his temper?

Chapter Two

"May the peace of God which transcends all understanding, guard your hearts and minds in Christ Jesus. Amen."

Roxanne raised her head. Pastor Downing's message had lifted her spirit. How had she made it as a teen without the Lord? She rubbed her temples, trying to rid herself of the memory of her mistakes.

She filed into the aisle with the rest of the congregation. The woman who'd sat beside her smiled. Roxanne grinned back and stepped toward the front altar, waiting until some of the crowd cleared.

The empty wooden cross on the wall meant so much now. Her thinking changed after she'd accepted the Lord that day at the shop. Thank God her co-worker hadn't given up sharing the gospel month after month. One day her words clicked in Roxanne's mind. Now she wished her friend still worked at the shop.

"Roxanne."

She circled back from the cross to the voice at the end of the row. Tim.

He shifted his Bible from one hand to the other. "I'm still embarrassed about my blunder the other day. Could

I make it up to you and take you to lunch?" His voice carried a quiet, cool tone, so unlike the first time she met him.

She caught her upper lip with her teeth. A harsh Tim offered her a meager welcome when he assumed she was a teen. But she had to admit, his handsome face now displaying a wide grin and shining white teeth, intrigued her.

She'd seen two Tims. Obviously the considerate one had asked her to lunch. But could she trust him after he'd been so rude? "Sorry. I need to go visit my mom this afternoon." It wasn't a lie, but she didn't have to go right away.

The light in his brown eyes faded. "Well, okay. Another time." He stuffed his hands in his pockets and curved around toward the foyer.

Sympathy for the guy caught in her throat, but just in case, it'd be better to prevent a dubious relationship before it ever began.

She clicked her fingers. Oh, yeah. Mandy had called last night. Said she wanted some sample supplies so she could practice on her mom and sister.

Roxanne headed down the hall toward the Sunday school room where they agreed to meet and pulled the extra kit from her purse.

The empty room contained a portable chalkboard. She walked farther in. *So this is where Tim teaches the Bible to his young flock.* The girls' complaints about his gruff ways still felt surprising.

"Trust in the Lord with all your heart and lean not on your own understanding." The printed words were written at the top of the board. Two hand drawn pictures of high-backed chairs appeared underneath. A stick figure sat on the first chair and a cross on the second. The question to the side of the drawings, "who's on the throne of your life?" must've challenged the kids.

She touched a fingertip to her cheek. *I get his message.* But the word *trust* tripped her up.

The Word said to put her faith in the Lord, not in man, and she'd trusted Him when she became a Christian. She shook her head. But she couldn't rely on her earthly father. How could she after he'd destroyed her faith in him?

Though she'd only been a girl, she remembered well the day he left.

She always told herself he'd come back, but when the months passed and he didn't, she convinced herself it was her fault. Only when her mother begged her to believe it wasn't did she accept the fact.

Roxanne squeezed her eyes shut. Most men fell in the same category with her father. None could love a woman enough to *stay.*

"Hi, Roxanne."

Leaving her dismal thoughts behind, she revolved away from the board toward the voice.

The pretty, dark-haired teen smiled at her.

"Hi, Mandy." Roxanne handed her the blue and white plastic bag with the samples. "Here you go."

"Thanks. I noticed you looking at our Sunday school lesson. Pastor Tim taught us how we need to live for the Lord, putting God first." The teen smiled at Roxanne and stuffed the little bag in her purse. "We learn a lot from him, usually on Sunday morning when the boys aren't giving him a hard time. He's a good teacher."

"So he loses his cool when they do?"

"Yeah, but mostly you never know when he's going to get angry."

"Hmm." Roxanne looked at the chart on the wall near the door.

A brightly colored poster decorated with fruit and entitled "The Fruit of the Spirit—Galatians 5:22" listed nine virtues from the Bible. "So, it's hard for your group to know when something will set him off."

"Yeah. But I still like him because he explains the Bible so well."

Roxanne figured she better change the subject. "Okay, practice with the makeup, and you can demonstrate your skill at our next meeting." She smiled at Mandy and followed her out the door. She wanted to express her negative opinion of the pastor, but that wouldn't be the right thing to do.

The teen grinned back at her. "See ya." She waved at a tall guy at the end of the hall. "Hi, Mike." Mandy beamed with pride. "That's my brother."

The foyer was empty except for a couple of teens and two women chatting near the church office. Poking her fingers down in her purse, she pulled her car keys out.

From the corner of her eye, she sensed motion in the sanctuary. Almost as if magnetized, she turned back and crept through the doors.

Tim knelt at the altar. He sat back on his heels, and his hands covered his face.

When she tiptoed closer, she could hear his mumbled words but couldn't distinguish their meaning.

He lifted his head and sat back farther on his haunches, then looked at the ceiling. Compassion replaced her doubts. She knew what it was like to be rejected. Hadn't her own father cast her away like worn out shoes?

Though red flags of misgivings still flew high, her heart told her to reconsider.

When he glanced up, he scrambled to his feet. Were his eyes glistening in the light or from moisture?

"Oh, Roxanne. I thought you'd gone." Tim shuffled from foot to foot, his gaze never finding her face.

"I... uh... wondered. Is that lunch invitation still open?"

JUNE FOSTER

Chapter Three

Tim held the door of his old blue Chevy as the petite blond slid in. He strolled around the back of the car eyeing her as she settled into the passenger seat. Why had she changed her mind and agreed to come to lunch? Whatever the reason, he was glad she did.

He squirmed when he thought of how she'd turned him down at first. Though he'd tried to disguise his embarrassment, he probably hadn't been successful. Maybe she changed her mind because she felt sorry for him. Or because she saw him praying. He tossed his head. Women. *I shouldn't even try to figure them out.*

He scooted into the driver's seat and stuck the key into the ignition. His glance traveled from her face to the blond hair she wore long, well past her shoulders. "Have you been to Lucio's? They have great Italian food."

"No, but Italian's fine." She smoothed a lock of hair off her neck. "Hey, Tim. Don't worry about the other night before the meeting. I love working with your girls. They're a sweet bunch of young ladies. I'm pleased with how well they're getting into this project."

"Thank you for volunteering. The senior kids raise

money each year to provide scholarships for three or four teens who can't afford to go to Camp Solid Rock during spring break."

"It gets them involved and helps them see the value of camp."

"Exactly." After wracking his brain as to what to say next, he punched the button on his CD player and hummed along to the pop tune.

Canyon Road led west through northeast Woodlyn in the direction of the restaurant. After a jaunt through an older neighborhood with ranch-style houses, he stopped in front of Lucio's then stole another glance at the attractive woman next to him.

Slender arms and legs peeked out from her blue patterned dress. She looked like she could use something to eat.

After parking in a slot at the end of the crowded lot, he rushed around to open her door. At least he'd show a few manners after his disastrous behavior the other night.

A red awning ran halfway down the length of the building covering the arched wooden doorway. Large brown pots on either side of the door held orange and yellow marigolds and chrysanthemums. A leafy vine grew up and over the entrance. With his shoulder, he propped the heavy door open.

A middle-aged woman glanced up from a hostess stand. "Table for two?"

"Yes, please." The aroma of garlic and freshly baked bread sent Tim's stomach into a growl.

The employee produced two menus from behind her podium. "This way." She ambled through the arched doorway to the main dining room and extended her hand to a table by the window.

Tim held the wrought-iron chair with a multicolored cushion as Roxanne eased down. Others dined at tables scattered among pots of indoor plants, two large columns, and a decorative basket with dried flowers.

A wide-eyed Roxanne glanced around. "I'm not used to this kind of restaurant. It's so quaint." She opened the menu. "My mom and I eat at fast food restaurants most of the time. Same with my friends at the shop."

The server set two glasses of water on the table. A lemon wedge rested on the side of each. "Are you ready to order, or should I give you a few minutes?" He took his pencil from behind his ear and held it in front of his order pad.

Tim lifted his glance to Roxanne. "What would you like?"

She flipped the menu shut. "Maybe we could split a pizza."

"No eggplant parmesan? It's their specialty."

"I'm not a big eater."

"All right then. Pepperoni okay?"

She nodded and raised her water glass to her lips.

"Okay, a large Lucio's Special Pizza with three kinds of pepperoni." He grinned and handed the menu back to the server.

Beyond their table, a familiar face—no, two familiar faces approached from the back of the restaurant. Jess Colton held Holly's elbow as she led the way with her belly.

"Hey, you two." With a wave, he tried to get their attention.

"Tim." Jess released Holly's arm to shake his hand. "Haven't seen you lately. How's everything?"

Tim stood as the couple beamed at them. "Excellent. Holly, Jess, this is a friend, Roxanne Ratner." His chest expanded when he introduced the pretty lady who'd accompanied him. Jess wasn't the only one with a good-looking woman.

Holly laughed. "Roxanne and I've already met. She's the hairdresser who made me beautiful for my wedding. How are you, Roxy?"

Roxanne giggled. "You've changed a little."

"Yup, I've put on some weight." Holly patted her tummy. "At least it'll come off in another few months, I hope."

The trim, muscular Jess reached his hand out to Roxanne's. "It's a pleasure. And speaking of Holly's middle, we've got someone to introduce you to." Jess rubbed her stomach. "Our baby boy is due in January." He slipped his arm around the expanse of Holly's waist and beamed. "His name is Timmy, after you, Tim."

Tim's heart almost pounded out of his chest cavity. "Oh, man. I... I don't know what to say."

"You were instrumental in helping me, and this baby would probably not be here if you hadn't ministered to me." Jess winked at Holly. "Coming to the hospital to see me, being my accountability partner. Hey, buddy. We're honored to name him after you."

Heat rose on Tim's ears. He'd been grateful for the opportunity to counsel Jess and befriend him.

Holly patted Roxanne's shoulder. "You're having lunch with one of our favorite people."

She looked up to the couple with large, round eyes. "I'd like to hear the story sometime."

Jess grasped Holly's arm. "You will, I'm sure. Well, we're on our way up to Greenwood to visit my folks.

Good seeing you again, Tim, and nice to meet you, Roxanne."

"Bye." Roxanne waved before turning back to him. "Wow. What an honor. And you're responsible for their baby."

"Whoa. That doesn't sound quite right." He guffawed. "I can't go into details, but since Jess mentioned it... he had a few issues with his weight and his health paid the price. Things have worked out well. But I'd like to hear more about you. You mentioned something about your mom."

The merriment left her face, and she stared at the table. "Oh, yeah. She works at Albright's, you know, the big department store. Most of the time I have to avoid the place. Their junior's department is too tempting." She twisted her cross necklace.

The waiter set the large pizza in the middle of the table and slid two plates in front of them. He served each of them a piece and turned to Tim. "May I get you anything else, sir?"

"No, this is fine. Thank you." Tim looked toward Roxanne's hand near her water glass. "Shall I say grace?" Since she didn't move her fingers away, he covered her hand with his. "Lord, thank you for the blessing of the new life in the Colton family, and please bless this food to our nourishment." He lifted his eyes to Roxanne's. When she raised her head, she scrutinized him as if sizing him up. Though he didn't want to make her uncomfortable, Tim couldn't take his eyes off her. What was she thinking?

Feeling shy, he glanced down at his pizza, cut off a piece, and chewed. "What about your father?"

She lifted a cheesy bite then took a breath. "Oh, he

left us when I was small." As if uncomfortable talking about the topic, she peered out the window. The words to an Italian opera on the speakers were as foreign as his understanding of her family.

Not a good idea to mention her father—unless she brought up the subject.

"My mom lives at the edge of town where I grew up." She twisted another link of her cross.

"It's okay. We don't have to talk about it."

"No, that's fine. My mom is alone. Well no. My dog, Teddy, lives with her. I've had him for years, but I couldn't exactly bring him with me to my apartment over the shop."

He'd always been able to size people up, to understand their behavior. Pain lurked behind her tough exterior. What had she experienced in her past to bring such hurt into her life? "I used to have a dog, too, when I lived at home."

She pushed a pepperoni, around on her plate. "I didn't want to move and leave my mom, but it was time." She sipped her water and set the glass by her plate. "Besides, the memories in that house, the arguing..." She furrowed her brow as she rested her chin on her hand.

Tim lowered his voice. "How did you come to ask the Lord into your life?"

"A lady in the salon where I work." Her face softened. "God gave me a sense of purpose after I prayed with my friend." A painting of a water taxi floating down the Grand Canal in Venice seemed to catch her gaze. "Like that little boat in the picture over there, I finally felt I was going somewhere and that I mattered." Was that a catch in her voice?

"You struggled with self-esteem before?"

"Yes. My earthly father made me feel worthless, but I found out my heavenly Father cared." The words streamed from her in one long breath, and she threw her hands up in the air. "Oh, Tim, why am I telling you all this? I barely know you."

Why do I always probe? He gave her a shy smile. "I want to work as a pastoral counselor one day—put my bachelor's in psychology to use." Heat rose on his neck. "Er, I don't mean you need counseling, but it's in my blood to care about people, especially Christians."

He wouldn't press her any more, but at least he knew how to pray for her. Then his heart fell. Another familiar couple walked in the front door. His sister Janelle and husband Ted.

Janelle glared at him without a word and glanced at Ted. Ted nodded, and they followed the host to a table across the room.

Beads of moisture broke out on Tim's forehead. How could he end this lunch quickly without inviting a confrontation?

*****

Roxanne lost her appetite for pizza. Thinking about her father always made her low.

Something about Tim—she couldn't put her finger on it. Though they'd had a rocky start the night they met, today he seemed to draw the words out of her. As if he cared. As if he had answers. How could the angry man she met that night be so compassionate now?

Tears had threatened when she told him about her father. Her eyes stung, and she was sure she'd messed up her makeup. She dabbed her mouth with her napkin. "Excuse me a moment. I'm going to the ladies room." Was her mascara perfect the way she'd applied it this morning?

Tim stood and pulled out her chair. What a gentleman.

Roxanne picked up her purse and headed toward the front of the restaurant near the hostess station. The sign over a room to her right pictured a woman and said "*Signore*."

She pushed the door. A long counter with a lengthy mirror behind ran along one wall. She examined her face. All she needed was a touch of eye shadow.

Makeup was her constant companion—a mask so the world couldn't see the real person behind. She prayed Tim hadn't observed the wounded, mistrusting woman.

The door swung open and an attractive lady with dark brown hair set her purse on the counter beside Roxanne's. The woman made no pretense about gawking or averting her eyes.

In an attempt to alleviate her unease, Roxanne rummaged through her purse, took out her eye shadow, and applied a bit of color.

"Excuse me." The stranger sidled up beside her. "I need to talk to you about the guy you're with."

Roxanne smiled. "Do you know Tim?"

She offered a sad nod. "Let me introduce myself. I'm Janelle Moore, Tim's sister."

Roxanne's throat tightened. Something wasn't right. Why didn't Janelle greet Tim when they came in? "I guess he didn't see you."

The lady shook her head. "Oh, he saw me all right. He just didn't acknowledge my husband and me."

Janelle touched her arm, her fingers pressing into Roxanne's shoulder blades. "You need to know something about the man you're having lunch with."

Roxanne pushed a strand of hair off her face. "Really, Janelle. I don't know if I should get involved in something that's not my business."

She stepped closer. "This goes beyond family concerns. It's for your own protection."

JUNE FOSTER

Chapter Four

Roxanne glared at Janelle in disbelief. "I can't imagine what you're saying is true. Are you sure we're talking about the same man?"

"Timothy Garrett, the guy you're sitting with. Yes, he's my brother." A shadow crossed Janelle's face. "There's something you need to know about him. He can put on a good act—like he's a nice guy, but he's not."

Roxanne wanted to walk out of the ladies' room. She needed to ignore this woman, but an eerie curiosity compelled her to stay, to listen to what Tim's sister had to say. Roxanne folded her arms over her chest. "I think you'd better explain."

Janelle gripped Roxanne's arm. "Tim's temper can blow out of control, and he can turn physically violent. While he attended seminary at Woodlyn Bible College, he beat up his fiancée one night in a fit of rage." Her shrill voice sent an disturbing chill down Roxanne's spine.

She gasped. "Surely you don't mean that."

Janelle nodded. "I do. Rena is my best friend. It's

been difficult for me. After the incident, my friend gave his ring back and called me in tears, describing the entire event in detail. I would advise you to be careful." She drew her hand away and hoisted her purse on her shoulder. "Please, be careful."

Roxanne's mouth remained open as the dark haired woman pressed past her. The door swung closed. Could the empathetic man she met really do something like that? A miniscule doubt niggled her, chipping away a tiny piece of her confidence in Tim. If he was the kind of person to strike a woman, how could Woodlyn church keep him on staff working with young people?

*****

Roxanne snipped the last section of hair, whisked Harry's neck with a soft brush, and flipped the plastic cape off. "All done. Now you can impress Janie."

He pulled his glasses out of his pocket and slipped them on his ears. With his head closer to the mirror, he peered at himself. A frown wrinkled his brow, and he brushed his hand over his newly trimmed hair. "I told you not to take much off. If Janie had been here today, she'd have done a better job."

"Janie called in sick. You know that."

"Yeah. She's never here when I need her."

"Well, maybe you'd better wait for your girlfriend next time." Heat traveled up her neck. She was doing this guy a favor anyway—taking him at the last minute. How dare he act so *haughty*?

If she ever got her own shop, she wouldn't have to endure guys like Harry. *My own shop.* She let out a long sigh. Would the day ever come? A glance in the mirror assured her she needn't worry about her makeup. It still looked fresh like this morning when she applied it.

Harry thrust a twenty in her face. "Keep the change."

Wow, big tip—nothing, since the haircut was twenty dollars.

Janie's boyfriend tromped out the door and piled into his car.

What got into him today? Roxanne checked her schedule. Her next customer should've arrived fifteen minutes ago, but the front area was empty.

She stretched her arms and yawned. Why was it always so hard to get up on Monday mornings? The encounter with Tim's sister yesterday afternoon still disturbed her. No way could she sleep last night with thoughts swirling in her head—the ugly picture Janelle painted of her brother.

The aroma of coffee in the break room enticed her. She sauntered to the back of the shop, picked up her mug from the shelf over the coffeepot, and peered at the picture of Mt. Rainier National Park on the calendar. When was the last time she'd been up there? The fall colors were exquisite this time of year, and the vistas spoke of the Lord's amazing creation.

The hot liquid's fragrance met her nostrils. She glanced in the mirror on the wall beside the coffeepot. Her hair looked fine. Making a good impression on clients was imperative.

One more check of the schedule indicated her client obviously had stood her up, and she had no more appointments until 5:00 p.m. Her heart pounded when a thought crossed her mind. She grabbed her purse and keys, locked the door to the salon, and headed out.

The morning had been stressful. The car seemed to drive itself to Albright's at the mall only three miles from the shop.

*****

Roxanne juggled the armful of bulky packages. She hadn't expected to find a sale in the shoe department.

Two oversized Albright sacks hung over her arm, and she carried the other. Her four-inch heel wobbled on the pavement. She stumbled but held on tight to her purchases. Setting a few bags down, she opened the trunk. Two shoe boxes slid out, and she stuffed them back into the plastic bag. Finally, she jammed all the packages in and paced around to the driver's seat.

Makeup and stylish clothes—the key to her success. Clients noticed her appearance when they sized her up as a stylist. But more importantly, she'd be more attractive to the opposite sex.

She tossed her purse on the passenger seat, and her charge slip dropped out. Two hundred sixty-nine dollars and twenty-three cents. With a gulp, she clutched her throat. How did she spend that much on shoes? But she couldn't deny the deep feeling of satisfaction. Her worries about Tim, the disgruntled client, and the no-show didn't seem as important now.

*****

Eighteen pairs of eyes stared at Tim from around the circular table. "Okay, people, you're in nine teams of two. Each team has a slip of paper with a Fruit of the Spirit written on it. I want you to read Galatians 5:22-

23. Then look at your paper." He pointed to the scripture reference on the chalkboard.

Johnny dropped his Bible on the floor with a loud whack. "Oh, sorry, Pastor." He gave Tim a smirk.

Best to ignore the *kid*. "As I was saying, look at your fruit. I want you to write a scenario for a journal entry. Create a situation encompassing the opposite of the fruit and tell how you'd react in the situation demonstrating the fruit. Each team will read theirs to the group."

"Pastor Tim." Tiffany folded her arms over her chest. "I don't get it. That's too confusing."

"Tiffany, if you'll kindly not interrupt and listen," Tim raised his voice, "I'm going to give you an example."

Tiffany nudged Betty and mumbled something to her.

He took a breath. Wednesday seemed to be a bad night. The kids behaved better on Sunday. What was the deal? "Look, guys. For example, if you have 'love,' write a situation about an unlovely person. That's the opposite. Someone who smells bad, cusses, maybe chews with his mouth open." He looked down at his notes.

"Like you?"

He jerked his head up. "Okay, who said that?" The muscles in his shoulders tightened.

Most of the teens rolled their eyes and shrugged.

His hands balled into fists. "Hey, if you guys don't settle down, you're not going to learn anything."

"Who said we wanted to learn?" This time Tim detected the source of the remark. Johnny. Hot blood sizzled in his veins. Another deep breath didn't calm him.

"Okay, so you've got your unlovely character. Now write about how you could reach out to that person in love. Act friendly toward him, invite him to a party, offer to help him with his homework."

Johnny sneered. "Hey, Tim. I've got 'self-control.' Can I make a scenario about two people losing self-control and making out, you know, kind of like the other day in your office?"

He drummed his fingers on the podium. "You can call me Pastor Tim. Let's keep this G-rated." He released his breath in uneven spurts. "Now get in groups around the room."

Beads of sweat formed on his forehead and hands. Most of these teenagers had no knowledge of good behavior. Time after time they presented him with a power struggle, and on every occasion he fell for it.

Their heads in a huddle, Betty and Mandy sat cross legged on the floor by the door.

When Tim neared, they waved their hands. "Pastor Tim, we've got 'peace.' We were thinking of writing a journal entry about how an earthquake hits and though we're afraid, we have the peace of God in our spirits."

Finally, someone was cooperating. "Excellent, girls. That's exactly what I was after."

Betty's mouth dropped open, and she pointed across the room. "Pastor, look behind you."

Tim twisted around. *What stunt would some kid pull next?*

Johnny lay on the floor next to Tiffany with one leg over hers. "How's this for the lack of self-control?" Johnny gave a loud guffaw.

Breath caught in Tim's throat. The teens appeared to

be shrouded in a red, glowing light. Another huff changed nothing. If he walked any closer, he'd jerk Johnny up and shove him against the wall.

Tim gasped for breath and turned toward the door, yanked it open, and slammed it shut behind him. The march down the hall tortured him. He'd left in defeat. But it was better than beating the kid up.

As usual, his occasional parent volunteer, Joe Brady, stood by the water fountain chatting with another parent.

Tim trudged up to him. "Joe. Can you look in on the kids?" A couple of deep breaths didn't calm the rage coursing through him. "I'm too angry."

Joe, his eyes wide, glanced up. "Sure." He strode down the hall and opened the door to the classroom.

Tim inched a few steps back down the hall and peered in as Joe lumbered into the room. Tim's young charges all sat around the table reading their Bibles.

A new wave of frustration scuttled through him. *Those young...* He walked toward the front entrance and shoved the door open. The clomping of his feet as he stomped to his car fifty yards in front of him kept time with his hammering heart. His hand shook as he tried to poke his key in the ignition. Finally he revved the motor and drove home. The thought of the kids acting like nothing happened tore his stomach to shreds. He could barely breathe.

Chapter Five

Tim's eyes stung and his back ached as he drove to work. Memories of Johnny and Tiffany messing around on the floor twisted his mind into knots. How could he teach with all the ridiculous tricks some of them pulled? He'd spent a miserable night. Tossing and wrestling with his bed wasn't his favorite pastime.

He pushed open the door to the main entrance and snuck by the office, hoping Pastor Downing or Nancy wouldn't see him. The secretary ran the church office with the skill of the CEO at Bank of America. What if she requested a report about last night? Dealing with the problem was more than he could take right now.

The incident with Johnny reemphasized why Tim's office remained locked—for the expressed purpose of preventing young pranksters from getting in. He turned the key and pushed the door open.

He had his faults, but keeping a messy office was not one of them. A bookshelf filled with the neat rows of titles he'd accumulated during college and seminary stood behind his mahogany desk. A closet on the opposite wall held his Sunday school materials. On the other side of his desk, a rolling chair provided seating for visitors.

Tim's attention drifted to the poster on the wall adjacent to the closet. The magnificent words from the book of Timothy, "For God did not give us a spirit of timidity, but a spirit of power, of love, and of self-discipline," appeared under a picture of a man standing on a mountain top with his hands raised to the Lord. Sometimes Tim wished he were as wise as the Biblical Timothy.

A knock on his door brought him back from his revelry. "Yes."

Pastor Downing stuck his head in. "Got a minute?" His face carried a pleasant smile.

"Sure." Tim pointed to the extra chair. A wave of heat traveled up his chest onto his cheeks. Did Pastor Downing come in to reprimand him about last night or to talk about a solution?

Pastor lowered himself into the seat and looked up with a smile he wished his dad would've offered. "I got a call from Johnny Thompson's father last night. As you know, Jack is one of our elders." Pastor Downing propped his ankle on his knee. "He mentioned something about a problem with the senior high group."

Tim bit his lip. Johnny actually had the nerve to complain. "Did Mr. Thompson tell you what happened?"

"Yes." Pastor Downing rubbed his chin. "He said you walked out on the kids thirty minutes before the class was over. Left them alone with Joe."

The volume of Tim's voice raised a notch. "Did he tell you why?"

"No. He said he didn't know the facts. That's why I'm

here."

"I guess Johnny didn't want to tell him about how he and Tiffany were down on the floor demonstrating lack of self-control, making a mockery of the lesson."

"I know Johnny is a handful. His Sunday school teachers have had problems with him since grade school. But you're the adult. I'm not excusing the boy's behavior, but it's your responsibility to deal with it."

"All right, but I need a meeting with Johnny's parents."

Pastor shot up in the chair. "Oh, no, not right now. I'd avoid it if I were you. Mr. Thompson can be... hard to get along with sometimes."

Tim focused at the green and white area rug in front of his desk. "All right. But I've got to get a handle on these teens." He couldn't tell Pastor Downing he left because his anger was out of control, and he was ready to hit the kid.

"Look. I appreciate all you do around here. Teens can be tough to work with at times. Let me pray for you." Pastor grasped his shoulder. "Lord, I ask you to bring my brother peace and wisdom. Just as Jesus calmed the raging Sea of Galilee, calm my brother's heart. In Jesus' name." With a smile, he patted Tim's arm and headed out the door.

Tim didn't want to admit it, but he'd struggled to keep his emotions buried when his boss prayed for him. If he could've chosen his earthly father, he'd certainly have requested one like the pastor, with his gentle spirit. But why did he say Tim shouldn't contact Johnny's father?

He locked his door and sank to his knees. "Lord, I know things aren't right in my life, in my ministry.

Please give me victory over these issues."

A stab of anxiety sullied him when he finally rose to his feet. Were Pastor Downing's words a *warning?*

*****

The winter schedule finally fell together. Tim assigned all his elementary and junior high teachers their curriculum and outlined their calendars. Even though they wouldn't be starting the winter quarter until after Thanksgiving, he liked to stay ahead. His boss hadn't mentioned Johnny and his father again since their chat yesterday.

The printer spit out the last form. With his hands on his desk, he pushed back in his rolling chair and stood to make a trip to the office to use the copy machine. As he reached for the papers, a bang sounded on the other side of the door. When it flew open, Johnny stormed in. The lean seventeen-year-old lifted his pointed nose and tossed Tim a smirk.

Tim's heart sank. Couldn't he just go one day without seeing the kid? "Hasn't anyone taught you how to knock before you enter a person's private office?"

"I did knock. Are you deaf?" The difficult teen plopped down into the chair where the Pastor sat yesterday.

Tim tried to breathe. "I don't think you should barge in here like this. Does your father know you're here?"

The boy tilted his head back with a half smile on his lips. "Of course, he's in Pastor Downing's office with the rest of the elders. And guess who they're talking about."

Tim's body felt as stiff as a robot. "Who?"

"You and what a lousy teacher you are." Johnny thrust out his chin.

The temperature of Tim's blood rose to a steady boil. Didn't the elders know how Mr. Thompson's son behaved? Maybe he'd crash the elder's meeting. But then he'd be reacting like he did most of the time, not acting with wisdom. Perhaps they weren't talking about him at all.

"Look. I think you should take some responsibility in this. You're going to be a senior next year, and you're acting like a little kid." Surely Johnny could see the wisdom in that.

He smirked. "Well, at least I'll still be here my senior year, which is more than I can say for you."

Tim's heart pounded triple time. Did the boy know what he was talking about? Why had they called an elders' meeting and not included him? Rage dared him to throw off all restraint. He had to remove himself from the teen's presence. "Get out."

The obnoxious teen turned with a smirk and stomped out of his office and down the hall. A glance at his watch told Tim it was time for lunch. Good. He had to leave before he lost control. Without waving at Nancy, he made his way to his car. If he could go home and be alone for a while, maybe he could cool off.

The drive home was a blur when he parked in front of his small rental he leased from Jess Colton.

A home with two bedrooms, a kitchen and a living room was plenty big. The entrance with its gray vinyl siding led to the living room. He plopped down in his easy chair near the freestanding fireplace.

Tim gripped the leather arms of the chair. How could the pastor have called the meeting without inviting him?

Memories of the past forty-eight hours piled up as his chest quivered. Finally, he caved, and the volcano erupted. Frantically searching for the closest item to destroy, he reached for the old book of poems. Page by page, he ripped them out. A growl emanated from his throat as he pursued his task. Each sheet landed crumpled on the floor until all that remained was a shell of a cover.

With a huff, he fell to the floor, no more energy to vent. His chest rose and fell with the air passing in and out of his lungs. How long did he lay there? He didn't know. When he finally got to his feet, he eased into the chair again, guilt encompassing every cell in his body. The precious book his grandmother had given him when he was a boy lay in shreds on the floor. And now she was gone. "Dear Lord God. What is wrong with me?"

For the first time in his life, the truth dawned on him. He'd suspected it before, but now the knowledge crystallized in his head. He had a problem—a big problem.

Before, he'd always blamed others, like Rena. She'd criticized him every time they were together, subtly expressing her disrespect.

He knew now he shouldn't have shoved her. Never again would he do such a thing. He'd repented before the Lord, not for losing his temper, but because he'd injured a woman.

Anger welled up in him so frequently and held him captive, his "thorn in the flesh." He'd revealed the problem to the hiring board for his job at Woodlyn Fellowship but assured them he'd brought the issue under control. Now he had his doubts.

The back of the chair cradled his head. His eyes opened with a start. Had he fallen asleep? An image of his father jarred him—the way he'd beaten his mother, and there was nothing he could do about it. Once he even tried to stand between her and Dad, to protect her. His father had slammed the ten-year-old boy so hard against the wall, his back had hurt for weeks. How could his mother still be married to the man?

A picture of Jesus calming the storm, like in Pastor's prayer this morning, filled his mind. He needed the quiet presence of the Lord, but God seemed just out of reach now.

He buried his face in his hands. *My life is so messed up. Will things ever get any better?*

*****

Tim sidled back through the door to the church office like a puppy with its tail between his legs. Nothing to do but talk to Pastor Downing. He raised a tentative hand to Nancy and proceeded to Pastor's door and knocked.

The sound of footsteps within the office grew louder until the door swung open. Wrinkles lined Pastor Downing forehead. They receded with his smile. "Come in, Tim."

Tim's heart pounded in his ears. "May I have a quick word with you?"

"Of course." Pastor pointed to a chair in front of his desk. "Sit down. Is something wrong? You look worried." He edged down opposite Tim.

Tim mopped perspiration from his forehead with the

back of his hand and slipped into the chair. "I'll come right out with it. I was concerned because the elders met with you today and didn't include me."

Pastor tilted his head as he squinted. "I didn't have an elders' meeting, just a short conference with Jack Thompson about the budget. He's the head of the finance committee."

"You didn't get together with the elders to discuss me?" He held his breath.

Pastor Downing stood and laid a hand on Tim's shoulder. "No. What gave you that idea?"

His face had to be scarlet. "I'm sorry. Just some wrong information." To have listened to that juvenile delinquent and believed him was embarrassing. "Sorry to have bothered you, sir."

He slunk back to his own office. Could defeat feel any worse?

*****

The cool, crisp Saturday morning brightened Roxanne's spirits. Fall was in the air. Only God could create such glorious colors. The foliage glowed with magnificent reds, oranges and purples. Some trees had totally lost their leaves now. At least she could count on the Douglas fir to stay green all winter.

Finally, she pushed herself out of the car and headed toward the main entrance. She hated to go inside the church building, it was so pleasant. With a sigh, she strolled into the foyer.

Some of her Saturday customers hadn't been too pleased about her cancelling her schedule today so she could come to Woodlyn Fellowship for the makeover event. But the bright smiles and animated conversation of the girls at the last training session made it all worth it. Makeup demonstrations, facials, and application of nail polish. She'd armed the girls with new skills.

It didn't take long to set up the largest Sunday school room last night and group the chairs according to what the girls were demonstrating. She breathed a sigh of relief when two mothers volunteered to supervise. Betty wanted to do little girl coiffeurs including braids and ponytails, which brought a smile to Roxanne's face.

She peeked into the room readied for customers. Though she still had an hour until the first appointment, she expected the girls any minute. A wave of doubt nagged her. Would they all show up? She couldn't let Tim down.

"Hey, Roxanne. How's it going?" She glanced from the Sunday school room to Tim as he ambled down the hall toward her.

"Hey."

His dark brown eyes twinkled.

She'd met a lot of guys before, but none made her feel like Tim did. Sure his warm smile kicked up her pulse, but it was more than that. Could he possibly be a man she could trust?

"Are you ladies ready for the big day?"

She hoped he didn't notice her burning cheeks. "Everything's under control. The girls were so eager when we got the room set up."

"Sounds like you have a way with them. Wish I knew your secret." He stared toward the sanctuary.

At first she thought he was teasing, but the bewildered look on his face told her otherwise. "Well, this is something they're very interested in. That probably makes a difference."

"Yeah, I guess. Anyway, let me know if you need anything. I'll be in my office." He ran his fingers over his chin.

"Okay." She attempted a reassuring smile. Tim held something back. He was the youth pastor, much more qualified than she to work with teens. But why did he have so much trouble with them?

*****

The greeter, sitting at a table in the main hall, maintained a professional manner. The teen girl didn't appear shy today as she checked off the women when they arrived.

Roxanne returned from the office and poked her head in the large room.

Mandy handed a tube of mascara to a woman and smiled.

Betty brushed a small girl's hair, separating it into three stands for a French braid.

In the area nearest the door, Tiffany sat on the floor applying nail polish to a lady's toes.

Roxanne's chest puffed out in pride. Everything was going well.

The morning zipped by. The teens hadn't let her down. The last happy customer left with bright red nails on her hands and toes.

Roxanne squared her shoulders, strolled into the sanctuary, and plopped down in the back row with her hands behind her head. If her days at the shop would go as smooth, she'd be happy. The only problem this morning was the extra women who showed up without an appointment. But she passed out her card and invited them to come to the salon for a service.

Joy filled her heart. She loved serving the Lord through her talents. Volunteering at the women's shelter downtown had been tough at first, but when she saw the smiles on the residents' faces, it was worth it.

Her hand landed on a piece of paper next to her, a bulletin from last Sunday. The announcements on the back mentioned senior high Bible study on Wednesday nights led by youth pastor Timothy Garrett.

Other than this morning, Roxanne hadn't spoken with him at length since the Sunday at Lucio's. She'd waved a couple of times at church when he'd visited the meetings with the girls, but he seemed to be so preoccupied.

She pulled herself up from the pew. Time to let Tim know they'd finished. She crossed the sanctuary and found her way into the hall opposite the Sunday school rooms. The plaque on the last door to the right said *Timothy Garrett, Youth Pastor.* She lifted her hand and knocked.

A smiling Tim peeked out. "All done? To be honest, I kind of stayed out of the way. Nail polish and little girls' hair styles aren't my thing." He laughed and opened the door wider. "Come in."

"I wanted to give you this." She patted the envelope and grinned. "Part of the proceeds. We'll be collecting the rest when my cosmetic order comes in."

"I'll turn this in on Monday." He took the envelope from her, placed it in the closet, and locked the door. "How can I thank you?" His face brightened. "Since this is such a beautiful day, do you want to take a drive up to Mt. Rainier this afternoon to see the fall colors?

Maybe we could stop at one of those country restaurants for dinner. It's the least I can do."

The story Tim's sister told her echoed in the back of her mind. Did she dare go anywhere with him? What if she said something that upset him, and he hurt her? If she went, would it encourage a relationship she might later regret?

She shook her head and looked into his handsome face. How could he have done the things his sister described? He was a youth pastor, after all. Youth pastors didn't lose their tempers. "Sure. I think I'd like that."

Chapter Six

The sign with "Mt. Rainier National Park" carved on a four-foot piece of board hung from a wooden structure over the road. The toll booth sat about one hundred yards beyond. Tim glanced at the woman in the passenger seat beside him. "I'm happy so many responded to the fundraiser. This takes us a third of the way toward the financial goal the elders set."

She chuckled softly and smoothed her jeans. "Your girls were great. And the women were impressed with their products. We didn't get one complaint."

He showed his yearly pass at the little shack and handed Roxanne the map the ranger offered. "I'm grateful to you." He inched his car forward behind a Jeep whose occupants stared and pointed out the window. "It was a success because of your hard work."

"Thank you." Roxanne grinned and turned toward the window. Douglas firs fifty feet tall lined the road, obscuring the view beyond.

The Jeep's driver pulled off on a turnout. Tim passed and followed the road, hugging the glacial river to the right. The landscape on either side changed to a forest of evergreen trees growing out of a carpet of orange and gold leaves from the bushes underneath. He peered farther into the woodland. The trees in the distance were veiled in a misty haze.

Tim couldn't shake the feeling they'd entered another world. The steep drop offs, the abundant evergreens, little mountain wildflowers and trickling waterfalls over the rocks lining the road all spoke of a peaceful existence, so different than his life in Woodlyn.

Roxanne drew her jacket around her. "Umm. Smells like fall. The season's changing."

"No doubt we have four of them in Washington state." The road curved again, revealing a thirty-foot waterfall cascading down a rock cliff past the turnout on the road. Water collected in a pool a few feet below. "There's a short path we can follow to get a better view. I've got an umbrella in the backseat."

His efficient helper gave a little squeal. "It's magnificent. Let's go."

He took the key out of the ignition and reached in the backseat for his blue and white umbrella. "I'll come around for you."

Tim offered his hand as Roxanne stepped from the car. The umbrella sheltered her from the droplets beginning to fall and spill onto the path. He juggled the curved handle with one hand and grasped her arm with the other. The boardwalk led down a gentle incline.

At the bottom of the short path, the ground leveled out into a grassy meadow. The runoff cascaded from a ledge along a fifty-foot precipice in front of them. The spray flicked a drop or two of moisture on his face.

"It's exquisite." She hugged her arms and shivered. "I should've brought my heavy coat."

"Let's get you back. It's wet and cold out here." He winked at her, glancing at her small frame and thin arms. Desire to protect her washed over him. He couldn't allow her to get sick.

Roxanne laughed. "This place is beautiful, but I can enjoy it better from your warm car."

He sheltered her again with the umbrella as the mist fell more heavily. The feel of her sweater-clad arm under his fingers kicked up his pulse as they climbed the path again. He opened the passenger's door, and she ducked into the car. When he sat in the driver's seat, he flipped the lever for heater, the warmth melting the damp coldness of the outside air.

"How about if we come back another day—if we can find a sunny one? But in the meantime, can I take you to supper in Ashford? It's the first town near the entrance of the park on the way home? I understand Arnie's has great fresh salmon and Caesar salad." He pulled out on the road.

"You're going to spoil me, but I'd love it." Roxanne dug in her purse and retrieved a mirror then took a glance.

Was she checking her hair to see if it got wet? She looked fine to him. Her enchanting eyes couldn't be more striking. He turned his face to the road.

After they exited the park, he caught his breath. "I marvel at how creative God is. The many colors of these trees are... are..."

"Resplendent." Roxanne's smile held a look of satisfaction, as if proud of herself for discovering the descriptive word.

"Yeah, resplendent. That's the word."

A log bed and breakfast came into view as they

approached Ashford. He patted his pocket when he heard a cell phone ring, but shook his head. Not his. His played "*Glorious Day*."

Roxanne dug in her purse. She looked at the screen of her smart phone. "My mom. What could she be calling about? Excuse me."

He slowed to the speed limit and looked for the restaurant he remembered up on the right when he'd been here the last time.

"Hi, Mom." She took a breath. "Yes, I'm just leaving Mt. Rainier." The smile faded from her lips. "Yes?"

Her mouth dropped open. "Oh, no." She grasped her throat. "Okay, Mom. Okay. I'll be there as soon as I can." She swiped a tear from her cheek. "You go ahead and go to work." The phone fell from her hand onto her lap, then she picked it up and slipped it back into her purse. As if dazed, she stared straight ahead.

"Roxanne, what's wrong?"

"I'm sorry to interrupt our trip, but... but I've got to go home—to my mom's. She's on her way to work and can't be late." She blinked and poked in her purse bringing out a tissue.

The heartbreaking look on her face sliced into his emotions. "Is there anything I can help you with?"

"Could you go with me?" She released a quiet sob and dabbed at her eyes. "I need to bury my little terrier, Teddy."

*****

Roxanne dreaded going back to the familiar neighborhood on the south side of Woodlyn. She had no choice but to give Tim directions. Her stomach remained in the same knot that had formed when her mother called. Mom had to be mistaken. Teddy wasn't dead.

Tim pulled up in front of the little three-bedroom house. As a girl Roxanne thought she would live in the home with Mom and Dad until she grew up. But all that changed.

After she'd put her phone back in her purse, the ache traveled through her stomach up to her throat, almost as hurtful as the pain she felt the day her father walked out of her life. Was her makeup a mess now, the tears causing her mascara to run?

As if he thought she couldn't face what she'd find inside, Tim grasped her hand as she led him through the front door. His touch brought the only comfort she felt.

The small living room looked the same—simple but tidy. Where was Teddy? He usually bounded into the front room when she opened the door, his tail wagging.

With a few uncertain steps past the couch, she inched toward the door to the kitchen tiptoeing over the squeaky mouse and the little red ball lying on the floor.

She struggled against her tears. Would Tim think her an idiot grieving over a dog? But one glance at him, tight frown, folded hands, told her he shared her concern.

She held her breath, dreading what she'd do next. Never had the view out the kitchen window seemed so ominous. A small brown lump lay by the fence, just as Mom said.

A tissue box sat on the kitchen counter. "He's out there," she said lifting the Kleenex to her nose. Her shaking finger touched the glass.

She clasped her hands and paced, staring at Tim as if

the answers to her questions were etched on his face. "Why didn't we make time to take him to the vet?"

"No, Roxanne. Don't think like that. What can I do?" His gaze followed her. Compassion colored his soft brown eyes.

She shook her head. "On every occasion when I visited Mom, I would always spend time with Teddy. He nuzzled me and licked my face and whimpered when I started to leave. I couldn't take him to my little upstairs apartment. I had to leave him here. Do you think he held that against me? Did he die of a broken heart?"

Tim peeked out the window. "No. Of course not."

Everything in the modest kitchen was in its place, the toaster on the counter, the flour, sugar, and coffee canisters on the shelf above the stove. And the floor spotless, Teddy's water bowl sitting in the corner.

Tim laid his hand on her arm and cleared his throat. "I lost a dog once, Sam, a chocolate Lab. I understand how you feel."

His attention made things worse, leaving no room to hide away her emotions like she always did. She gulped back her pain and tried to save it for when she was alone. Backing away from him, she headed to the kitchen door. "He was fourteen years old. I... I guess it was time." No putting off any longer what she had to do. With a flip of the latch, she unlocked the screen. The doggie door swatted as she stepped into the backyard. "I got pretty attached to him."

"Would you like me to do this? If you'll tell me where things are, like the shovel and where you want to put him, I can get started."

She looked up at the man who exuded tenderness.

His offer to help her tugged at a place in her heart. He seemed sincere. Something she wasn't used to from a man. "Maybe we can do it together. I think I can take care of things if you're here to help. The shovel's in the shed."

She took another gulp of air and moved down the length of the wooden fence running next to the greenbelt. A chill passed through her heart as she stared at the pile of brown fur lying near the corner where the fence angled toward the back perimeter of the yard.

Tim nodded and headed to the metal structure her father had left behind. His yard equipment and tools still remained inside.

Her father used to mow the lawn and play with Teddy when he was a puppy. He'd throw the ball out and command Teddy to run out for a pass. Her dog would bark, wag his tail, and dart out as fast as his little legs would carry him. A sigh escaped. She had to stop remembering.

Tim pulled the outside handle, and the door squeaked open. He took a step forward and poked his head inside.

With reluctance, she peered into the small building. "The shovel's in the back."

He grasped the spade and pointed into the interior of the shed. "Can I use the box on that shelf? We can put him in it first."

She hadn't thought that far. "Okay." Bile rose in her throat. "There's a good place to bury him, over by the trees."

He craned his head out and scanned the area. "Teddy would like that." They walked around to the end of the yard opposite the greenbelt between a Douglas fir and a cedar.

"At least, he'll be here by these trees that stay green all year long." She pushed a tear off her eyelash and pointed to the ground. "That spot with no grass."

Tim thrust the end of the shovel into the soft earth and stepped on the blade. As he worked, dirt piled up beside the hole. Finally, the opening grew large enough for the box with Teddy's body. "Let's go get him."

She struggled against the tears gathering in her throat. How could she go through with the next step, putting him in the cold ground forever?

Tim's focus lingered on her. "Come on." He picked up the box and slipped her hand in his. The warmth of his skin against hers offered her hope to believe everything would be okay.

The lifeless body rested next to the fence. She squeezed Tim's hand tighter as they neared.

All too soon, Teddy's remains lay in front of them. The emotion she forced back refused to be restrained any longer. She hadn't realized it would be so hard to look at the form of her dog she'd loved for so many years. *God, I don't know if animals go to Heaven or not. But if they do, I surely would love to see Teddy there.*

The tears slid down her cheeks as her grief hemmed her in. "I don't think I can..." Her hands covered her eyes. Then strong arms about her shoulders tucked her into the safety of his chest, and his warm breath fell on her neck. She leaned into him, inviting his strength.

"Shh." He ran his hands over her back and tightened his embrace. "Now let's give him a proper send off."

When Roxanne moved away, he placed a thumb on her cheek and wiped away a tear. His gentle smile brought her peace. The urge to return to his arms almost overpowered her.

She looked away—toward the greenbelt behind the fence before she embarrassed herself. Tim was a friend, helping her out of a difficult circumstance. Maybe if she said that a hundred times, she'd believe it and not the truth.

The youth pastor had found his way into her heart. Why? Other guys had tried to come into her life but only wanted one thing. She winced when she thought of the times she'd given in. They hadn't been concerned with her as a person. Tim was the first Christian man she'd befriended, and she marveled at the difference—a man who cared more about serving God than himself.

He grasped both of her hands and bowed his head. "Lord, please bring Roxanne the courage to do what we have to do. Bless her and strengthen her by Your mighty power."

She'd always dealt with her problems alone. It felt so good to have the support of this man who knew how to pray for her. She nodded, hoping he perceived her heart of gratitude. What would she have done without him today?

He caressed her hand and reached down toward Teddy. "Are you ready?"

Her heart told her no, she wasn't ready to put Teddy in his grave.

Tim knelt and gently slid her dog into the box and secured the lid. As he curved around with the little parcel in his arms, she held onto him. The journey to the hole seemed to be over all too soon.

He bent down, laid the box in the opening, and squinted up at her. "I have an idea. Is there anything you want to put in here with him?"

She glanced around at the house and knew just what she wanted to get. "Wait a minute."

Through the back door and down the hall took her into her old room. On the top shelf of her closet, she found the small decorative box, set it on her bed, and opened the lid. A little piece of metal shaped like a bone from his old collar was inscribed with the word "Teddy."

A picture of her dog when he was barely more than a puppy lay next to the bone. Maybe Tim would like to see it.

She held her treasure secure in one hand and the picture of Teddy in the other and glanced out the kitchen window.

Tim stood guard over the hole, his head bowed, his hand over his forehead.

She guessed he was praying for her—the first man as far as she knew to ever speak to God about her. The thought brought joy into her lonely heart. She placed her hand on the backdoor and pushed it open.

Tim glanced up when the door closed behind her.

As she neared, she held out her hand. "I want to leave this with Teddy."

He nodded with a half smile.

Did she see a hint of mist in his eyes? She knelt down to the little box in the hole, raised the lid, and dropped the bone nametag inside. Now she wasn't sure she could watch what Tim would do next. "Oh, and here's a photo of Teddy... before."

With a raised eyebrow, he stuck it in his shirt pocket. "May I keep this?"

"Well, yes, if you'd like." What did he want it for?

Slowly he shoveled the dirt on top of the cardboard

container until soil filled the hole. Her Teddy was gone, under the ground.

Her behavior must've appeared childish to Tim, but she couldn't stop the tears and her quivering shoulders. As she gained a fragment of control, she lifted her eyes to her friend. "I hadn't planned on getting so emotional."

"It's okay." A smile sat on his lips. "I'm grateful I could be here for you today."

If she could feel his arms around her again, it would ease her pain. She closed her eyes. "Please hold me, Tim. I need you a moment longer."

"You mean like this?" He slipped his arms around her shoulders and tugged her near.

She felt safe there. The breeze of the cool early evening didn't chill her as it usually did, his embrace so warm and sturdy.

His presence soothed her. "It'll be okay in time, Roxy."

She whispered in his ear. "You called me Roxy."

He chuckled. "It seemed like a good name." He allowed her to remain next to him until she felt ready to pull away. When she did, he glanced back to the grave. "Maybe we can find a headstone for Teddy one of these days."

His words touched her heartstrings. The guy sounded like he meant all the kind things he said to her. Was she falling for someone who'd dedicated his life to serving the Lord, this youth pastor?

*****

Tim drove back to his house after dropping Roxanne

off at her upstairs apartment. His heart wrenched out of his chest at the sight of her with her hands over her face, sobbing. He touched his pocket. The picture of Teddy was still there. He knew what he'd do with it.

He understood loss. Understood the absence of a decent relationship with a father and sister, the death of a dog when he was ten. Defeat defined his life. He couldn't even learn how to control his anger.

He parked the car in the carport and unlocked the front door. His easy chair and the empty table beside it reminded him of another loss—the book of poems his grandmother had given him. He sank down and rubbed his forehead.

Did he dare admit it? Roxanne was stealing her way into his heart, and he wasn't ready for it.

He'd damaged Rena's life by the way he'd treated her, and he didn't want to take a chance on doing it again. A relationship with a woman was out of the question. He'd live his life as a bachelor. Well, hadn't the apostle Paul gotten along just fine without a wife?

He meandered into the kitchen and pulled a bottle of water out of the refrigerator, tossed the cap in the garbage, and sat down at his table. A shudder ran down his spine. He couldn't bring Roxanne into his angry life. Would she be safe with him? A quiver careened through his body. His mind screamed the answer. *No. No.*

Chapter Seven

Roxanne leaned against the wall and gazed out the glass windows. Most of the trees in the salon's landscaping next to the sidewalk had lost their leaves, except the evergreens. Larry didn't insist on putting up Halloween decorations all over the walls, which was a blessing. Looking at ghosts and goblins every day until November didn't appeal to her.

She lifted her eyes to the gray sky and back to the sidewalks. Water ran in rivulets toward the underground drains. Woodlyn wouldn't see many sunny days until next July.

As if to create a barrier from the reality she didn't want to face, she closed her eyes. Tim only waved or smiled when he caught a glimpse of her at church. No attempt to strike up a conversation or suggest they go for the dinner they'd missed.

He'd held the umbrella that day at Mt. Rainier, protecting her from the drizzle, and showed kindness when they buried Teddy. She twisted away from the window. The good-looking pastor mystified her.

Doubt rifled through her chest. Was there something about her he didn't like? She held her breath. When she finally released it, her heart still pounded.

Tim's cell number was still tucked in her purse since the day of the fundraiser. But she wouldn't call. He'd only think she was chasing him.

In the past she'd held on to a guy by giving him what he wanted. Would she have to do that to get Tim interested? But what about her new faith? Did God really care about intimacy in a believer's life?

She strolled back to her station and whisked up the remains of her last client's haircut. Maybe Tim was too busy to think about her, or he didn't like crying women.

Her heart ached. He showed her attention one day and disappeared from her life the next. When would she learn? Guys couldn't be trusted. A pesky tear escaped the corner of her eye.

A gust of cold air rushed inside the shop as a man in jeans and a blue jacket strolled in. He glanced around as if he unsure of himself.

She didn't mind greeting customers since her station sat closest to the door. "May I help you?"

The guy had one hand stuffed in his pocket. "I don't have an appointment, but could I get a haircut?"

Probably in his mid-twenties, and a little scruffy, the fellow did need a trim. His disheveled blond mane grew close to his shirt collar.

She checked her appointment book. Nobody for an hour. "Yes, have a seat. I'll be with you in a minute."

With a broom, she finished sweeping clumps of hair into a dustpan and dumped the remains in the garbage pail. In the waiting area, the man picked up a magazine, set it on his lap, and turned the pages with his other hand.

She gasped. The guy shifted in his chair revealing

the outline of a gun beneath the hand in his pants pocket. She clutched her throat. He probably planned to rob her when he sat down at her station. That was why he hadn't taken his hand out.

She gripped the edge of her counter. Beads of moisture formed on her palms. *Dear Lord, please help me.*

What were her options? If he sat down in her chair, he'd be close enough to pull a gun on her without making a scene.

Did he intend to rob all of them? Janie placed foils in her customer's hair on the other wall near the break room.

Larry's station was empty. *He must be in the back.* To sneak to the employee room and alert him might be the best thing.

She risked another glimpse at the man.

He moved from one side of the chair to the other then slammed the magazine shut and tossed it toward the table with the other periodicals. His hand remained jammed in his pocket.

She didn't dare walk any closer. "Uh, sir, I'll be with you in just a moment." She circled around to the break room. Would the young guy guess she was on to him?

He glared at her and stood, pacing the floor.

Roxanne could barely keep from running. She darted through the open door. Larry stood at the counter stirring a cup of coffee and glanced up.

"There's a man out there." She hissed and sucked in a breath between her teeth. "He's... he's trying to rob us. He's got a gun in his pocket."

Her middle-aged boss surveyed her with wide eyes. He edged nearer the entrance to the salon and glanced out. "How do you know?"

"He hasn't taken his hand out of his pocket. I saw the outline of a gun."

Larry circled back to her with a frown. "Yeah, I see who you mean. Okay, go ahead and call him to your station, and I'll keep my eye on him. There's a weapon in my bottom drawer. I'll watch for him to make a move. If necessary, I'll call the police."

She shivered and wished Larry had offered to take the customer but supposed it'd be better for her boss to observe the man's actions instead.

Mustering all the courage she found inside, she crept back to her station. Her throat caught in an involuntary swallow. "O... okay, sir. I'm ready for you."

The man avoided eye contact and eased down in her chair.

She clutched her chest when the guy drew his hand out of his pocket. A ghastly fear gripped her. She shot a glance at Larry, but he sat in his chair motionless.

The customer scooted farther down as if trying to avoid attention.

One glance at the sight in front of her drew a gasp from her lips. The young man had nothing but a stub for a left hand.

Heat filled her face. *Lord, I thought him a thief. Forgive me.* "How... how much would you like me to take off?"

"Well, I don't want it as short as the army barbers whacked it. Wearing those GI haircuts for four years was enough."

The truth began to dawn on her. "Where were you stationed?"

"Mostly at Ft. Bliss in El Paso. But I did twelve

months in Iraq. That's where I got my hand blown off by enemy fire." He lifted his arm. "I'll feel better when I get my prosthesis."

Words formed in Roxanne's heart. No way she could keep them back. "Thank you for serving our country." Her heart clenched.

"You're welcome." He tossed her a half smile. "Just don't shave off all my hair."

"Don't worry. I'm giving you the spiked look." *Like Tim wears.*

After the cut, she dabbed some gel on the top and tousled his hair. "How do you like this?"

The man displayed white teeth when he offered her another smile. "Looks great. Thanks." He stood and reached in his pocket with his good hand and pulled out some bills. "This should cover it."

Her head moved from side to side. "No, I'm sorry. I can't take your money. Please let me thank you for defending us." With effort, she tamped down the emotion in her throat. If she gave into tears, the guy would see her sentimental side.

"Well, thanks, ma'am. But next time, I insist on paying." He saluted her, thrust his stub into his pocket, and pushed the door open using his shoulder.

With a hot face, she dared a glance at her boss to see his reaction. He dug in the top drawer of his workstation.

"Guess I've been watching too many detective movies. The guy had a war injury."

"Yeah. He wasn't a notorious killer after all." Larry lifted out a notebook filled with a bunch of papers. "Ah, there it is—my product receipts. Sometimes I wonder why I hang onto this shop. You never know what's going to happen next."

Some help he was. If the man had been a gunman, Larry probably would've run out the door to save his own skin.

In her seven years at the shop, he'd changed. He didn't seem interested, leaving for hours or even days at a time and making no improvements in the salon. She jerked the broom off the hook on the wall to sweep up her area.

Janie finished her customer and sent the woman off with a smile, probably oblivious to the drama. She strolled toward Roxanne's station. "If my boyfriend comes in this afternoon, tell him I'm going shopping. He said he might be in for a haircut later. But I'm not waiting around for the dude. You never know about him."

"Harry, right?" She swept the remains of the soldier's haircut into a dustpan.

"Yeah, Harry Dickson." The slender brunette pulled out a set of keys and clutched the faux-leather bag.

"Well, okay, but the last time I cut his hair because you weren't here, he got ticked."

"He can be like that." Janie headed out the door and hopped into her car parked in front of the shop.

Roxanne fought the urge to cancel all her appointments for the rest of the day and go shopping with her co-worker. The tension surrounding the injured soldier lingered in her gut, and she still couldn't get Tim out of her mind.

If she and Tim spent more time together, maybe he'd take an interest in her. Maybe if she showed up at church in a new outfit, she could get his attention.

She ran a shaking hand through her hair. If she could

buy some of those stylish Gucci sweaters or Prada boots, her anxiety would go away. Only thing. The balance on her credit card mounted higher.

*****

Joe's ringing cell phone caught Tim's attention. His volunteer looked at the instrument. "I gotta take this, boss. Be back in five."

He nodded and turned back to his rowdy students. "You guys calm down." Sheer determination didn't help to control the volume of his voice. "Roger, that includes you." With two fingers, he rubbed his temples. "Now the Bible tells us followers of Christ must be imitators of Him. None of us can reach perfection like He did, but we can aim for the goal of being like him."

Snickers and giggles interrupted the lesson. *What now?* Switching his thoughts from his notes to the kids, his mouth fell open. Blood rolled down Roger's forehead and onto his cheeks.

Johnny bolted up from his seat. "Look, Pastor Tim. I need to get him to the doctor." He grabbed Roger's arm and raced out of the room.

Following his first instinct, Tim ran out into the hall behind them. The boys stopped about ten feet away, laughing. "Hey, Pastor Tim. Like our theatrical blood?"

Another disruption. Unbelievable. "Okay, you slackers. I've had enough. Go wash up in the restroom." It took all his restraint not to grasp both their arms and escort them out of church. "I think it's about time to call some parents."

"Won't do you any good." Johnny sneered as he and Roger jaunted into the boys' bathroom.

What did the kid mean? Pastor Downing had said Mr. Thompson could be difficult to deal with. Tim mopped beads of perspiration from his forehead. But was there another reason why the pastor didn't want Tim to contact Mr. Thompson? If Tim didn't communicate with Johnny's parents, nothing would be accomplished. Surely Pastor Downing didn't have a specific motive why he advised against it. *Could the preacher be setting me up for failure?*

"Everything okay?" Joe hurried down the hall. "Sorry. The call was from work."

Tim nodded. "I have two young men in the restroom cleaning up a mess they made. Would you check on them, please? Thanks, Joe."

*****

Tim stepped out the church's front entrance and darted to his car. The heavy rain soaked his hair and jacket. Why did he always leave his umbrella at home or in the back of his Chevy?

The deluge hadn't let up since before the youth meeting. He splashed through a couple of puddles. A cedar tree released a barrage of raindrops on his head as he dug in his jeans pocket for his keys. Shaking his hair, he unlocked the car, slid into the driver's seat, and started the ignition.

His nerves played hardball in his stomach. He punched the CD player's start button and laid his head back on the headrest. Maybe the quiet worship music would calm him.

Control over anger had defied him year after year. Though he still hadn't gained victory, God had used the struggle for good. Beginning in seminary, he'd discovered the desire to help others who could benefit from counsel. Didn't the scriptures say that God comforts us in our troubles so we can in turn comfort others? Maybe Tim could help people who dealt with rage—that is if he overcame the problem.

But the thought didn't change his situation. The disruptions were getting worse by the week. He sucked in a long stream of air. Where was his job headed? He had to show a measure of success before he could arrive at his true calling, to serve as a pastoral counselor.

The wipers whished back and forth clearing the rainwater from the windshield. He peered out toward the church. The only area of his performance the elders seemed pleased about was the girls' fundraiser. They'd brought in more money than any other project.

Roxanne had been instrumental in that—not him. Could she be the right person to stand beside him—the woman God wanted him to love and serve as Christ served the church?

Roxanne. Just the sound of her name and her bright blue eyes were enough to quicken his heart rate. He couldn't deny the compassion he'd felt for her when they buried her dog—the first time he discovered an attraction to her and the first time he realized the need to end any further association. He couldn't risk it. Not after Rena.

He settled his head back again and tried to concentrate on the words of "Our God Is an Awesome God." *Lord, let me keep my ears and eyes on You, the awesome God.*

"Glorious Day" sounded from his pocket, and he pulled out his cell. When he looked at the screen, his heart fell. Roxanne. Why was she calling him?

"Hi, Roxanne."

"Tim. Tim." Her voice rasped across the line.

"I can hardly hear you. I think we have a bad connection."

"Can you come to the shop right now?" She sounded hoarse.

He glanced in his rearview mirror and pulled out of his parking place. "What's wrong?"

"Everyone left when I finished up my last customer." Her breathy voice brought eerie chills to his spine. "Janie's boyfriend came in ... asking for a haircut. He's, he's drunk, and I'm scared. He grabbed me then I ran to the bathroom and locked the door."

"I'm on my way now. Just stay where you are. Be there in five minutes."

"Please hurry."

He clenched his fist around the steering wheel. Some ignorant drunk trying to bother Roxanne. He ground his teeth as he sped down the street and turned off on Cedar Drive toward her shop. *Lord, please protect my Christian sister and keep her from harm.*

After two more stop lights, the road curved onto Smith Avenue. Though he couldn't become involved with her, ignoring her wasn't an option if she needed help. He dimmed his lights and stopped in front of Larry's Hair Design.

The car door banged when he slammed it shut, and his heart pounded. The salon lights were off. Had the creep done that? He squinted and cupped his hand to the glass.

Roxanne shoved a blond guy wearing glasses. She must've disregarded his advice to stay in the restroom.

The jerk reached for her again, moving his head toward hers.

Rage gurgled up in him as he pushed through the doors.

Roxanne glanced at him, tears streaming down her face. "Tim." She screamed.

The guy turned around—obviously not expecting him.

Tim grabbed the man by his shirt and pulled him away from the quivering woman.

"Hey, whadya doin' here?" The man's slurred words turned Tim's stomach.

Roxanne wiped at a tear on her face. "I was stupid for coming out of the bathroom before you got here."

His heart thudded as his breath came in short spurts. The idiot gave Roxanne a hard time—just like his father had done to his mother.

Once again, a red haze formed in front of him. "Aargh." He pounced on the man and landed a blow to his face. The guy fell backwards as his glasses skidded across the floor.

The drunk struggled to his feet and reached for his spectacles. He leaned toward Tim as if he intended to shove him but stumbled and dropped his arms.

"I'm warning you now, if you ever come anywhere close to this woman, you'll answer to me." Tim snarled at him, his muscles tense.

"Who ya think you are? Da owner dis place?" The guy hooked his bent glasses behind his ears and lifted one side of his mouth in a smirk.

"No. I'm Tim Garrett. Roxanne is a good friend of mine. So get out of here." There. The man would know who he was dealing with.

The scrawny drunk scowled, whacked Tim with his shoulder, and staggered out the door.

"Maybe I should've called the cops." Roxanne clutched her throat. "But something told me you'd still be at church."

"Tell me what happened." His heavy breath slowed.

She rubbed her forehead. "I thought he'd be okay since I cut his hair before." She collapsed in her chair. "He came in looking for Janie to give him a haircut. When I told him she'd already left, he started flirting with me. I could smell alcohol on his breath." She glanced toward the mirror, brushed a strand of hair away from her face, and lifted her focus to him again.

"Is that when you called me?"

"No, I resisted him for a minute but realized he was too strong. I kicked his leg, and he backed off a moment. I ran to the bathroom and locked the door. Then I called you." She placed thin arms around her shoulders and shook.

The sight of Roxanne trying to comfort herself tore at his heart. He held out his hand to her. She grasped his fingers and stepped up from the chair. He closed his eyes as he brought her into his embrace. She was so slender, he could almost wrap him arms around her twice. A fire burned in his soul. His desire to protect her inundated him again. But if he didn't walk away, he could repeat his past mistakes.

Sorrow surged over him as he pulled back and gazed into her sweet face. With all the self-control he could muster, he refrained from doing what he wanted—to kiss her.

The whoosh of the door opening caught Tim's attention. The guy poked his nose back in. "Jush want ya to know, Tim Garrett. Ya gunna hear from me 'agin." Harry made an offensive gesture and stomped toward his car, the rain beating down on his head.

JUNE FOSTER

Chapter Eight

Tim raised the umbrella over his head and sidestepped puddles of rainwater. Only two more blocks to The Grape Vine. The ornate wooden front door of the downtown Woodlyn restaurant came into view on his right.

He squeezed under the awning. The steady downpour had persisted for three days now. Next time, he'd wear something heavier than this leather jacket. The cold air blasted his arms and chest.

A healthy-looking Jess Colton hurried down the sidewalk. He stuck out a gloved hand. "Hey, Tim. How are you?"

"Good." Tim opened the glass door for his friend. "Glad you could make it for lunch. We haven't talked in a long time."

Jess removed his Indiana Jones hat and shook the raindrops off before he entered the building then turned back to Tim with a grin. "Yeah, it's nice to get out once in awhile." He smirked. "My home office is confining sometimes."

"How's Holly?"

"She's still at the dental office for a few more

months, since the baby's due at the end of January." His face lit up like the stadium lights at a Mariner's game. Then his eyes widened as he lowered his voice. "To tell you the truth, the idea of becoming a father is scary."

Tim chuckled. "I wouldn't know, buddy." He'd love nothing more than to be married and have a child to raise and nurture. But he knew better than to get his hopes up. He'd only train the kid how to become angry, like his father taught him.

Jess stepped up to the hostess station.

"Yes, sir." The hostess smiled.

"Table for two, please," he said.

"Sir, we have a waiting list today. It could be up to a half hour." The lady perused her seating chart. "But if you're in a hurry, I can seat you at the bar. It's non-smoking."

Jess turned to Tim. "Is that okay with you? Sorry, but I need to get back to work."

Tim didn't frequent bars, but in this case, they didn't have much of a choice. "Sure. I understand."

The hostess pulled two menus out and led them into the lounge. She set the lunch specials down on the bar in front of two high stools.

A mirror reflected a variety of bottles lined up on a shelf in front. Glasses hung from hooks on the ceiling. Tim lifted himself up onto the chair. He'd expected another kind of music besides classical tunes.

The bartender placed two cardboard circles in front of him and Jess. "Yes, gentlemen, what can I get you?"

Jess gave him a quick glance. "I'll have an iced tea. We're here for lunch."

"Yes, sir. The waitress will be right over. And you sir, what can I get you to drink?" He peered at Tim.

A craving hit him for a drink he hadn't consumed since he was a kid. "I'll have a root beer, please."

From a carafe, the bartender filled a glass with ice tea. He set a tall goblet, long-handled spoon, and square ceramic container of sugar packets in front of him. Jess opened the Splenda and stirred it into his drink.

The man behind the bar popped the top off a tall, brown bottle of Hayes Root Beer and placed a glass filled with ice in front of Tim.

Lifting the bottle's long neck up, he took a swig, not worrying about the ice.

Jess surveyed the menu. "Guess I'll have chicken Caesar salad." He closed it and glimpsed at Tim. "Have you seen any more of the lady you were with at Lucio's?"

Why did his buddy ask that question, and how much did Tim really want to tell him? "Oh, uh, not really." He didn't want to go into the incident last week with Harry Dickson.

"Oh yeah? She seems like a nice person." He jabbed Tim's shoulder. "Good looking, too." Jess squeezed a slice of lemon in his tea.

Tim scanned the room. Only a few people besides him and Jess appeared to be ordering lunch. Everyone else at the bar and the tables had a glass of wine, beer, or a mixed drink.

No one would overhear their conversation, and he wanted to open up. Jess had certainly confided in him at one time. "I... to tell you the truth, I've avoided getting to know her better though I'd like to. It's a long story."

A girl in jeans and a white tee shirt rushed toward them. "Sorry to keep you gentlemen waiting. We're really busy today. What can I get you?"

Tim motioned with his thumb toward Jess. "Same as him. Chicken Caesar salad."

"All right. Two Caesars." She set two placemats and two rolls of silverware in front of them and scurried away.

Jess scratched his head. "Look, Tim. There was a time when you listened to my long story, wrenched me out of a dark hole. I'm ready for anything you want to tell me."

Tim raised the root beer bottle to his lips again. The crisp, bubbly flavor elevated his spirits. If he could trust anyone, it was Jess Colton. "I've had issues with controlling my emotions at times, you might say. I gave into the behavior modeled for me as a child." He gulped. Could he go on? "Are you sure you want to hear this?" He bit his lip.

"If you're afraid I'm going to judge you, forget it. I'm your friend."

He nodded. "When I was in seminary, I got engaged to a woman my sister introduced me to. Rena Telles. She was an exchange student from Brazil attending the same university as my sister. We dated, and eventually she agreed to be my wife."

Jess sipped his tea. "Obviously, it didn't work out."

"No." He ran unsteady fingers through his hair. "This is hard, Jess. To talk about my failures."

"I remember a time when I confessed everything about my miserable life to you—nothing but putty in your hands." Jess laughed. "Go on, brother."

"The problem was we were too much alike, our fiery personalities." He coughed into his fist. "One night we had an argument. I—I lost my temper. I did something I was sorry for later."

"What, man?" Jess's eyes bore down on him.

Tim's shoulders rose with his deep breath. "I raised my hand to her as I yelled in her face and just about hit her. We were in the park. I wound up shoving her, and she fell to the ground." Tim shook his head, and his breath caught. "Thank God she wasn't hurt. My temper is so bad, she could've been." His throat tightened. The vision of Rena on the grass, the anguish in her eyes, still haunted his dreams. No, she wasn't physically hurt, but he'd wounded her in another way.

Jess rubbed his forehead. "Do you ever speak to her now?"

"No. She threw the ring at me. I violated her trust. I don't think she'll ever believe a so-called Christian man again. My sister has hated me ever since." He dumped the remaining root beer down his parched throat and caught the bartender's eye. "I'll take one more."

Jess tilted his head examining Tim's face. "So you have feelings for Roxanne, but you're avoiding her because you're afraid of another relationship."

"That's about it. I fear letting someone down like that. I don't trust myself." Admitting his apprehension out loud made him breathe easier. He tilted the bottle for a long swig.

"That's a rough place to be. I know. I was there once with Holly. I kept thinking I couldn't saddle her with a diabetic husband, a man with no self-control. But the Lord—through your counseling I might add, broke my addiction. If He could take a hopeless food addict to a normal-size guy and keep me there, He can work in your life."

"Yeah, you were pretty much a blimp." Tim chuckled. *When was the last time I laughed?* The Lord had freed his friend and given him a beautiful wife and a baby on the way. Would God do that for him?

Jess offered him a wide grin. "And you've got a listening ear any time you need it. I'm not kidding. After how you helped me, it's the least I can do."

Jess's reminder of God's mighty power lifted his spirit. "Thanks. You're a good friend." He raised his bottle of root beer to his mouth and drained it when the waitress brought the salads.

"Let me bless this, brother." Jess bowed his head.

When his friend finished the prayer, Tim looked up and laughed. "I think this was the first time for me to pray in a bar."

Jess laughed. "Yeah, well, next time let's make reservations."

*****

Tim knelt at the altar and bowed his head. He'd dealt with another difficult Wednesday youth group meeting last night. No pranks. Just inattention by almost all the kids except for Mandy and Mike.

His chest clenched, and he gulped down the urge to yell with his frustration. He leaned back on his heels. In desperation, his shoulders fell forward, and he covered his eyes with his hands. "Dear Lord ..." If God could heal a glutton, He could bring him victory, too. "You are the Author of my life and the new Spirit within me. I beg You, resolve these issues. Show me what to do."

The emotion was almost more than he could bear. Was he a man or a wimp? He hesitated a moment looking at the wooden cross above the altar.

Turning from the stage, he crept down the aisle. His

breath caught in his chest. On the back row, a lone figure sat so still Tim wondered if someone was asleep. Halfway down the aisle, he identified the person—Pastor Downing. Had he heard Tim's pleas to the Lord? He opened his mouth but couldn't find the words. Why was he afraid for Pastor to see his struggles?

"Got a minute?" Pastor scooted over and patted the seat next to him.

"Sure." What now? Surely he wasn't going to chide him for praying too loudly.

His boss raised kind eyes to him. "Uh, Tim. There's something I need to talk to you about."

"Yes, sir?" His palms became damp.

Pastor Downing perused his face. "I'm aware you're having trouble with the teens. If there's anything I can do to help, let me know."

Tim released a breath and laced his fingers. "The main instigator is Johnny Thompson. He pulls a prank almost every Wednesday. Having Joe there helps, but he sometimes leaves the room. Johnny knows how to time his antics."

"Would you like me to sit in on a lesson? I'd be happy to do anything I can."

If Pastor Downing showed up, the teens would act like angels. "I don't know what it would accomplish. But you're welcome to visit any time."

"Remember, call Johnny's parents as a last resort. They'll defend Johnny all the way." He patted Tim's shoulder. "You need to reach the boy."

"I'll remember that." He had to find another way to resolve the issue.

"All right. Let me pray for you." Pastor bowed his head. "Father, I pray You will give my brother in the

Lord wisdom as he deals with these kids at this difficult age. Please put Your calming presence upon them. In Jesus' name."

God heard prayer. But when would things change? "Thanks."

"Oh, and Tim, let's start the plans now for the Christmas craft-fair fundraiser. The hordes of shoppers will be here before we know it."

"Yes, sir." If the project were even half as successful as Roxanne's makeover, he'd be happy. Maybe she would be willing to help again.

He mentally kicked himself. What was he thinking? He couldn't keep reaching out to her.

A smile crossed Pastor Downing's face, then faded. "Oh, and one last thing. I usually don't put much faith in rumors, but I think you should know about the visitors I had yesterday in my office."

Tim's breath snagged. "What visitors?"

"Harry Dixson came in with his girlfriend Janie Cavanaugh. She apparently works with Roxanne Ratner, the young lady who so successfully conducted the makeover fundraiser."

Just the name Harry Dickson sent a chill down his spine.

"Harry says he had lunch in The Grape Vine a week ago with Janie and saw you at the bar guzzling a beer." Pastor Downing replaced a hymnal into the rack.

Tim's heart plummeted, aggravation lodged in his throat. Maybe it looked like he was drinking, but the guy who probably had animosity toward him could've been getting revenge.

Pastor put his hand to his mouth and coughed. "I don't believe in listening to every piece of gossip, but let me ask you, were you at The Grape Vine sitting at the bar?"

Tim clenched his teeth. He needed to speak up for himself but only nodded. What was wrong with him? For a second, the authoritative figure in front of him was his father, accusing him of something he never did. His tongue froze in his mouth.

Pastor Downing leaned forward clasping his hands in front of him. "Were you drinking?"

Tim nodded again. What was he doing keeping his mouth shut? He was a pastor, too. If he'd done anything wrong, it was sitting at the bar so that someone could accuse him of doing something he shouldn't. At least he had a Christian brother as a witness. He lifted his head. "Yes, sir, I was."

Pastor Downing straightened in the pew.

"Hayes root beer. It comes in a brown bottle. I didn't even give it a second thought."

"But at the bar—didn't you know how it would look?"

Tim held up his hand. "I know it gave a look of impropriety. The couple who saw us had every reason to believe I was imbibing. It won't happen again."

"All right. Let's file this under the heading of an unfortunate event. Now go get started on the fundraiser, and I'll continue to pray for you.

He nodded. Words failed him, his body so weary from stress. He stumbled back to his office, locked the door, and fell into the chair behind his desk.

Though he desired to help hurting people, he had to complete his service as youth pastor first. The chances of getting the recommendation from Woodlyn for a position as a pastoral counselor dimmed.

His breath came faster. How dare Harry try to get him in trouble with his *boss*? The familiar rage began building in him. The boiling sensation started in his stomach and lifted to his throat. His limbs trembled—no outlet for his anger here.

He rose from his chair and paced to the window opposite the door to look out at the dreary, dismal day. The familiar volcano within was about to explode. His fingernails dug into the palms of his hands until it became painful. *Dear God, I'm in trouble. I need your help. Things are getting worse, not better.*

Chapter Nine

Roxanne shook the plastic cape and swept the floor around her station. The very pregnant Holly Colton sat in the waiting area up front, her face glowing. If Roxanne were to guess, pregnancy agreed with her.

"Okay, Sweetie." Roxanne winked. "I'm ready for you."

Holly pushed herself up from the chair. "It's not hard to figure out Thanksgiving is only a few weeks off with all the scarecrows, stalks of hay, and cornucopias on the walls. Are you sure you and your Mom don't want to join us for dinner?"

"Oh, Holly. Mom wants to spend a few days up on the peninsula, you know, to kind of get away." She exhaled a deep sigh. "We'll probably eat our turkey, dressing, and pumpkin pie at some restaurant. But thanks, girlfriend."

"Okay, Roxy. If you change your mind, Jess and I will be at home. His folks went on a trip back east."

She patted the seat and swiveled her chair making it easier for Holly to sit.

The attractive woman smiled into the mirror.

"You said you wanted to try some highlights?" She picked up a strand of Holly's hair, examining it.

Jess's wife laughed. "I've got to do something to perk up my self-image. I'm as large as the national debt." Holly gave her a playful poke. "Hey girl, you look like you've never had to worry about weight."

"Well, if the Lord ever brings me a husband, I might have a reason for eating. I could eat all the potato chips I wanted, for the baby, of course."

Cocking her head, Holly offered her a sideways grin. "Have you seen Tim lately?"

"No." Her cheeks grew hot. What? Was she still in high school? She could hold an adult conversation about her feelings. She cleared her throat. "I thought we were becoming friends, but he hasn't called. I guess he's not into me."

No more phone calls. He disappears after the service. She didn't need a wall to fall on her to figure out he wasn't interested in her. She cupped her hand beside her mouth. "I'll tell you the truth, Holly. He makes my heart sing, just looking at him. He's a solid Christian and knows so much about the Bible."

Holly leaned back in the chair and wiggled her right shoe as if she'd seen it for the first time today. "I fell in love with Jess while he was still chubby. I know you see Tim in the same way. You care for the man he is inside."

She rubbed her silver cross. "You're right, but I can't run after him." She swung the cape over Holly and tied the strings behind her. "I shouldn't have picked out his Christmas present. Who knows if I'll get the chance to give it to him?"

"God's in charge of your future." Holly patted her

arm.

"Yes, thanks for the reminder." She picked up a few more strands of Holly's hair.

"Okay, Lady, I'm using a formula that's safe for the baby."

"I appreciate it. Fix it however you think is most flattering. I trust you."

She wove the comb handle through the section of hair, placed the foil under it, and brushed the strands with the color. Good thing Larry left before Holly came in. They'd have more freedom to talk, especially about girl stuff.

When she put the last piece of foil on Holly's head, she set the timer. After the bell dinged, she removed the foils, washed her hair, gave her a haircut, and styled it with the blow-dryer and flat iron. Transforming Holly from nice-looking to gorgeous tickled her insides. "You're beautiful, Lady. Jess will be impressed."

"Now if I can style it as well as you did." Holly rolled her eyes and using her palms, hoisted herself slowly up from the chair. She reached to Roxanne and gave her a hug. "I'll be back one more time before the baby comes."

"Okay, Honey. See you at church." She accepted the check Holly held out to her.

Holly maneuvered out the door and turned to wave at her as she lowered herself into her car.

A tug on Roxanne's sleeve brought her attention back into the shop. Janie stood next to her, the corners of her mouth turned down.

"Roxie, can I talk to you for a minute?"

"Sure, is something wrong? You look worried. Didn't you like my last customer's style?"

"Of course. Nothing like that." She cast her gaze to the floor tiles. "I heard you and her talking about God."

"Yeah?"

"I'm feeling guilty after the other day."

Uncertainty gripped her. Janie looked so serious. "What do you mean?"

Her friend caught her upper lip between her teeth. "I always thought you Christians were stiff, straight-laced people. But I see how special you two are. That's why I'm sorry for what Harry and I did to your friend, Tim."

What she and Harry did to Tim? Was it anything about the other evening when Harry made advances? No way had Roxanne planned to tell Janie. "What are you talking about?"

Her co-worker swallowed hard. "Harry and I, well mainly Harry, tried to get him fired."

The words pelted her like a hailstorm. "Fired?"

"Yes. The other day when Harry and I went out to lunch at The Grape Vine, your friend sat in the bar with another guy." Janie sipped a breath through pinched lips. "He guzzled something in one of those brown glass bottles. Harry claimed he was drinking beer, but we could see the label, Hayes Root Beer." Janie pulled a strand of hair through her fingers. "Harry wanted to get back at him. He told me some story about Tim beating him up, but I believe about half of what he says. Anyway, he made up a lie and went to your pastor. Unfortunately, I'm the one who told Harry Tim worked at the church you attend." Janie placed her hand on her forehead. "I'm sorry we caused him trouble."

Roxanne clinched her fists, fighting against anger for what Janie and Harry did. But the emotion faded as she saw regret in Janie's face. Tension subsided and she took a cleansing breath. Now what should she do? Was Tim's job in jeopardy? Should she tell him what Janie said?

*****

Tim stretched his legs in front of his computer and downed the last of the coffee in the mug. Thanksgiving dinner at Paxton's Diner yesterday stirred the loneliness in his heart he didn't want to admit to. He'd considered calling Roxanne but decided against it because she probably had plans with her mom.

Of course, his folks didn't call. No surprise. Who knew how they celebrated the holiday? Anyway, he welcomed the few days off. He'd felt like cheering when Pastor cancelled his Wednesday night youth meeting.

The L-shaped desk stood in the corner of the small spare bedroom—a good place for his computer. His internet connection worked well the last hour, something it didn't always do. He grabbed his coffee cup, ambled out to the compact kitchen passing the stove and refrigerator to the coffee pot on the counter.

The steam from the hot java warmed his face when he took a sip. He strolled back to his desk, eased down in his rolling chair, and typed in "anger" on his Google search page. The first article didn't tell him anything he didn't already know, a couple of unpleasant repercussions of anger—inappropriate behavior and alienation of friends.

The hardest part of dealing with the debilitating emotion was learning to control it. He even knew the root cause—bitterness toward his father. It didn't help that his dad had modeled the behavior as Tim grew up. Maybe the prayers he offered up to the Lord for two hours last night would.

He still wanted to get Teddy's grave marker—ever since the day he and Roxanne buried the dog. He typed "pet gravestones" into the search engine.

A website popped up. All he needed to do was put in the order and send in Teddy's picture. If nothing else, he wanted to do it as a thank you for Roxanne's help with the fundraiser.

He flinched. The next fundraiser, the craft fair, would take place in less than four weeks. If he were honest, he'd admit his inept ability to raise money. Sure, some of the parents offered to help, but he needed better organizational skills for the event, like Roxanne's.

He stroked his chin. Maybe he'd call her, and she'd take pity on him. His desperation trumped his fear of being around her and falling harder for the woman. He'd deal with his feelings the best he could.

The newspaper lay on his computer table. An ad for the Tacoma Zoolights appeared toward the bottom of the page. Since the *holiday happening* opened this weekend, maybe he could combine his mission of asking Roxanne to help with a trip to the Christmas event he'd wanted to visit. Roxanne would probably enjoy it, too.

His cell lay on the end table in the living room. His throat tightened when he remembered his missing book—Grandmother's book of poems. His hand hovered a moment then he pushed her speed dial number.

He heard three rings.

"Hi, Tim." The halting note to her voice took him off guard. Maybe she didn't want to talk to him.

"Are you busy? I wasn't sure if you were working today."

"Yes, but this is a good time. I'm between customers. How are you?"

"I'm fine." He'd better get right to the subject before she got another client. "I need to ask you a favor. And I'm going to bribe you by seeing if you want to go to the Tacoma Zoolights tonight—before the holiday crowds descend."

"I... uh, sure. It's been a while since we've talked."

He winced. True, he hadn't called her. She'd probably wondered why. As much as he hoped it didn't matter, it probably did.

"And Tim, I've got something to tell you, too."

He listened as she relayed the story about Janie and Harry going to the pastor.

"Thanks for the information, but my boss and I have talked. Everything's fine." Not entirely true. The allegations undoubtedly hadn't helped the elders' opinion of him.

"I'm so glad. Janie's really sorry."

I bet she is. He clenched his fist. But another concern jarred him. He'd probably be less successful at cooling his romantic feelings for her than suppressing his irritation toward the couple who'd caused trouble.

*****

Tim's heart softened at Roxanne's *ooh's* and *ahh's*. "Look at the green spider and its web. Can you imagine all the work that went into this?" She tightened the belt on her knee-length dark-blue Parka and pulled her matching scarf closer around her neck.

"It's chillier out here on Point Defiance than in the city." He shivered as he grasped her gloved hand. "Look at the long line to get in."

"People don't want to miss this amazing sight even if it is freezing."

He circled her waist and tugged her closer as they strolled along the concrete path meandering through the zoo.

"Wow." She pointed to a toucan and walrus created out of brown, gold, silver, and green lights.

He could watch her pretty face all night. "They use over a half million lights on this event."

"The display takes my breath away, like the sky on a starry evening. There's a Santa's sleigh and a Christmas tree."

Maybe the lights took her breath away, but she stole his with her petite red nose and bright eyes.

He released her and rubbed his hands together. Smoke streamed out of their mouths into the frosty air.

A splash of light lit the sky when they wound around on the trail toward the park entrance and snack bar. Tiny bulbs flashing with every color in the rainbow illuminated the tree in front of them. Instead of leaves, the branches were strung with hundreds of miniature globes wound around the bare branches. Even the trunk displayed a mass of glimmering green.

He clutched her hand, so small in his. "Would you like to get some cookies and hot chocolate?"

Her cheerful smile and nod gave him the answer.

He slid the snack bar's glass door open.

Roxanne stepped in front of him into the warm cafe.

"It's so cold outside. We might be in for some snow." Her teeth chattered as she rubbed her hands together.

Only two people in line in front of them. "Two large hot chocolates with marshmallows and some chocolate chip cookies," he said when it was their turn. He gave the cashier a ten. The next attendant passed the steaming cups of cocoa to him and two bags of cookies. He handed a cardboard cup to her as they made their way out to the deck.

Empty of other visitors, plastic tables covered the wooden deck overlooking the path to the lions' cages. He set his drink on the table and drew a chair out for her. Scooting his seat so his shoulder touched hers—for the warmth he told himself—he took a sip of his cocoa. The comforting heat of the hot liquid abated the chill in the air.

Her eyes caught the twinkling lights. "Have you visited the animals in the summer?"

"No. Maybe next year." If he allowed himself to dream, he'd be here with her.

She pulled her fuzzy blue cap down further over her ears and rubbed her gloved hands together. "Next year." She stared at a spot over his shoulder.

A sip of hot chocolate created a warm path to his stomach. His heart soared, like Santa's sled skyrocketing through the sky when he gazed at Roxanne's face, but he couldn't sit here all night gazing at her. "Uh... Roxanne. There's something I'd like to ask you."

"Oh, yes. You mentioned a favor."

He gulped and forged ahead. "I need your help with the Craft Fundraiser coming up right before Christmas. I'd feel a lot better if you'd work alongside me on this."

She peered out at the sea of flickering lights for a moment. Turning to him again, she grinned. "I'd be happy to."

He released the breath he'd been holding. She had a way of looking at him as if he were the only man in the world. Did she have feelings for him, too? The thought made everything seem twice as hard.

She tapped her chin as if pondering some great mystery. "I have tons of ideas, not just for girls, but for guys, too. Things like woodcarving, photography, models of ships, even painted sneakers. The girls could make their own lotions, create bath salts, knit, design cards from rubber stamps—"

"Whoa, you're hired. And if you'll come to the Wednesday meetings with me, you can help get the kids started on their projects. I can't thank you enough."

Something about Roxanne—she seemed so determined about the things she wanted to accomplish. The way she held her mouth and fixed her eyes on him. It made his heart race. He didn't want to admit it, but his feelings for the woman sitting next to him hadn't disappeared, only multiplied.

Should he tell her the truth about his anger issues and ask for her prayers? Maybe one night, in front of a cozy fire, the lights turned low, soft music in the background... He shrugged his shoulders. Where would he come up with that? His freestanding fireplace would have to do.

"Tim, why did you ask me?"

His focus returned to her questioning face. "Ask you what? To come to the Zoolights?"

"No, to help you. Was it because I'm good with crafts?" She peered at him, a query on her face.

He suspected she wanted to know how he felt about her, but could he tell her? Could he confess he had strong feelings for her? He gave himself a mental reprimand. No. He couldn't allow himself the luxury. "I'm confident when you're helping me. I asked you, yes, because of your abilities. But you're my friend, too." How could he give her more?

She blinked her large blue eyes. "Oh." Her breath turned to vapor as she blew out a sigh. Disappointment spread on her face.

"I... I want it to be more, but the time isn't right. There are things in my life... maybe I can explain one of these days." He reached for her hand.

She lowered her gaze as she pressed her lips in a straight line. "It doesn't matter. I'll help because I care about you. Even if you don't feel the same."

"You're wrong. It's just that..."

Her chest rose and fell. She stared down at her hot chocolate. "No. It's okay. I get it. I'm not your type. You were nice to me when we buried Teddy because you felt sorry for me."

His churning emotions stirred in his stomach. Did Roxanne really believe that or was she pressing him into admitting his real feelings, which she probably suspected? Or was she playing games with him? It didn't matter. She was hurting, and he'd take a risk in letting her know he *did* care. But would he be opening a door for her to meet the real Tim, the angry Tim?

"Maybe you should take me home," she whispered.

His lungs constricted at the pain in her eyes. He gave in to his heart and slid his fingers over her chin. "Not yet." He moved closer, and his lips touched hers. Soft. Warm.

Reaching behind her woolly cap, he permitted his arm to slide around her shoulder. Though she pressed him, he needed her to know her conclusions weren't true. When his lips met hers again, he laced his other arm around her.

Their kiss lasted longer then he'd intended, but he couldn't pull away. When he finally did, he slowly opened his eyes to her lovely face only inches away. "Roxanne, someday..."

Chapter Ten

Tim flipped the switch on his electric freestanding fireplace, the warmth a defense against the cold, rainy winter day. He rotated around to warm his backside. A twinge of sentiment scudded through him. Had the final day of this challenging year actually arrived?

The best decision he'd ever made was to ask for Roxanne's help with the craft sale. Not only was she an organizer, but the kids seemed to take to her so much better than him. What was her secret?

She never let him down, not missing a single Wednesday. She'd orchestrated every detail. The day of the event almost ran itself.

He turned his face and chest toward the heat. The Christmas fundraiser made even more money than the makeover day. He couldn't believe the painted sneakers did so well. The girls' bath salts and lotions sold out after the first two hours. The corners of his mouth lifted. The group had built up enough funds now to bring four needy teens to camp.

Though he took Roxanne to lunch the next day to

celebrate, they hadn't been alone—hadn't enjoyed another kiss. Heat traveled up his neck to his ears. What was he doing? If he wanted to avoid getting serious, thinking about kissing her wasn't the way.

Like turning pancakes on a grill, he twisted around again, extending his fingers toward the fire. He had to finalize his plans for his last major responsibility for the school year, spring camp. Since the project was organized by Woodlyn Fellowship and three other churches, he had little say in what his role would be, but at least the administrators of Camp Solid Rock put him in charge of sports—better than crafts, organized games, or even ministry.

He sank into his easy chair. Once camp was over, he'd have plenty of time to get ready for a new job as a pastoral counselor, his heart's desire. But first he had to regain the trust of the elders and get their recommendation.

The three positions he'd found yesterday on the internet looked promising, all opening next fall. The one in Woodlyn caught his eye, but each asked for a written evaluation from his previous employer.

Right now he doubted Pastor Downing would give him a positive referral. Pastor had downplayed the issue with Harry, and he'd been patient concerning Tim's problems with Johnny, but if things didn't get better, Tim might even have to leave the ministry. Not because of his own choice but because of the troubles at Woodlyn. The thought brought a wave of uneasiness. How could he turn his back on the work the Lord had called him to do?

The congregation didn't think much of him. He might as well face it. After all, he hadn't received any invites for Thanksgiving or Christmas. Guess the story about Harry must've spread.

He rose from the chair and padded into the kitchen in his old cloth house shoes and poured another cup of coffee. Something to keep his insides warm. Stirring in some cream, he set the spoon in the sink and shuffled back into the living room.

He sat down again in the chair and set his coffee on the end table, propping his ankle over his knee. Though he hadn't heard from his family, the thought hit him. He needed to pay them a visit, whether he was up for it or not.

His father wanted to punish him, to exclude him from family events now, but did he blame him? The memory of the night before he left for seminary when he told his dad he hated him always remained lodged in his gut. His father resented him because he thought his son too religious and a hypocrite for wanting to be a pastor. His dad hadn't spared his opinion. Tim was a fraud. But if he had shown more patience...

Mom may have wanted to invite him over, but his father would never have allowed it. He brushed aside the resentment. *Dad would be happy if he never heard from me again.*

The empty feeling in his chest depressed him. He couldn't call his parents.

The box with Teddy's grave marker sat on the side table near the front door. He'd wanted to give it to Roxanne for Christmas, but with the holiday rush, UPS delivered it two days after.

He scratched his head. Since today was New Year's Eve, did she have a date for tonight? Maybe he could suggest they get together, and he'd give her the gift.

Could he see her and keep things platonic? He could try. And what about calling her at the last minute? The worst she could say would be no.

He pressed her speed-dial number and reached her voice mail. "Hi, Roxanne. This is spur-of-the-moment, but I was wondering if you'd like to go to dinner tonight. Give me a call." It dawned on him, New Year's Eve. Probably the busiest day for a hairstylist.

The study Bible lay on his end table with the plastic marker at the second lesson on the book of Revelation. He scratched his head as he finished another section. The book turned his brain into a pretzel, especially with so many interpretations. His stomach growled so he strolled into the kitchen to fix some breakfast.

He reached for the pancake mix, and his pocket vibrated. With one glance at the caller ID, he saw her name. "Hi, Roxanne."

"I'd like to go to dinner tonight, but I have another idea. Since the restaurants are so crowded, do you want to come to my house? I'm not the best cook, but I can whip up something."

Her offer warmed him more than the heat from his fireplace. "Not after you've worked all day." He wasn't the most experienced of chefs either, but he'd been in the kitchen a few times. "I'm fixing dinner for you. Do you want me to pick you up?"

"No, that's okay." She chuckled. "I didn't know you could cook." Though her voice sounded serious, a giggle gave away her intentions to tease him.

"We may be having macaroni and cheese from a box, but I'm going to give it a try. I'd like to pray together, too. Maybe ask God's direction in the new year."

"I'd like that."

Her calm, sincere voice echoed in his heart. At this rate, he'd have to work overtime trying to ignore the knowledge that he'd be spending New Year's Eve with a beautiful woman.

The notion dawned on him. He'd be alone with Roxanne in his house. Should he invite another couple? With all the trouble at Woodlyn, he couldn't afford any more problems. But if he couldn't be obedient to the Lord, he wasn't a mature Christian. He'd call Jess, his old accountability partner, to be on the safe side, and tell him he was having company on New Year's Eve and ask for prayer.

He sat down at the kitchen table. Now what was he going to cook?

*****

The front bell dinged, and Tim rushed to the door. The sight of Roxanne, her long blond hair visible under the hood of her white, down-filled coat tripled his heart rate. The hood's fur trim framed her lovely face. How many hours had she spent applying her makeup to look so flawless? "Come in out of the cold."

"I brought some homemade Christmas cookies." She handed him a shoebox tied up with a red ribbon.

"Thank you, Roxy. My first of the season."

After she pushed her hood back and unzipped her coat, he set the cookies on the bookshelf and reached toward her shoulders to help her wiggle out. "You've got more jackets than anyone I know." He laughed and hung the garment in the closet in his computer room.

She looked like a model out of a woman's fashion

magazine in her long sleeve coral sweater and white jeans. Looking at her made his knees weak. He couldn't restrain his wide grin. "Come on in the kitchen."

She set her purse on the end of the couch and followed him, a silly smile on her face.

"What? You don't think I know how to cook? I bought a cookbook and taught myself." He chuckled. "We're having broiled salmon, pasta, and green salad. And Roxanne's Christmas cookies for dessert."

"Oh, that sounds good." She clapped her hands. "If you decide to retire as a youth pastor, you could become a chef. It sounds wonderful."

The grin on his face disappeared as he pressed his lips together. She didn't know how close to the truth she'd come. His job at Woodlyn Fellowship could be over soon if he didn't start making a positive impression on the elders. Faith. In the Lord. The only aspect of his life which sustained him now.

The tray of salmon with lemon slices and capers looked pretty professional, in his opinion. He set it on his dining room table in front of the fire he'd built.

"Can I help?"

"Grab the bread basket, please. Oh, and those two glasses of ice water with lemon wedges." The bowl of tossed greens sat on the shelf in the refrigerator. He grasped the wooden container and set it on the table. "May I say the blessing?"

She grinned and bowed her head.

He grasped her hands. "Lord, bless this food to our nourishment. And be the Shepherd over our lives in this New Year, transforming us according to Your perfect will."

She slipped into the dining room chair when he

pulled it out from under the table. Cocking an eyebrow, she blessed him with a smile. "Not only can you cook, you're a gentleman."

Not always. To cast away thoughts of his failures was imperative now. Roxanne sat across from him, not Rena. He passed her the bread basket, and she placed a roll on her plate then set her napkin in her lap.

With amusement, he watched her as she devoured lots of dainty bites of salmon and pasta—the most he'd ever seen her eat.

She finished a bite of salad. "You show me up in the kitchen. Now I can't have you over." She dabbed at her mouth with her napkin.

Was she kidding? "Why do you say that?"

"Because. I'm a lousy cook." Her smile evaporated. She was serious.

"I bet you're not as bad as you think."

She bit the tip of her little finger. "I watched my mother go to great lengths only to fail." The last piece of salmon disappeared from her plate.

Her mother's failures? In the kitchen? The expression on her face told Tim she meant more than culinary failures. "What happened?"

"Dad said..." Roxanne's words seemed to lodge in her throat, and she took a sip of water.

He had to know more. "You mentioned he left when you were a child." Tim scooped salmon on his fork.

She pinned him with a hard look then stared at her plate. "I don't usually share this with everyone."

"I'm not everyone. I'm your friend. Tell me what happened with your parents." His gaze fixed on her face, his counseling heart kicking in.

She sighed as she heaved her shoulders then dropped

them. "My dad used to promise me he'd always be there, that he loved me. He used to say it over and over." Pink filled her cheeks.

"But he stopped?"

She nodded. "One night, my mom made a special dinner." She ran her finger along the rim of her glass. "After that I didn't want anything to do with the kitchen."

"Go on."

She reached into her pocket and retrieved a tissue. "She burned lamb chops, and the odor of charcoal and grease filled the whole house. Dad came home from work and threw his car keys down on the table. Even today, I still hear the clink. I'd never seen him so agitated. He went upstairs and packed. Said he was leaving." She bit the side of her lip. "When he walked out the door, I tugged on his coat, begging him not to go. Always before, when I cried, he'd hug me and tell me everything was fine. This time he didn't. He gave me an odd look and walked out. My mom cried, not loud crying, but soft tears, and let him go. No coaxing him to come back. Nothing."

"I'm sorry." He reached for her hand.

She dabbed her eyes with the tissue. "At the time, I thought he left because of the burned meat. Of course I found out later, the incident was the culmination of many years of problems between my parents. But my distaste for the kitchen remained."

Her disclosure made his words easier. "I had some rough times with my father growing up as well. He didn't leave my mom but sometimes I wish he had. Dad's a very angry man. But, hey, this is not the way to celebrate New Year's Eve." He rose and picked up their plates.

She followed him into the kitchen with the water glasses. "I'd like to leave those memories in the old year."

"Definitely." Maybe he shouldn't have encouraged her to talk about her past. Compassion tromped through his heart. Now a better idea of her childhood formed in his mind. He wanted to protect her from more than loud-mouthed drunks.

His kitchen never got so clean, so fast. They cleared the plates, stuck the dishes in the dishwasher, and wiped down the counter tops.

"Want to try some of your cookies?" he said.

"How about if we bring in the New Year with them?" She patted her stomach. "I'm too full right now."

"Good idea." Roxanne's gift sat on the side table by the door. "Come sit on the couch. I have something for you." Joy rose in his chest. What would she say when she saw Teddy's marker?

She sat on the couch and drew a small box out of her purse, the kind that held jewelry. "I have something for you, too." With a coy smile, she set the package next to her.

He hadn't counted on getting anything from her. In fact, it was the first Christmas present he'd received this year, even if it was on New Year's Eve. "Who goes first?" He retrieved the package from the hall table and set it on the floor.

"You." Roxanne nudged the small box wrapped in gold paper toward him.

He lifted off the red bow, removed the outside wrap, and lifted the lid. His heart beat faster. He had no idea what to expect. Tissue filled the box, so he peeled it back and pulled out a silver ID bracelet.

"Well, what do you think?" She clasped her hands under her chin.

He turned the bracelet over. Silver links connected a flat band with engraving on the front. "'The Lord is our refuge.'" He flipped it on the other side. "'To Tim, from Roxanne.'"

Words wedged in his throat. He swiveled his knees to face her. "Would you put it on?" He couldn't remember a time he'd received a gift that meant more. The scripture said so much.

She leaned closer, her flowery fragrance intoxicating. With soft hands, she wrapped the bracelet around his wrist and attached the clasp.

Her thoughtful gesture touched him—in a place where distrust and anger usually dwelled. "I'm not sure what to say, Roxanne. Just... thank you."

"Oh, Tim, you're welcome. Now, I can't wait any longer to see what's in that package." Roxanne pointed to her gift.

A chuckle bubbled out of his chest as he lifted the present and passed it to her. "I hope you like it."

After she turned the box around, she set it on her lap and unwrapped the silver paper. With a slow movement, she reached in. Her mouth opened and closed again. She took a breath and read the inscription. "*Teddy Ratner.*"

The day he died appeared under his name. To the right of the inscription, the small green frame displayed the weather-proof picture of Teddy. "I'll be happy to install it for you."

She only stared at it and turned it over a couple of

times in her hands. Maybe she didn't like it. He leaned closer to look at her face.

A small tear ran down her cheek.

"I didn't mean to give you something that would make you cry."

She lifted moist eyes to him. "This is the most special gift I've ever received." The marker rested against her chest as if it were a great treasure. She leaned her head on his shoulder. "Thank you."

He relaxed onto the couch.

Roxanne made no effort to move. Finally, she sat up to face him. "You said the night at the Zoolights, you might be able to share something with me at another time. Is this the time?"

Was it time? He wanted her to know, wanted to make a commitment. But did he dare?

He rose from the couch and ambled to the fireplace, the warmth bringing him courage. Turning, he faced her. The acceptance in her eyes prompted him to continue. "My life growing up was less than ideal. Many times I'd witnessed my father's anger and cruelty toward my mother. And to me, too."

Could he go on? Should he? He ran his hand through his hair. "I haven't... how should I say it? I haven't found victory over my past. Sometimes I'm just like him." He heaved in a breath.

She rose from the couch and glided toward him, her face mere inches from his.

He pulled her near as if she'd shield him from the part of his nature he abhorred. "Sometimes I don't trust myself not to lose my temper." How could he explain a lifetime of turmoil to her?

She stepped back and peered into his face. "Don't

you think through the Lord you could overcome it?"

Her childlike faith warmed him, yet brought frustration. "I—I don't know. I would hope so, but I'm afraid I might do to you what..." Tim clamped his mouth shut. *What I did to Rena.*

She furrowed her brow and studied his face as if she could glean the meaning of his words there.

He grasped her hand. "Roxanne, I have feelings for you." He hadn't planned to say this. But they were out now.

Her fingers traveled around his neck, and she whispered in his ear. "Me, too."

Truth washed over him as he gazed into her radiant eyes. The way he felt about her was deeper than his feelings for Rena. Rena was his first romance, and he'd been more in love with the notion of having a girlfriend than actually loving her. With Roxanne, it felt solid and real.

How easy it was to cup both her cheeks. His lips met hers, tentatively at first, but when she pressed against him, he allowed his mouth to discover hers more deeply. His hand roamed along her silky tresses from her head to her small shoulder blades.

How long had his fingers roamed over her shoulders and arms or his lips explored hers before reality broke in? *I shouldn't be doing this.* Her nearness set him on fire. *Stop.*

He tried to regain the willpower to step away, but Roxanne held him tighter. Her lips trailed to his neck, then his ear. A stroke of lightening stabbed him.

"Tim, I... I want you. This one time," she whispered.

"Roxanne." He desired her more than he could say. Would God look the other way? What would it hurt?

He put both hands on her face, and when his lips met hers again, he could barely breathe.

Her fingers played with the top button on his shirt.

He had to resist... for the sake of his job but most of all in submission to God. He drew her hands away from his chest. *What was I thinking? God forgive me.* "Roxanne, we can't do this. It's wrong."

"But if two people really care about each other..."

His heart raced as he walked to the window and opened the mini-blinds. The Christmas lights up and down the street shone, in celebration of the season. "In the Word, it says intimacy before marriage is wrong. If I went to bed with you, it would be a willful sin."

"Don't you like me? Am I not good enough for you?"

He couldn't deny the pain in her voice, but she hadn't perceived a word he said, hadn't even tried to understand. Frustration built in him. Didn't she know right from wrong? "You'd better go home and read your Bible."

The minute the words were out of his mouth, he knew he'd said the wrong thing. He hadn't let her down gently, but he couldn't stop the words. She needed to know how disobedient it would be. "If you've been a Christian for a while, you might've read the part of the Bible that speaks about purity before marriage."

She picked up Teddy's grave marker and stuffed it in the box. "I need my coat now." Each word was a sword cutting the air. She glanced at her image in the mirror in the entryway and fluffed her hair.

"Forgive me, Roxanne. I was too harsh."

"I need to go." Her tense voice chilled him.

The thought struck him like a blow to his head. Had Roxanne been with another man? She was a new

Christian. He prayed God would place His gentle hands on her and work in her life.

He brought her coat from the other room and held it up so she could slip her arms in, but she grabbed it and threw it over her shoulder picking up her gift and purse.

"Please, Roxy. Try to understand." There was nothing he could say now to redeem the evening, yet his commitment to the Lord exceeded everything else.

She whirled toward him. "Thank you for dinner and for Teddy's marker." Her stiff words echoed in the entryway. A tear rolled down her cheek as she turned the lock and glided through the threshold. "Oh, and Happy New Year."

*****

Roxanne woke up early on a morning when she could've slept late—New Year's Day. Even a deep breath didn't bring energy to her tired body after only four hours sleep.

Last night after she drove back from Tim's, she'd plopped down on the couch and nosed around for her Bible. At midnight, when she read the scriptures, she remembered how she and Tim were going to bring in the New Year and eat cookies. Disappointment grabbed her heart.

She identified the passage she wanted in I Corinthians after a glance in her concordance. The words *The body is not meant for immorality, but for the Lord* hit her upside her face. But the next scripture disturbed her the most. First Thessalonians told her the Christian should avoid intimacy before marriage. Each must learn to control his own body in a way which is holy and honorable, not in passionate lust.

The truth became obvious. Last night she'd been aware of what the Word taught, but reading it again solidified her understanding. Why did she think it wouldn't matter? Heat filled her cheeks. She knew the reason—she longed for affirmation from a man, and Tim's attention would provide that.

She rubbed her eyes with her fists, swung her legs around the side of the bed, and stood. Muted daylight peeked through her blinds. Probably another rainy morning.

Maybe a cup of coffee would clear her mind. She stepped into the kitchen, pulled out the container with the fragrant ground coffee, and placed a few scoops along with water in her coffee maker. Her wide yawn spoke of fatigue from sleep loss. She added one more scoop to the filter and slumped down into the kitchen chair, hands over her face.

Reality seeped into her thoughts. After Dad left, she missed his pats on the back and kisses on her cheek—the times when she sat on his knee, and he listened to her childish stories. The coffee maker's sighs drew her attention. Her sighs were louder. She'd tried to use Tim's affection as a replacement. An icy chill careened down her spine. Though she missed Dad's love as a child, she couldn't make up for it with a sinful act. And that obviously wasn't the way to a healthy, godly relationship with Tim. Thank God he hadn't given in when she offered herself.

She ignored the coffee maker and stumbled back to her bedroom kneeling on the carpet beside her bed. "Dear Lord, forgive me for what I did last night. My motives were all wrong." Her heart refused to stop aching.

Pushing up from the bedside, she cleared her dry throat. She knew what she needed to do. With a shaking hand, she picked up her cell from her night table. Nine-thirty. He'd be awake.

Fear raced through her chest. She set her phone down again. The small amount of courage she had after her prayer disappeared. She paced to the kitchen and back. Tim would ridicule her or maybe even laugh at her.

She strode the perimeter of her bedroom more times than she could count. What would the Lord have her do? Surely it would be to apologize to Tim. She peered at her cell and picked it up again. With trembling fingers pushed his speed dial number.

The phone rang so many times she suspected he hadn't awakened or else didn't want to talk to her. His voice mail would come on any second. Then she heard him. "Hello, Roxanne." Did she detect a note of disgust in his voice?

Her words stuck in her throat for a second, and she cleared her throat. "Tim. I... I need to tell you I'm sorry." Only the sound of his breathing carried over the line. She bit the inside of her cheek. "Please forgive me. I was wrong last night. I didn't sleep. All I could think of was what a position I put you in and how I'd ignored the Word of God. At least say you forgive me."

A raspy cough met her ear. "I forgive you, but I need to ask your forgiveness as well. I should've been gentle with you. You're new in your Christian faith, and I lost my temper."

She couldn't believe it. Tim apologizing? "I take all the blame, but thank you for saying that."

"I haven't changed my mind about you. Let's just take it slow. And pray for God's direction."

"I want that, too. Happy New Year again." A weight lifted from her shoulders as she hung up.

She poured herself a cup of coffee and thumbed through the piles of credit card bills. If she was lucky, she could pay half of the balance due this month.

The knock on her front door startled her. She pulled it open as far as the chain would allow. "Larry, happy New Year." She unclasped the lock. "What are you doing here?"

He scowled at her. "I've got some bad news. I'm selling the shop and the new owners have their own staff. You and Janie are going to have to find new jobs."

Perspiration covered her forehead despite the cool day. "You don't mean it. When?"

"I've been working on the transaction for a while but didn't want to mention it until I was sure. You have to be out of the shop and the apartment by tomorrow night. Since you're on month-to-month here, and your rent is due on the first, we'll call it even." He turned around on her porch and marched down the stairs.

Chapter Eleven

Larry's words bounced off Roxanne's brain. She didn't want to grasp their reality, yet she couldn't deny the meaning. "You sold the shop, and I have to leave?" In an attempt to clear her thinking, she shook her head.

"You heard me." He shouted from halfway down the outside stairs from her apartment to the ground level.

She tugged her sweater closer and moved onto the small porch. "How could you do this? I thought you liked Janie and me."

Larry stopped at the bottom of the stairs and swiveled around to her, palms up, as if he couldn't be held responsible. "Of course, I like you both, but when a financial opportunity comes along, I can't turn it down. That's life. You'll find another shop easy enough. You're a good stylist."

"But... but you didn't give me much notice."

He shrugged and headed to the front door of the shop.

Her body and emotions froze as the significance of his words infiltrated her brain. Could New Year's Day start off any worse? She twisted around slinking back into the kitchen and sank into the chair at the small wooden table. No job, no home, and she'd made a mess out of her relationship with Tim.

Reality struck her like an electric shock. She had to pack up. Her kitchen supplies were meager—a few dishes and some silverware, a couple of pots in her cabinet. Then her mind flipped through the contents of her bedroom, and her hands grew icy. The dozens of sweaters, jeans, jackets, and shoes in her closet and drawers weren't skimpy.

With her eyes closed, she rested her head in two hands. The brunt of Larry's words burrowed into her mind and sent tears rolling down her cheeks.

Where would she go? The only thing to do was move back home with Mom—for now. Thank God she had the option. But a job? What was she going to do about employment? And what about her goal of owning her own shop?

Maybe she could turn an unfortunate situation into something beneficial. She'd read the verse in her Bible about how God works all things for good for those who love Him. She snapped to her feet and paced the kitchen floor.

First she'd have to call her mother and see if she could come home. Afterwards she'd phone Tim to help her move—if he really hadn't held last night against her. She pinched the bridge of her nose and reached for the phone.

"Hi, honey. Are you coming over today?" Her mother's voice soothed away some of the tension.

"Mom." *How do I approach the subject?* "I'll just come right out and ask. My boss is selling the business. Can I move back home for a while?" She tightened her shoulders and marched around the tiny living room.

"You know I'd love to have you. You're always welcome. What happened?"

"He's selling the shop." She tamped down the emotion as she relayed Larry's order. "I need to bring some things over today."

"I'll be here."

The muscle in her jaw twitched. "Thanks, Mom. I'm going to see if I can get a friend to help me."

"Okay, honey. I'll go check your room to make sure it's ready."

Her dear mother. What would she do without her? Maybe the Lord could use Roxanne to nudge her closer to Him. "Thank you, Mom."

She looked around her living room and bedroom. All she needed would be a few boxes. The furniture stayed with the apartment. It might take a truck when it came to her shoes and clothes, though.

Maybe she should rent a moving van. Ha. How could she do that? Her credit card was maxed out.

She'd have to rely on their cars. Between hers and Tim's, she could make it—if he'd help her. First she had to ask him. Her palms grew damp when she picked up her cell again. He answered on the second ring.

"Tim, it's me again."

"Hello, again."

The sound of his deep, calm voice brought a wave of self-pity. "I need a huge favor."

"What's up?"

Explaining what happened was hard, but she couldn't cry. "And I've got to find a job as soon as possible." No way would she tell him she couldn't place any more charges on her card.

"Let's start by getting you moved to your mom's.

Afterwards we'll worry about a job."

We. Tim said we. Did he see her as part of his life?

"But first, let's pray."

Tim sought the Lord first. He had his priorities right as far as she was concerned.

"Lord, I pray for my sister, Roxanne. You said to seek first the kingdom of God and all these other things would be added to you. I've witnessed her seeking You first."

Her cheeks flamed. She hadn't sought the Lord first last night.

"So I ask You to provide for her, but more than that, bring her victory in every area of her life. I care about her, Lord, and I know You do, too. Amen."

She released a sigh of relief. "Thank you."

"I'll be over in about an hour."

The tension in her stomach relaxed a little. "I appreciate you."

"You just like me for my muscles." His chuckle sprinkled sunshine on her unpleasant situation.

Roxanne freed the slow giggle in her throat and filled her lungs with fresh air. But then her hopes plummeted to a new low. How could she get her own shop? She didn't have money to buy anything—no resources for a down payment to a bank. God wasn't going to send her money from Heaven.

*****

Roxanne grabbed the flattened boxes she and Janie left next to the dumpster behind the shop and juggled them up the stairs to her soon to-be-empty apartment then winced. What would Tim say if he saw all the garments she'd stuffed into her closet and drawers? If she started in the bedroom first, maybe she could pack most everything before he got there.

It didn't take long to reassemble the boxes with cellophane tape. Kenneth Cole and Versace shoes came flying from the top shelf of her closet. She pulled folded Dior sweaters and Donna Karan shirts from her drawers and stacked them in a neat pile in the larger container. Afterwards she'd fill other cartons with the rest of the stuff—pajamas, scarves, tee shirts, underwear, and a couple of Coach purses.

The buzzer made her jump. She dropped the down-filled jacket on the bed and headed toward the door. A glance through the peephole told her Tim had arrived. She checked her hair and makeup in the living room mirror and released the security chain.

He stood on her small porch at the top of the stairs, drew his shoulders up near his ears, and shivered. "Hi, Roxanne." No smile.

"Please, come in." She backed away from the door.

He scuffed his shoe on the doorstep. Maybe he decided not to forgive her after all.

"I can't tell you how grateful I am—because you're here but also for your forgiveness."

He lifted his eyes and nodded. "You're welcome. I... uh, I guess I had an awkward moment." He scratched his head and walked in. "Of course, I forgave you." Looking around the kitchen, he rubbed his hands together. "Okay, let's do this." A smile lit his face. "Last night is in the past."

Heat filled her cheeks. She wished last night had never happened. "I'm still working on the bedroom. Would you mind packing up the kitchen items?"

"Sure. Everything goes?" He poked around the room opening cabinets and drawers.

"Yes. There are a couple of boxes over by the couch in the living room." She pointed to the last two she'd collected. "I'll finish in the back."

The rattling of pots and pans told her he made progress. She filled several more containers in the bedroom, emptying part of the contents of the drawers. The clothes on hangers resting on the bed could lie in the back of hers or Tim's car. She headed through the living room to the kitchen.

Tim beamed as he grabbed a sheet of newspaper. "I took the liberty of bringing these from my car to wrap breakables in."

She tapped her forehead with her fist. "How ditsy can I get? I didn't even think of it."

"I packed everything from the kitchen in two boxes, and there's still room in the second one. Hey, this isn't too bad. I'm taking these downstairs."

The open doors displayed the empty cupboards. "Can I help?"

"No, thanks. You can finish in the bedroom." He bent down and picked up a container.

"Be careful." She rushed toward the door to open it.

With clenched teeth, she tried to catch her breath. In a few minutes he would see what she'd packed so far. Would he ask questions or make any negative comments?

She snuck back to the bedroom and hauled five large boxes into the living room, the weight of her clothes as heavy as her unpaid bills. She panicked. This didn't include the rest of the things on hangers.

The door swung open as Tim marched into the

kitchen. He rubbed his bicep on his right arm. "We're almost done, right?"

The lump in her stomach turned rock hard. "Just the rest of my clothes," she gulped.

His eyes gaped when he strolled into the living room and saw the boxes. "These... all these are your clothes?"

"There's more." She raised a restraining hand. "I'll... let me go get the rest." If she allowed him into the bedroom, he might feel awkward. Her heart fell when he stood in the living room with his mouth hanging open. She set the last five cartons in front of him. Then she gathered the hanging clothes dropping them to the couch.

He gasped. "You've got to be kidding."

*****

Tim draped the last load of garments over his shoulder and tramped down the stairs. Never in his life had he seen such a collection. His mother and sister together probably had half the wardrobe Roxanne did.

He'd filled the trunks, backseats, and passenger seats of both their cars, and there was still more. Since they'd left several piles of clothes on hangers in the apartment, they'd have to make a second trip. A nagging thought worked into his head. How could she afford all these clothes? Did she make that much money as a hair stylist?

On the porch, she pulled the door shut and locked it then ambled down the stairs. She glanced back at the apartment for a moment. His heart ached for her situation and at the same time, he feared she might be in debt—saddled with too many payments.

Her usual smile was absent as she juggled a couple of shoeboxes under her arm.

"We'll come back for the rest." He stuffed the shoes into the backseat.

"Thank you for not saying anything."

"About what?"

"You know about what. We don't have to pretend."

"You mean your clothes? Do you want to tell me about it?" *She's right. We don't need to ignore the truth.*

"You've guessed my problem by now. I overspend."

He strode beside her into the salon. "More like a shop-alcoholic?"

With her eyes squeezed shut, she nodded. "I'm working on my issues. But thanks for not ridiculing me." She cleared out her station stuffing the items in a large shopping bag.

Memories of the night he protected her from Harry followed him as he walked out the door with Roxanne. His fingers fell on her arm. "Granted, you've got a tough problem. And an expensive one. But look, all things are possible with God."

"Somehow that doesn't make me feel any better." She ran a finger under her eye.

"I always seem to come on too strong." He circled her shoulders with his arm. "I can't criticize you. My struggles carry more impact than yours. We'll talk it over, get the problem out in the open. God's got the answers, Roxy."

Chapter Twelve

Tim backed away from his computer and stretched. A week into the new year already. He took a sip of morning coffee. Saturdays were a lifeline to his sanity.

He'd started off right doing a couple of good deeds—helping Roxanne pack up and move and installing Teddy's grave marker. He might as well complete the list—visit his parents, his New Year's resolution.

His watch indicated ten o'clock. What was stopping him? He'd always adhered to the philosophy that procrastination only made things worse. His stomach lurched as he threw on his coat, picked up his keys, and locked the door.

The CD player would serve as a distraction. He punched the *play* button. Might as well settle back for the hour's drive to Timberwood. If he prayed the entire time, could he control the scorching anger he feared would erupt when he reached his childhood home and talked to his father? Maybe this time he and his dad could find resolution. He could always hope.

He pulled onto I-5 North. Too soon he entered the city limits, his nerves a jangled mess. How would his parents feel about him coming unannounced? If he'd called first, they'd probably leave before he got there. Dad would anyway.

He parked his car at the curb of the two-story home with the familiar gray and white vinyl siding in their quiet neighborhood, his dad's SUV parked in the driveway. How hard would it be to talk to him? *Who am I kidding?* He blew out a stream of air.

Ringing the bell seemed crazy since he used to live here, but the door was locked. When his mother appeared, she gasped and clutched her throat. Did it seem *that* offensive for him to knock on his parents' front door? After a moment, she relaxed and a bright smile spread on her face. She stepped out on the porch to hug him.

"Tim. This is a surprise." She squeezed his hand. Had she lost weight? Streaks of gray appeared in her dark brown hair. He didn't remember the tiny creases around her eyes.

"I didn't call ahead, Mom."

Her eyes traced his face, and she wrinkled her brow as if his presence presented a problem. "Uh... do you want to come on in?" She stepped back into the entry.

"Is it okay?" He had to ask permission to walk into his childhood home.

Again, Mom surveyed him as if assessing a task she had to tackle. "Sure, honey."

The house hadn't changed much since he'd lived there. Beige carpeted stairs ran along the wall straight ahead, and the bright kitchen with large windows overlooking the backyard and greenbelt jogged his memory. The formal living room with walnut paneled walls, the room reserved for guests only, sat empty with a couch, coffee table, two chairs, and a few pictures on the wall, the space his father forbad him to enter as a kid.

Tim caught a breath. Wasn't hard to figure out where his father was, in the darkened den on the other side probably watching ESPN, if the cheering was any indication.

Mom squeezed her hands together. "Do you think you want to see Dad, or would you like to come into the kitchen with me?" Her face held lines etched into her forehead and the sides of her mouth, reflecting the strain of the years she'd endured.

"Mom, I missed you at Christmas." He blurted the words out and wrapped her in a hug. What was he, a child again? He forced back his emotion.

The rims of her eyes reddened. "Son, I missed you, too. But you know how your father is." She bit her lip. "Go on in there if you want. I'll be in the kitchen." She pointed to the den and squeezed her hands again.

Why couldn't his mother stand up to Dad just once? If Tim had ever seen a case of codependency, Mom exemplified it.

Dad, his dark hair graying like Mom's, sat in his easy chair with feet propped up on the footrest. A pouch in his midsection protruded under his tee shirt. His eyes remained on the TV screen, though he didn't seem too excited about the game.

Tim hesitated then shuffled into the den, his heart pounding. "Hello, Dad."

His father gawked at him a moment and glanced toward the door. "Marion. You didn't tell me Tim was coming." His shouts must've carried to the kitchen.

Like Edith Bunker, his mother ran into the den out of breath. "Oh, Raymond, he just arrived a few minutes ago."

Dad snatched his attention from Mom to the TV and raised the volume.

Not exactly welcome, am I? "I didn't give either of you any warning. I won't stay long."

The unfriendly man folded his hands over his chest and gaped at the screen, no words for Tim.

Mom ran a hand through her hair and backed out of the den.

"I came by to tell you Happy New Year." He took a risk and eased down on the couch.

Dad kept his eyes glued on the game.

Rocks pelted Tim's stomach. The TV apparently held more importance than he.

"You made it plain the last time I saw you that you didn't have much use for me. You said you hated me."

Maybe Tim fared better with silence than Dad's cutting words. "I... I'm sorry. If there's any way we could make amends, I'd like that." He fidgeted on the couch. "Maybe a new start in a new year."

"Humph." Dad still hadn't taken his eyes off the TV. "You've got all that religion now. You'd start nitpicking, telling me all my faults." His father kicked the footrest back into place and sat up straight. "You're a hypocrite. Acting pious and yet so spiteful to your own sister."

"What do you mean?"

The older man gave him a quick look. "Well, the minute your fiancée breaks up with you, you stop talking to Janelle because she and Rena are friends. Your sister told me a real nice story, too."

"No. It's not like that." He studied his fingers in his lap. "It was all an awful mistake." He couldn't go on.

He'd fallen into his own trap and couldn't possibly tell his father the details. Dad would have no sympathy and probably wouldn't believe what he said.

"I don't want you coming over here with some holier than thou attitude."

"You're not willing to give me a chance, are you?" Heat rose on Tim's neck and traveled to his ears. He should've known better. His father didn't care to try, and his sister hadn't helped. "If that's the way you want it." He spoke a few decibels louder than he'd intended.

"Yeah, that's the way I want it." Dad pushed the lever to recline his chair and leaned back.

Fury rose in Tim's chest. He'd hoped he would work things out at home, but he couldn't have been more wrong. To make an exit before he said anything else—that's all he could do. He marched from the den into the entry. No sense in saying good-bye to his mother. It would only stir up too many emotions in both of them. He jerked the front door open and slammed into Janelle.

"Leaving so soon?" She took a step back, her hostility mirroring their father's.

"Hello, Janelle. Looks like you won't have to worry about any unpleasant family reunions. I was just going."

"Going to see your girlfriend, or did she take my advice and dump you?" She pushed past him into the house.

His jaw muscle twitched. Could she be talking about Roxanne?

She whirled around to him, her hands on her waist. "Answer me. Are you still dating that cute little blond?"

A pang of sorrow gripped his heart. Two members of his family and he couldn't even be in the same room with them without an argument. "If you mean Roxanne, yes, we're still friends."

"Well, if she didn't believe me, she'll find out soon enough about how you treat women. I think your boss needs to know, too."

"What are you talking about? She didn't take your advice?" He gritted his teeth. "And what does Pastor Downing need to know?" A searing pain roiled his belly.

"I see she didn't tell you. We had quite a little chat awhile back about you and Rena."

*****

Tim waved at Nancy when he trudged by her office on the way to his. Three weeks had lapsed, and he still couldn't put the day at Timberwood out of his mind. He'd only made his family situation worse.

He hated to avoid Roxanne now, but he didn't want to find out what Janelle had told her about him and Rena. Too, he was afraid Roxanne might want to discuss it. His situation with his father was worse now. How could he explain all that to his friend?

He still didn't trust himself not to lose his temper with her. The visit home had confirmed how unprepared he was for another relationship... his lack of control over anger. He swiped a hand across his mouth.

Roxanne must be thoroughly confused. Every time he saw her at church, he had no choice but to wave and walk away. Maybe she'd think he was busy with the teens. He opened the door, switched on the light, and ambled to the window to gaze out at the gray skies and the tall Douglas fir growing by the side of the church.

The weather reflected his mood. Would the day ever come when his family would be free to love each other?

He circled around at the knock. "Yes, come in."

Pastor Downing stuck his head around the door, a smile noticeably absent. "Tim, do you have a minute?"

"Sure." He wanted to think Pastor needed to talk about the order for the new Sunday school books, but he doubted it. "Sit down."

The older man eased into the extra office chair. Pastor sat for a moment peering at him, as if formulating what he wanted to say then cleared his throat. "Tim, once again, I've had a disturbing visitor in my office." He pulled on his shirt buttons. "Yesterday, right after you'd gone to lunch."

His shoulders slumped. Surely Harry hadn't come back with another tale. As far as he knew, Janie's boyfriend left town. "Who was it?"

"I'm afraid it was your sister."

His heart stopped. Janelle had threatened to talk to the pastor. Guess it took her three weeks to get up her courage.

"I'm so sorry to come in here like this." He shifted in the chair. "But would your sister lie about you?" Pastor pinched his lips together in a firm line.

What Janelle said wasn't hard to figure out. Shaking his head back and forth didn't make the situation go away. "No, she probably wouldn't."

"When you came before the board, you mentioned you'd struggled with anger issues but didn't disclose any details. You said you'd resolved your problems." Pastor scratched his head. "But you didn't mention the extent of your concerns. I realize this was before you came to us, but the accusation is serious. I'd like to believe you've overcome the past." He chewed on his lip then took a breath. "Did you hit a woman when you were in seminary?"

"Please. Try to understand."

"Understand what?" Pastor's words were hot, searing knives.

Tim had no choice but to confide in the man. In a few minutes, the pastor would administer his punishment for his mistake with Rena. He'd better face up to it. "It's true what my sister said. In a moment of frustration, I..." It'd been so much easier confiding in Jess. "I shoved a woman, and she fell." He could no longer disguise his emotion. "I've repented and asked God so many times for freedom from my compulsive temperament."

Now he couldn't restrain the volume of his voice and his building fury. "Pastor, I want you to understand, not pity me. I need your help, your counsel, not your reprimand."

Pastor Downing's scrutiny pierced him as his words spilled out. What was his boss thinking? He prayed Pastor filtered his evaluation with compassion. Would the elders want to keep him on?

His mentor gripped his shoulder. "I understand and trust you, but how about asking Rena's forgiveness?"

He stroked his chin. *Why didn't I think of that?* He was afraid he knew the answer. Fear of her reaction.

Pastor folded his hands in his lap. "There's one more distressing accusation your sister made."

He jolted in his seat. What more could Janelle say? She had nothing else on him.

"Are you having an intimate relationship with Roxanne Ratner?"

Chapter Thirteen

"Is that what my sister told you?" Tim bolted up from behind his desk. "Certainly not." He stormed around to face the man.

Pastor Downing nodded his head. "Your sister's accusation worries me."

Tim fought to recapture his breath. "I admitted to having problems in the relationship with my former fiancée. And thank you. You were kind to listen. But what my sister told you is a lie." He raked his hand through his hair. "I'm concerned, more for Roxanne's sake than mine. I'd never want her character muddied. No, sir. Janelle's words are not accurate."

In truth, Janelle's claim came close to becoming reality New Year's Eve—if he hadn't stood up for what he knew to be right. The thought brought a chill down his spine. *Thank you, Lord for Your strength.*

Pastor Downing nodded with a half-smile. "I have no doubt you're telling me the truth. But I felt I needed to relay to you what your sister said."

"I'm glad you told me—if nothing else, to protect Roxanne's reputation in your eyes." The gray day outside the window didn't cheer him. He'd stood up for her, yet he was the stronger of the two on this.

The spare chair sat facing the pastor, and Tim slumped down. "There is something I'd like to talk to you about." He cleared his throat. "I do have feelings for Roxanne, but I'm afraid of a relationship because of my past."

The kindly man grinned. "Son, I'll admit you've had some hard breaks and difficult struggles, but from all my observations, I believe your heart is in the right place." He sat up straighter. "Allow the Lord to work His will in you through the Holy Spirit."

His look caught Tim's and held it. "I generally don't share this, but the Lord brought me out of a deep pit one time. I nearly lost my family, my home, and my job because of it."

The pastor had struggled like Tim? He'd never have suspected it.

His boss's toe tapped a nervous beat. "I nursed an addiction to gambling." He paused then cleared his throat. "But you see, God was able to set me free, and He's able to do the same for you, rescue you from the turbulent emotions inside."

Pastor's name for him—*Son*—felt like warm water washing over him on a cold day. How different his life would've been if he'd had an earthly father like Pastor Downing to love him. *No.* He couldn't fall into childish self-pity and the *if only* game. "What you told me will go nowhere. I promise." He found a glint of encouragement in the man's words. "I'm sorry to hear it, but your story brings me hope. That's something I need right now."

His boss stood, patted his shoulder, and walked toward the door but turned back to face Tim. "Don't forget my suggestion about your former fiancée."

Rena's number was still in speed dial. It'd be easy enough to call her, but would she get the wrong idea? Maybe she'd think he was trying to make up with her.

He swallowed a few times then dug the phone out of his pocket.

The familiar voice answered on the third ring.

"Rena." Silence stretched between them. "It's Tim."

"I don't think we have anything to talk about." Her voice trailed off. At least she didn't hang up.

"Please, Rena. I'm not trying to start trouble. I know it's been a long time... too long. I should've made this call months ago." He paced his office, his hand on his forehead.

"Well, what do you want to say? Get it over with."

He didn't blame her for her harsh tones. Did he dare ask her? "Can I meet you somewhere?"

"Are you kidding? I don't trust you anymore."

"Okay, I deserved that. Maybe somewhere in public?"

"What's it about?"

"I need to bring closure by asking you for forgiveness... in person. I need to see it in your eyes."

"You want me to forgive you? I guess that's something you never said before. Okay, but definitely in public. How about in front of Anderson's Grocery? I'm heading there in a minute anyway."

"All right. I'll be there." He took in a gulp of air. Now to figure out what he'd say.

Nancy curled her fingers in a wave when he passed the office. Since it was lunchtime, he wouldn't have to explain where he was going. He gripped the steering wheel with icy palms. They hadn't warmed by the time he arrived at Anderson's.

The cold, misty day didn't help his mood. He pulled up in a parking place in the second row closest to the doors and plodded to the front of the store, then decided to move away from the entrance, which wasn't conducive to conversation. The sidewalk along the windows was protected by the roof's overhang. Rena could see him here.

Was she involved with someone else now? Did she still work the night shift at the hospital?

His heart pounded as the dark haired, dark eyed Brazilian walked toward him, her long brown coat wrapped tightly around her. "Hello, Rena. Is this public enough for you?"

"You don't have to get sarcastic with me." She pulled her coat's hood down revealing her shiny, long strands of hair.

Puddles of rainwater intruded on their space under the overhang. "I can't even say a word without sounding like I'm starting an argument."

She shrugged. "What did you want to say? Make it quick, because I'm cold out here." She wrapped her arms around her shoulders.

Maybe they could at least go to the snack bar at Anderson's and get a hot coffee. "We could go..."

"No we can't. I'm not going anywhere with you." Her glare shot him down.

The old anger threatened. What was it about her? "Look, Rena, I didn't come here for this—to get in a fight."

A teenage employee pushed a long line of shopping carts into the store and glanced back at her.

She put her hands on her waist. "If this is a trick to get us back together, you can forget it. I'm dating someone."

He breathed through his nose and exhaled with his mouth. The woman riled him, his patience tested to the limit. *Could you shut your mouth and listen.* He tightened his jaw so hard it hurt.

Rena folded her arms over her chest and stared.

"I've told God a hundred times how sorry I am." *This feels like lifting weights.* "But for some reason, I never told you." He peered into her eyes praying she'd see his sincerity. "I am so sorry. I never meant to harm you." The cold air penetrated his jacket. "That's all I came to say today. Not to try to reestablish our relationship. I need to know you forgive me."

Rena stared at the ground. Her face softened as she blinked up at him. "I can see you mean it. There was a time when I was very much in love with you. It wasn't all your fault." The corners of her mouth lifted. "You know how fired up we Latinas can get."

His mind echoed with the memories of him and Rena before the nasty end. "Can you say you forgive me, and mean it?" Whether she did or not, at least he'd asked.

She reached her gloved hand and ran her fingers over his cheek. "Sometimes I wish things had been different. I forgive you, but I'm not sure I could ever learn to trust you again."

He nodded. "I understand. You've given me all I need."

Rena stepped closer to him and placed her arms around him in a loose hug. "I feel better, too, Tim. I wish you the best."

As if by instinct, he slid his arm around her waist. Relief flooded his soul. Until she said the words she'd forgiven him, he hadn't realized the burden on his heart.

A tiny broken piece of his angry life fell into place.

"Good-bye." Rena hoisted her purse's leather strap onto her shoulder and curved toward Anderson's front entrance. Over her shoulder, she looked back at him. "Oh, and Tim, I'm sorry, I embellished things a bit when I told Janelle about us."

*****

No parking places in front of Anderson's. Everyone must be shopping on their lunch hour, including Roxanne. But it would only take a minute to grab two cans of tuna and some bread she promised Mom she'd pick up.

Finally—a place on the third row opened up. She took the keys out of the ignition and grabbed her purse. The front flap held her money. She fished around in the little pocket. Yes, she had enough.

With her steady paycheck from the job her sweet mom got her at Albright's, her finances benefited. But the store manager had placed her in the juniors department. What was the irony in that? She had to seek God's strength every day not to purchase any of the cute clothing.

She glanced out her front window. A familiar face—Tim, stood near the end of the building next to a very attractive woman.

Roxanne gaped, transfixed by the scene in front of her. They seemed to be in animated conversation.

Who was the woman? Couldn't be a relative. She didn't look a thing like Tim. The person reached her hand to Tim's face.

Roxanne's mouth fell open.

The dark haired lady pulled Tim to her in a hug, and his arms slipped around her waist. Long strands of hair brushed his coat.

The hug went on too long. Certainly didn't seem like he minded her attention.

Roxanne's lips trembled. She opened the car door and rushed into the grocery store to the canned foods section. Breaking down in the middle of the parking lot wasn't something she cared to do.

Another woman embracing the man she loved. Was this the reason he'd been avoiding her?

Her heart broke as she whipped out her compact and glanced at her image. Her makeup was still perfect. Was the other woman prettier than she?

*****

Tim checked out the pink and red hearts some of the girls taped up around the Sunday school room. A poster with a bear dressed in a crimson and white skirt with one hand on her heart and the other holding a valentine was taped to the wall by the door. The caption said "Bear with one another in love." A little girly for his taste, but half the kids in the group were girls.

The teens conversed in groups of two and three at the large round table.

Tim lifted his hand. "Okay, guys. Time to get quiet."

As if he'd never said a word, the chatting continued.

His dry erase board stood behind him, his markers in the tray. Would those kids ever settle down?

Johnny looked up from his conversation with Tiffany. "Hey, Pastor Tim, are we having a Valentine's party?"

"Don't you guys think you're a little too old for passing out Valentines?" He shot Johnny a glance. "Besides we've got our bowling event coming up."

Tiffany waved her hands in the air. "Come on, Pastor Tim. We want to have a dance."

"You know that's against church policy. Now I'd like to start with prayer." He bowed his head but stole a peek at the kids. They all had their heads down. "Heavenly Lord, I ask you to put Your words in my mouth tonight. Open up the hearts of these young people to hear Your message."

He glanced up. "Okay, people. Valentine's Day is coming, and we think of love, but the kind of love your school friends talk about is romantic love. There's another kind of love, referred to in the Greek as *agape*, meaning love of God."

For once the kids paid attention.

"Agape love is pleasing God and loving others the way He loves us." He cleared his throat.

Mandy raised her hand. "But Pastor Tim, what about romantic love? What does God say about that?"

He looked at his notes. "The world will tell you the purpose of a relationship is to get your needs met, but God says to consider the needs of the person you love. There's a big difference."

Mike waved his hand in the air. "So God doesn't want us to have our needs met?"

"Mike, ironically when we put the needs of others ahead of ours, our own desires are fulfilled." Did Tim live up to his words? Did he want to put Roxanne first? He'd avoided her for the last three weeks, but could he risk a relationship with her?

"Now tonight, we're moving on to something else.

Are your peers showing you love when they tell you it's okay to take drugs? Or should you listen to One who loves you more than anyone else and tells you to honor God with your body?" Only the Holy Spirit would impress this truth on the kids.

"Whose advice will you take—the so-called friend or God's? In the long run, who are you accountable to?" The lack of distractions amazed him. Had they really heard what he was telling them? They'd remained glued to his remarks through the entire lesson.

"Mike, will you close in prayer?"

"Sure." The boy bowed his head. "Lord, I pray that we will learn to love each other with agape love and put You first in our lives. Please bless Pastor Tim. In Jesus name."

His heart thudded at the simple prayer. How he agreed with Mandy's brother, that God would bless him and make him whole.

"All right, guys. Have a good rest of the week." *Finally, a meeting without incident. Maybe the kids are beginning to take an interest.*

Mandy and Tiffany were still chatting about passing out Valentines when they walked out of the room and into the hall.

He locked up the Sunday school room after them. If he crossed through the large sanctuary, he could arrive at his office faster to leave his materials off. He headed down the hall then took a right into the worship center.

"Pastor Tim, can I talk to you a minute?"

A feminine voice behind him whispered as he neared the door to the hall leading to his office. He circled back.

Mandy stepped away from a potted plant near the

altar. "I just wanted to ask you a question." She cleared her throat. "How much older do you think a guy could be than his girlfriend? I mean, how much older is too old?"

"I'm not sure what you're asking, Mandy?" Why did she save the question for now instead of in the youth meeting?

"I mean do you think a guy could be ten or twelve years older than the girl in a romantic relationship?" A wistful smile lightened her face.

Mandy was one of the girls he could trust. He didn't doubt her sincerity. "Wow. That's a tough question. I mean, if a guy was forty-five and the woman was thirty-three or something like that, it might work. It all depends on the people. And God. Personally I believe if people listen, He will direct them."

"What if the guy is twenty-eight and the girl is sixteen." Her eyes were bright with interest.

Now he had a good idea of what she was getting at. He took a step back. "No, Mandy, a sixteen-year-old is still a teenager and a twenty-eight-year-old is an adult. It wouldn't be appropriate."

The rims of her eyes grew red. "Yeah, but what if they waited until the teenager turned twenty?"

He scratched his neck under the collar of his shirt with wet palms. "I really think this is something you should discuss with your mother."

She stepped a few feet closer to him and threw her arms around him. "I think I'm in love with you."

The flash blinded his eyes. He blinked, then his jaw dropped at Johnny's laugh.

"Now that's a pretty picture." The troublesome teen leapt up from a pew behind them.

Tiffany popped up beside him. "Good job, Johnny."

Mandy threw her hands up. "Hey, you guys. I told you not to do that. I really do have feelings for Tim, and you wouldn't believe me."

"Too late now, Mandy. I've got the picture," Johnny said.

Chapter Fourteen

"Johnny, give me that camera." Tim's temper threatened to explode. And he'd thought things had gone well tonight.

"Sorry. I've got a use for this." The troublemaker snickered and pranced out of the sanctuary toward the front doors.

Mandy froze, her eyes the size of dessert plates.

He glared at her. "You need to tell your mother what happened. This could look bad for both of us. I'm going to have to report the incident to Pastor Downing."

She buried her face in her hands. "No. I can't tell Mom. She'll kill me."

A sardonic laugh bubbled from his lips. "I'm going to get killed, too, if someone misconstrues that picture."

Mandy voiced a loud sob and rushed toward the sanctuary door.

His emotions jostled in his throat, ready to erupt. Another doubt piled high on the mound of reservations the church elders probably had against him.

At the last meeting, he could've brought up the subject of the difficult teens, but they'd adjourned early. After that, they didn't meet because of the holiday season. He'd had no opportunity to speak words in his defense.

He unlocked his office, placed his materials on his desk, and backed out the door, closing it after him. With his churning stomach, the trek to the main church office seemed like miles. The only option was to tell the truth about the matter and pray that Pastor believed him. If he didn't, Tim would have to face the consequences.

An involuntary swallow almost choked him. A sliver of light shone from under Pastor's office door. With a shaking fist, he raised his hand, took a breath, and tapped lightly. "Pastor Downing, it's Tim."

"Come in." His voice sounded tired.

The mix of emotions ripped through Tim. What happened tonight was not his doing, yet his sister's accusation, his problems with Johnny, even Harry's report might influence opinions about him.

With a wet palm on the doorknob, he turned it and poked his head in. "Got a minute?"

Pastor Downing returned a thick book to the shelf behind him. "Yes," he grumbled.

The office chair supported Tim's weight as he rubbed his forehead, cleared his throat, and relayed what had transpired in the sanctuary.

His boss squeezed his eyes shut and opened them, his face without expression.

Telling the story was almost worse than experiencing it the first time. Why didn't the man say anything? Tim squirmed under his scrutiny. Moisture formed on his brow.

"I'm sorry this happened. And we'll deal with the picture when we see it. In the meantime, we need to call

Mandy's mother." The harried man rubbed his neck and looked at Tim with wary eyes. "Let's work on this tomorrow morning." He huffed. "I've got a lot of other things on my mind now."

A shock of fear ran through Tim. What if his boss doubted him? "You do believe me, don't you?"

Pastor closed the Bible on his desk and rose from his chair. "As I said, let's talk tomorrow."

In shock, Tim stood and gawked at the person he thought was his friend. Though the pastor of Woodlyn Fellowship showed no emotion, apprehension rose. What if Pastor Downing didn't believe Tim told the truth?

*****

Tim leaned back in the pew, allowing the rest of the congregation to exit after the Sunday night service. He rested his head in his hands. True to his word, Pastor met with him after Wednesday night concerning the picture incident. Mandy's mother, Mrs. Jones, said Mandy denied putting her arms around him.

What about the picture Johnny had? If he used it against Tim, Mandy would have to confess the truth.

How could things get any worse? Now the Pastor thought Tim was an idiot and probably didn't believe him. He dreaded the elders' meeting tomorrow night. The thought of their questions that would undoubtedly come brought moisture to his forehead. Yet he had done nothing wrong—except where Rena was concerned.

Why did the teens give him such a hard time? Where had he lost their respect? He closed his eyes, placing his head on the pew in front of him.

"Hey, Tim. Can I disturb you?"

The soft purr of Roxanne's voice brought him back to the room. She leaned against the end of the pews to his right.

He cared about Roxanne—even fallen in love with her, but the weight of his problems had occupied his mind and his heart for weeks. If she ordered him out of her life, he wouldn't blame her.

"Hi, Roxanne. How are things going at your mom's?"

Her long blond hair framed her pretty face. She tucked a strand behind her ear. "I wanted to give you some good news."

"I can use good news." He chuckled.

"My mom and I—we've had a lot of time to talk. About God and things." Her eyes sparkled. "She prayed with me to give her life to the Lord."

Joy catapulted through his heart. At least something had gone right. "Praise the Lord, Roxy." The soft cushioned back of the pew supported his back. He scooted toward the end of the row and patted the seat next to him.

She slid down beside him. "I'm trying to get her to come to church soon. She said until she'd prayed with me, she hadn't realized what she missed—God in her life."

"That's a blessing." His pulse thudded in his chest. Her presence soothed him. "Roxy, I've missed seeing you." The words were out before he thought. How easy it was to listen to his heart instead of his mind.

"On New Year's Eve you said we needed to take things slow. You must have meant that."

Heat filled Tim's cheeks. "So slow a snail could do

better. I'm sorry. My life is complicated."

The last worshiper had filed out of the sanctuary. He reached for her hand, but she pulled away, turning to face him.

"This may not be any of my business, but I need to know. Who was the woman with her arms around you the other day in front of Anderson's?"

"Anderson's?" He quirked a brow. She must've seen him with Rena. After all, Rena had chosen a public place.

Though he dreaded the thought, he'd probably have to discuss his past relationship with her. Janelle said she told Roxanne about Rena, and now he was surprised Roxanne didn't mention her conversation with his sister. "That was...someone from my past. I needed to ask for her forgiveness."

"Your fiancée?"

He sat up straight facing her. "My former fiancée. Things ended badly. I take the full blame."

"She must've forgiven you. Her arms around you like that." Roxanne's face took on a shade of red.

This probably looked bad to her. He doubted she'd understand. "The hug only sealed Rena's promise she no longer held anything against me for what I did. Our relationship is over." He dared to hold Roxanne's hand again. "There's only one woman I have feelings for—you." He tugged her into the circle of his arm. Closing his eyes, he nuzzled her hair, breathing in the flowery aroma.

"Pastor Tim. You sure have a way with women. Hugging one and trying to kiss another." The brash voice of Johnny Thompson blared at him from the back of the church.

Johnny made his way down the center aisle and waved a piece of paper in his hands. He scooted into the pew in front of them and stopped. A sarcastic laugh rolled from his throat as he thrust a picture toward Roxanne but jerked it back before they could look at it. "You may be interested in this. But I'm keeping it for now." He gave a surly laugh.

She stared at Johnny as if processing his words.

Tim reached in front of her to grab the picture, but his nemesis took two steps back.

"Yeah, you're quite a Romeo." The teen continued his taunt.

With a pounding heart, Tim stood to his feet gasping for breath. "I'm giving you two seconds to take a hike." How was he supposed to control the force of his emotion threatening to emerge? "You know that picture was a set up."

"Yeah, but no one else knows that. Well, maybe your girlfriend here, but who would believe her?"

He despised making a scene in front of Roxanne. "Why do you hate me?" The question was out of his mouth before he could clamp his jaw shut.

"You think you're so smart. You know so much about God, but you can't even keep from getting mad. Chris wouldn't..." Johnny put his hand on his mouth and coughed. "You're the biggest hypocrite I know." The teen lifted his chin and sneered.

Wrath seethed in Tim's stomach, and his jaw clenched. "Regardless of what you think of me, you need to accept some of the blame for our disagreements. Just leave." His breaking point loomed, and Roxanne witnessed the whole sordid event.

"Okay, I'm going, but your day is coming."

Roxanne moved her head closer to the wayward teen and squinted. "Wait, Johnny. Come here."

He twisted around and stared at her, slowly squinting his eyes to little slits.

"Johnny, don't you remember me?"

*****

"Mom, tell me again how the Thompsons are related to us." Roxanne sat down opposite her mother at the tiny kitchen table with its blue flowered tablecloth.

Monday morning. One cup of coffee and Roxanne had to leave for work.

Mom took a sip from her Northwest Trek mug. "Yes, the Thompsons." Her smile faded. "We used to get together with them when your father was still at home." She nibbled a bite of toast and wiped her mouth.

"Didn't they have two sons, Johnny and Christopher? Christopher was just a couple of years older than me. I remember playing with Chris during family dinners. His little brother used to jump right in the middle of what we were doing." Roxanne's eye twitched. "So how are they related?"

Mom traced her finger along the pattern in the tablecloth. "Marty Thompson, the boys' mother, is your father's sister."

A chill careened up her spine. "I thought I recognized my cousin last night in church."

"Who, dear?"

"Johnny. Johnny is in Tim's youth group. Apparently he gives Tim a hard time during their meetings." Mocking the youth pastor as he did seemed plenty daring for a teen, nothing she would've dreamed of doing.

Mom sighed. "You know, Marty always did have a harder time with him than with Christopher. Chris behaved himself—a little angel." Mom rested her chin in her hand. "I heard he went to seminary to become a pastor and already graduated."

"Like Tim." She sipped her french-vanilla flavored coffee. Tim's thorn in his side—her cousin. How would that influence his feelings about her? And where was Christopher these days?

Chapter Fifteen

The middle chair of the semicircle in front of Pastor Downing's desk remained empty, probably reserved for Tim. He glanced around the room then edged down. To his left, Rich Jones, Mandy and Mike's father, smiled at him with kind eyes. Next to Rich, Jack Thompson cut his gaze to Tim with one of those *let's hurry and get this over with* looks.

On the other side, Sherwood Baker, Betty's father, cleared his throat. If Tim was in the middle of a herd of buffalo, he couldn't have felt more trapped. Perspiration dampened his underarms. He tried to ignore the beginnings of the headache forming between his eyes. *Lord, I wonder if this will be my last day as youth pastor at Woodlyn Fellowship.*

Pastor Downing looked up from the notes he'd scanned. "Gentlemen, let's open with prayer." He bowed his head. "Lord, we ask you to be God over this meeting and bring us Your wisdom as we try to best serve You. Amen."

Tim raised his painful head. He hadn't done anything to warrant termination. Surely the elders would see that.

Pastor fidgeted in his chair. "Jack, I believe you

wanted to begin the session."

Mr. Thompson cleared his voice. "Yes. Pastor Garrett, in your favor, the fundraisers exceeded expectations. However..." he waved his hand in the air and glared. "As you know, we've had questions about your handling of the teenagers." He shuffled the papers in his lap. "There have been numerous concerns."

As if raising a bottle of ammonia to his nose and taking a long whiff, Mr. Thompson's presence made him flinch.

The senior pastor perused his notes again as if trying to avoid eye-contact with Mr. Thompson.

Mr. Jones cleared his voice. "At your first interview, you told us you didn't know of any personal matters we should be aware of. You grew up in an unstable home but said things had settled out." He craned his neck towards Tim raising an eyebrow. "Would you say that's still the case?"

Tim gave an involuntary swallow. "Gentlemen, I'm working hard to...."

Mr. Thompson pounded the table and waved a paper in the air. "Let me reiterate some of the concerns the elders have." He pulled out a pair of glasses from his pocket and hooked them behind his ears. "A Harry Dickson reported he saw you drinking."

With lips clamped shut, Tim restrained the heated response he almost allowed. Instead he grasped the sides of the chair, his knuckles turning white.

Pastor Downing looked at Tim, frowned, and then dropped his gaze to the paper in front of him. Tim never dreamed Pastor would report the incident to the elders. He thought they'd cleared up the situation. And why didn't his boss allow Tim to speak after Mr.

Thompson's interruption?

"Then your own sister relayed a regretful story about how you mistreated your former fiancée. In addition, she said you were sleeping with Roxanne Ratner."

Air huffed from his mouth as he leapt to his feet. "That's not true." What if Tim lost control? *Dear, God.*

Johnny's father lifted a restraining hand. "Sit down, Garrett. You'll have your say." He cleared his throat. "You barged in on Pastor Downing with a story about how Mandy threw her arms around you, and Johnny took a picture. Which, I might add, everyone involved denied. Lastly, I need to mention the night you walked out on your class and left them unexpectedly with a volunteer and no Bible study."

"Please, Jack, you sound like you're reading his offenses before he receives a jail sentence. Let Tim speak." Mr. Jones's quiet voice commanded more authority than Mr. Thompson's railing. Finally, someone stood up for Tim.

Mr. Baker opened his mouth. "Go ahead, Tim. We'd like to hear your side. Can you refute any of these accusations?"

Pastor Downing gave him a quick look and glanced at a poster on the wall. Instead of anger, sorrow welled up in Tim, like the time when he was six years old. He'd scraped his knee and started to cry. All he wanted was some encouragement. Maybe the words, "It's okay, son. Don't cry now." Maybe a soft pat on the back.

But Dad showed him hateful eyes and said to act like a man and stop blubbering. Tim cried then and took refuge in his room, the loneliest spot in the world at that moment. But the next time, he didn't allow tears, only resentment. And the time after that, bitterness. Finally, anger ruled his heart.

Once again, he raised his eyes to the senior pastor. "I suppose if you want to fire me, you have every right. Yes, I had problems with my former fiancée, and I did walk out on the youth group. But Mr. Thompson, did Johnny tell you anything at all about the many distractions he caused...?"

"How dare you blame your lack of ability to lead our teenagers on them? That's wrong." Mr. Thompson chopped one hand into the palm of the other.

The man spoke the truth. Tim hunched his shoulders. If he couldn't control the class, he had no one to blame but himself. He nodded. "You're right. If you need to dismiss me now, I'll understand." His eyes stung. Where was the usual anger? He liked that emotion better. "As far as the other accusations, they're all false. I only wish I had a copy of the picture Johnny took."

Mr. Jones's kind voice captured Tim's attention. "I suggest we allow our youth pastor to stay on until summer barring any major problems. Let's call it a probationary period and give him one last chance."

For the first time during the meeting other than the prayer, Pastor spoke up. "I agree, Rich. Is that acceptable to you, Tim?"

Eye contact with Pastor Downing became impossible, and Tim focused on his shoes. His boss had betrayed him. "I promise to do my best. Believe it or not, I do have the best interest of the teens in my heart. If you don't mind, I need to go to my office." If he didn't leave now, he'd probably display an unmanly emotion. The elders might see a grown man cry. His reputation couldn't take any more hits.

*****

Roxanne sighed, stuck her key in the front door lock, and traipsed into the house. Mom wouldn't be here since her shift started at three. Laying her purse on the hall table, she plopped down on the couch. Her feet ached and stung at the same time.

With her head back on the pillow, she closed her eyes and slipped off her shoes. Tim hadn't told her the whole story about his fiancée. She needed to hear it from his mouth. What really happened? *Did he actually care about me like he said?* He avoided her most of the time, and she'd seen him hugging Rena. What about Johnny's allegations? She wanted to trust Tim, but it was hard.

The old restless urge welled up in her. Maybe she should go downtown despite her aching feet—so many cute boutiques with tons of shoes, jewelry, winter coats...oh, the possibilities were endless. She rose up and searched for her purse.

No Roxanne, no. Her credit card balances didn't look any better than when she moved in with Mom. *Lord, please be strong for me. I can't do it by myself.*

Pacing the living room brought little comfort. She had to find another way to cope with life. Maybe she should clean out her closet and go through some of her keepsakes. Anything to distract herself from shopping.

Mom had always kept her old bedroom like Roxanne left it. On tiptoes, she reached up to the shelf in her closet above the tightly packed hanging dresses. She pushed past the Coach bag and her new leather boots to the cardboard containers of mementoes she'd kept through the years. Her hand landed on the box where she'd found Teddy's doggie tag the day she and Tim buried him.

An ache ran through her. Tim. She loved him and cared for him. But he never showed much interest in her unless she approached him. *So hot and cold. Just like my father.* Holding onto Dad was like trying to capture water with one's fingers spread wide. She rubbed her eyes and set the box on the floor, dropped down with crossed legs, and slowly raised the lid.

Memory after memory spilled out on the carpet—her Girl Scout pin, a lock of hair in a plastic bag, an old charm bracelet, a photo of her first boyfriend. After thrusting her hand to the bottom of the box, her fingers touched something brittle, perhaps a piece of paper, and she pulled it out.

Her name was written in her father's scrawl on the front of a yellowed envelope—a letter she'd never seen before. She slipped her fingers in and pulled out a creased piece of paper. She unfolded the correspondence dated the year she was ten. *He must've put it here before he left.*

My Roxanne,

I hope you find this letter someday, and it helps you make sense of things. Maybe you'll understand—I left your mother, not you.

I was a coward. I should have stood up to my responsibilities at home, but my relationship with your mother squeezed the life out of me. I couldn't face it any longer.

I'm asking you to forgive me, Roxanne. I love you now and will always love you. If and when you marry someday, just give the guy a little breathing room.

Please forgive me.

Dad.

The letter fell from her hands. Lifting herself from the floor, she sat on the side of the bed. She had to process his words.

What had Mom done to make him leave? Yet didn't he say he was a coward? She leaned over and collapsed on her pillow. But the tears were bittersweet. Her dad loved her.

She pulled her stuffed bear to her chest until her tears stopped. Her dad cared for her but left because his life with mom strangled him. Could she ever forgive a man who'd never looked back?

Chapter Sixteen

Roxanne peered across the kitchen table at her mother's glowing face—a change she'd noticed about Mom since she gave her life to the Lord. Did Roxanne dare bring up the subject that had preyed on her mind for days? She swallowed the lump in her throat. "Do you ever think about the time when Dad left us?"

Mom eyed her coffee cup then looked up. "Yes, honey, I often think if things had been different—if I hadn't made so many mistakes, he'd still be around." She fixed a steady gaze on the wall. "But mostly if I'd known the Lord in those days, I think our marriage would've survived."

Rising from the chair opposite Mom, Roxanne took a few steps toward the coffee maker. "You weren't responsible for his behavior." She filled her empty cup with more of the hot liquid.

Mom clasped her forehead. "I tried to dominate him. Now I see it's wrong to try and control someone's life." She laced her fingers. "I pray you don't make the same mistake."

"I may never have the chance. Tim's so unpredictable, and I'm not interested in anyone else." She eased back into her chair and took a sip of coffee.

"Maybe he'd abandon me like Dad did us."

A slow smile stretched across Mom's face. "I'm new in the faith, but let me share this with you. Last night I read something in the Bible about trusting the Lord and not our own wisdom." Mom's eyes twinkled as she reached for Roxanne's hand. "Allow God to be in charge."

The corners of her mouth curve up. "Thank you. I needed to hear that. God has a plan." She tilted her head to one side. "There's something else on my mind."

"What is it, Roxie?"

A glimmer of faith brought the courage to say the words. "I'd like to find a way to start my own business."

*****

Blood pounded in Tim's temples. He had to allow enough time between the elders' meeting and the visit he'd make to Pastor Downing's office. For one thing, he needed to let the anxiety in his soul subside before he confronted his boss about the lack of support. Despite the meeting, he found a deep affection for the man and craved his attention as a mentor.

Four days since the Monday night meeting. The anticipation of his task at hand ransacked his stomach. Might as well get it over with. He turned off his computer, moved around the other side of his desk, and reached toward the door then heard a knock.

Pastor Downing, as if reading his thoughts, stood in the hall. "We need to talk."

Tim squared his jaw. "Yes, sir. Come in."

Pastor's face held a look Tim couldn't quite interpret, maybe regret, even contrition. He sank into the chair opposite Tim's desk and rubbed his forehead. His smile faded when he opened his mouth. "I suppose this conversation is overdue."

Tim pulled up the spare chair and shifted in his seat a couple of times. Undoubtedly his boss had thought about the strained relationship they'd endured over the last four days. Tim waited for the final blow when Pastor Downing would pronounce his edict against him. His words lodged in his throat.

The other man picked up the conversation. "I've procrastinated in talking to you." He gripped his hands, staring at his feet. "I've got to ask your forgiveness, as well as make a confession."

Tim's jaw dropped as he gaped at Pastor. Where was he going with this? Tim's actions were being questioned, not the other way around. "I'm listening."

The older man cracked his knuckles and glanced up. "Forgive me, Brother. I acted like a coward. I'm praying about what to do next. It could very well result in my dismissal."

"What are you talking about?" His heart clenched at Pastor's announcement, the space between them tense.

"I was unfair to you at the meeting. All because I was afraid." He swallowed hard, probably searching for the courage to go on. "Do you remember when I told you how the Lord freed me from a gambling addiction?"

He nodded. "Yes, but... "

"When I came to Woodlyn Fellowship, I didn't report it to the hiring board as I should have. Jack Thompson found out after making a few inquiries. He, uh... came to me and threatened to tell the congregation if I didn't cooperate with him."

With open palms, Tim gaped at Pastor. "Why would he do such a thing?"

"There's something you don't know." Pastor coughed into his fist. "Johnny's older brother, Christopher, was on the list of youth pastors we were considering. When you were selected, Jack became furious. I think he poisoned Johnny's mind against you. Encouraged him to act up, intent on running you off." He shook his head and stared at the floor. "I kept silent all those months when you had your problems. I was a coward—afraid of allowing Thompson to carry out his threat. Afraid that the congregation would rule against me. I'm so sorry, Tim."

So that's why Johnny always gave me a hard time. He must've influenced some of the other teens as well. Tim slowly moved his head side to side. "Unbelievable." He'd suspected something more was going on with the pastor. The way he didn't support him some of the time and discouraged him from calling Johnny's parents. The old anger fumed inside. The man had betrayed him. How dare he do this? Tim balled his fists.

Yet Pastor's words tapped at the door of his heart. *I'm so sorry.* How could Tim stay angry with the guy? He took a deep breath. The man was like the father Tim never had. "How did Mr. Thompson find out about Harry Dickson?"

"Unfortunately he was in the office the day Harry made an appearance. Harry said a few things about you drinking before I shut my door, and Jack heard him. Jack demanded to know what that was about." Scarlet spread across Pastor's face. "He also demanded to know any other complaints or negative incidents about you, said he was preparing a report for the elders. I filled in the blanks. The rest of the events, he heard from Johnny and no telling what the boy said."

Pastor Downing had let him down—put his own fears first. He was weak, allowing Jack Thompson to control him. Tim swiped a hand over his eyes. But hadn't Tim exhibited his own weaknesses day after day? Tim needed to forgive the man. "Whew. Johnny's father has it in for me." He lowered his head. "But I need to take credit for the majority of the problems."

"As much as we Christians love the Lord, we're still flawed. Can you forgive me for not speaking up in your defense?"

He gave his head a scratch. Christ had forgiven him of his sins. Though anger surged when he thought of Jack's conspiracy and Pastor Downing's cooperation, he chose to forgive instead of getting mad, surprising even himself. "Yes, I forgive you." Calm settled on his spirit.

"And Tim, I'm praying about how the Lord wants me to handle my situation with the congregation. I know God would have me to reveal my past and the way I've allowed Jack Thompson to run God's church. I've even permitted the man to harm your ministry. It's time to come out from under the hold this man has on me and on the church. I'll step forward with the truth as soon as I have clear direction from the Lord."

Though Tim's heart became saddened, he realized the validity of the Bible passage that says everyone is susceptible to problems and temptations. He hadn't been singled out from other Christians to endure his out-of-control emotions. Hope filled his heart—whatever happened, God was in charge. "We've got a compassionate congregation here at Woodlyn. They'll receive your confession with open hearts. But I'll tell you the truth, if they don't accept your disclosure, they probably won't allow me to stay on either, and I'll be dismissed with no recommendation for a counseling job. It could be the end of our careers at Woodlyn."

*****

Tim locked his office, his heart a little lighter after his conversation with Pastor. He smiled and waved to Nancy as he walked out the front door. Forgiving Pastor instead of bearing a grudge felt good.

Though Tim hadn't conquered his explosive anger, he desired to become more transparent before Roxanne. But was he ready? He wanted her to know he loved her, but would she risk a relationship with him, despite his past?

She'd witnessed the ugly scene with Johnny. That night in church, the kid had shrugged and walked out the sanctuary. First thing Tim would do—find out what she meant about the teen remembering her.

Tim unlocked his car door and crawled in. He fished out his cell, but stuffed it back in his pocket. Should he do this? He shook his head, pulled the cell out again, and punched in her number.

After the second ring, he heard her voice.

"Hello."

Did he imagine the hint of uneasiness in her tone? "Is this a bad time?"

"Actually, I'm on my break."

"I'm sorry about last Sunday." He pinched the bridge of his nose. "Let me make it up to you and take you to dinner tonight." He wouldn't be surprised if she had another date.

"Tonight? Yes, I'd like to see you." Though he detected her wary tone, he felt encouraged. She lowered her voice. "I found out about Johnny."

Tim clenched his hand into a fist. Even the sound of the boy's name made him cringe after all the pranks he'd played this year. "Do you want to tell me now?"

He couldn't imagine what she would say. "No, tonight."

*****

The stone walkway leading through the gardens behind The Mediterranean meandered around a willow tree to a ceramic fountain next to a concrete bench. Beyond that, ivy spilled over the sides of a wooden planter. Tim smiled down at Roxanne. "What did you think of the moussaka?" The aroma of tomatoes and garlic emanated from the restaurant. He could eat another serving of Baklava with the flakey crust and layers of honey and nuts.

"It was delicious." Her blue eyes glistened. A warm pink painted her cheeks. "I enjoy being with you." She squeezed his hand and drew her jacket closer around her shoulders.

The slender young woman by his side brought him joy. Would the day come when he'd feel free to put his whole heart into their relationship? He slid his arm around her shoulders and drew her down on the bench. "You know, it seems like we're the only people in the world out here. I could look at you all evening. Roxanne. I wish..." *No use talking about it.*

She folded her hands between her knees. "I want the

same thing."

"How do you know what I was going to say?"

She only smiled.

To feel her lips on his—his pulse raced.

Roxy touched his shoulder, ran her hand across his back, and his lips met hers. Her nearness made his heart pound harder than Rena's attention ever did. He desired Roxanne to be a part of his life. But when would the time be right?

A shadow crossed her face when she pulled back. "I waited to tell you something. I didn't want to spoil our meal."

Probably about his troublemaker. He knit his brow.

She cleared her voice. "I found out... Johnny Thompson is my first cousin."

Not what I expected to hear. "Your cousin? That includes Christopher, too."

"Yes, on my Dad's side."

Fatigue threatened. Johnny, his *thorn in the side*, Roxanne's cousin.

"Mom said Christopher had gone to seminary like you, and that Johnny was always the pest in the family. I'm sorry. He's made things miserable for you." She rubbed her hand over his.

"Don't worry about it. You have nothing to be sorry about. We've all got people in our families we don't get along with—like my sister Janelle."

With narrowed eyes, she tucked a blond strand behind her ear. "It's too bad she thought it was her duty to tell me about Rena." With a few taps of her foot, she blinked. "I've always wanted to ask you about her...about what happened?"

"It's hard to talk about." Janelle had already filled her

mind with the sordid facts. No need to repeat them.

She cocked her eyebrow. "Did you love her?"

What he would do to avoid that question. "Yes, in a way, but I wasn't ready for a serious relationship. Sometimes I wonder if I am now." The minute the words left his mouth, he realized she'd take them the wrong way. The old lingering doubts about himself still hung on, but she might not understand that. "I mean... I... uh..."

She slipped her hands on her waist. "What did you mean?"

Why did he always seem to jam a foot in his mouth and make a statement that sounded divisive? "I'm afraid of repeating my past mistakes, that's all. Nothing to do with you." He held out his open palm hoping she'd understand. Somehow, he didn't think she would.

"Why did you break up with her?" She pressed on as if she didn't know the story.

The waterfall's cascading droplets fell from one ceramic tier to the next. Was it his imagination they descended faster now? "She broke up with me."

"Why?" Roxanne wouldn't let the subject go.

He folded his arms over his chest. "I don't feel right talking about it. Janelle told you anyway, didn't she?"

"Yes, but I want to hear it from your mouth." She scowled at him. "Or maybe you mean you can't talk about it because it's private between you and Rena."

He emitted a low growl. "No, that's not it at all." He'd never heard her speak with such a harsh tone.

"Why won't you tell me?" She was pressing him, insisting on answers—so much like Rena, with frustrating, infuriating demands.

His voice rose. "Because it's embarrassing. You want

me to say it?" His emotions were out of control. "All right. I shoved her, and she fell to the ground. Are you happy now?"

Roxanne looked at him through tiny slits. "So what your sister told me is really true?"

His heart pumped hard in his chest, and he could barely catch his breath as if Rena sat on the bench. "Stop pressuring me."

"For a while I thought Janelle exaggerated, but if this is the way you treated Rena, I can understand how she felt." Her shrill voice rose to a crescendo.

"Just shut up." Tim jumped up, his fisted hands drawn near his face.

Roxanne gasped and clutched her throat.

He wasn't going to hit her. He jerked his hands back to his side.

Wide-eyed, she lifted from the bench and took three steps back. "Get out of my life, Tim Garrett."

*****

Tim took a breath and tried to put last night out of his mind. It was over with Roxanne. Though his heart ached more than he could say, he had to admit the truth. He should've known. He wasn't ready for a relationship and probably never would be—with Roxanne or anyone.

Though she pressed him to his limit, he couldn't blame her. In fact, it only showed he couldn't handle confrontation. Sure, her interrogation wasn't warranted, but he couldn't hold her responsible for the outcome. Most of the blame lay with him.

He tried to ignore the pain and disappointment and

leafed through the catalogues on his desk, his order for the spring Sunday school materials almost complete. Diving head first into his work was his best option now. The boxes on his computer screen waited to be filled with an x. How much longer would he have this job? If Jack Thompson had anything to say about it, his days were limited.

A knock on his door drew him back from his thoughts. Probably Pastor Downing again. "Yes, come in."

The door squeaked, and someone with dark brown hair peeked in.

His mouth dropped. Janelle. He bounded up from his computer to meet her at the door. "Uh... hello, Janelle."

She took faltering steps into his office. Her features held an expression he couldn't interpret. Not angry, not resentful, yet somber. What did she want?

He braced for another altercation. *Lord, are you testing me?*

"Got a minute, Tim?" His sister glanced from one side of his office to the other—from the poster on his wall to the computer on his desk then lifted woeful eyes to him.

"Yes." How was he to act or react to her presence? He didn't want to cause a scene that everyone in the office would hear. With an opened palm, he extended his hand to the chair in front of his desk training his eyes on her. He drew up the seat across from her.

She fingered the strap on her purse, took a deep breath, and met his gaze. "Tim, I need to tell you, Dad isn't doing well."

"What's wrong?"

"He went in for a test. The doctor scheduled a heart

bypass operation for next month—coronary artery blockage."

His shoulders dropped forward. The thought of losing either parent without the opportunity to say good-bye made him sick inside. "I should try to see him again. The last time, I didn't get anywhere."

"I remember the day. Maybe it would be a good idea. No one can say you haven't made the effort." She twirled a strand of her dark brown hair around her finger. "We're the only kids Mom and Dad have, and... we're family." She dabbed at her eyes.

His sister didn't have to tell him that. Perhaps it would take something like this to bring peace between them. "I appreciate you letting me know."

"I... I wanted to tell you something else." Janelle glanced at her folded hands. "I talked to Rena a couple of days ago, and I've done a lot of thinking."

Tension rose in his chest. What now? Would she chide him again about his treatment of her or maybe try to get them back together? "Oh, yeah?"

"We talked for a long time. She told me about how you sought her out a few weeks ago to ask her forgiveness. She admitted her responsibility in the breakup and said she made you look like an ogre when she should've taken part of the blame."

"Well, it's good to hear somebody saying something nice for a change." He tried to suppress his sarcasm.

She hadn't stopped staring at her lap. "I took her side from the first and didn't try to understand your feelings."

"Yeah, well, what I did was wrong."

"No one is perfect. Certainly not me." She brushed a tear from her cheek and cleared her throat. "I was too harsh after New Year's when you came to see Dad. And I... I'm sorry about trying to cause you trouble with your job." She put her hands over her face. "The lie I told Pastor Downing..." She pulled out a tissue and wiped her tears. "I'm prepared to tell him the truth—as soon as I leave your office."

Skepticism hovered in his mind. "What brought about this change of heart?"

She finally lifted her gaze to him. "Maybe Dad's illness, maybe I'm finally growing up. I used to resent your interest in religion. To be honest, I thought you were a hypocrite because you acted so holy, and yet I knew all your faults. I'm starting to see that we all have imperfections—human failings, me included." She pushed up from the chair and stood before him.

He rose and peered down at her. "My faith tells me we don't have to wait until we're perfect to reach out to God."

She paused, searching his face. "I think another thing that's caused me to dwell on this is Dad's failing health, thinking about where he might go when he dies—where I'll go for that matter. I don't know, Tim. These notions are all new to me."

Despite their differences, he loved Janelle and prayed she'd come to faith in Jesus as he had. "I'm glad you're seeing these things. Let's treat each other with respect."

"You're right." She patted his shoulder. "If nothing else, to show Dad we've made peace." Her voice caught. "Tim... I honestly don't think he's going to be around much longer."

Chapter Seventeen

Tim attempted to focus his rebellious mind on his office computer screen, but the sound of Roxanne's voice even after two weeks still echoed in his brain. *Get out of my life.* He suspected she'd stopped coming to Woodlyn Fellowship since he hadn't seen her on Sunday mornings.

His small office hemmed him in now as he paced the perimeter. The view from his window revealed the typical Washington rain. His heart stuttered in his chest. Now he didn't have to worry about getting involved with her when he wasn't ready. He wouldn't see her now—or ever. Roxanne. He'd never kiss her again or hold her.

The poster on his wall with the scripture from the second book of Timothy reminded him of God's available power, love, and self-discipline. Yet he'd still failed.

Had Roxanne picked a fight on purpose the other night? Surely not. Another thought wounded him. Maybe her loyalties now lay with the Thompson family since she discovered Johnny to be her cousin. The thought held him like a vice, and he gave his head a shake.

Rubbing the tense muscles in his neck did little good. He stuffed the emotion threatening him—had to get his mind on his work. He plopped down in his office chair, adhering his foot on the floor to keep it from swiveling.

The long drawer in the center of his desk held his black leather organizer with his important church documents. He needed the church credit card for Friday night when he took the kids bowling and the trip to Pizza Palace.

He lifted the folder out and thumbed through the contents—the budget for this year and next, brochures for outings, notes he'd taken in past elders' meetings, receipts he hadn't turned into the office yet.

Where was the credit card? He poked his fingers into the flap where he usually kept it. The little compartment appeared empty. He flipped through the notebook, removing everything. His frustration built—no card. Maybe he forgot and stuck it in his wallet. He reached for the back pocket of his jeans. Only his personal credit cards there.

After a thorough search of his desk and office, he allowed the truth to wash over him. The card was missing.

With a furrowed brow, he pushed up from his chair and lumbered through the door. Nancy might know something. A cold chill ran down his spine as he stopped in the hall. His office remained unlocked. How many other times had he neglected to secure it? He stuck his key in and turned it, pulling it shut.

His stomach knotted into a hard rock as he walked down the hall to the main office. Nancy frowned at the computer screen and shook her head, tossing her short brown hair from side to side.

The edge of her desk served as an anchor when he gripped it. Before long he'd see that *I'd never lose a credit card* face. "Sorry, Nancy. I need to bother you a minute."

Her frown changed to a smile when she looked up at him with navy blue eyes. "Sure, Tim. What can I help you with?"

He relaxed a muscle or two and cleared his throat. "Have you seen my church credit card? I've searched everywhere in my office."

"Hmm. Your church credit card? I don't believe so." She squinted as she placed a finger on her cheek. "Let me look where I keep mine." A notebook similar to his surfaced from a side drawer. She shuffled through papers. "No, no, it's not here. Maybe the pastor might have an idea."

A shiver of apprehension shot through his stomach. Another shortcoming to add to his long list of failures at Woodlyn Fellowship—irresponsibility. *How could I have lost the stupid piece of plastic?* "I'll pay for Friday out of my pocket. I can't disappoint the teens."

Nancy stuck the notebook back in her desk drawer. "Don't do that. Let me give you some petty cash." She stood and walked toward the safe.

"Let's just wait. Maybe the card will show up between now and then."

She nodded and returned to her desk. "In the meantime, I'll inform Mr. Thompson. As you know, he heads the finance committee. Jess Colton just started as his assistant, but I don't think he'd know anything."

Tim refrained from doing what he wanted—to slam

the office door. One thing he always prided himself on, his sense of responsibility. Could he be failing in one of the few areas he got right?

*****

Roxanne punched the button to raise the resistance on the elliptical machine. Her tennis shoes peddled faster as beads of perspiration formed on her brow. The gym helped her work off her tension and to forget—forget Tim was no longer in her life. She never knew she could miss anyone this badly.

The Sound Fitness wall clock said she'd been there an hour. No wonder she had to wipe all that sweat off her face. Thank God the owner, Diana Harkins, allowed her to pay month to month. No surprise Diana was so nice. Any sister of Holly Colton's had to be.

Roxanne peddled backwards and wiped her brow again. The memory of the night two weeks ago at The Mediterranean chilled her though her body temperature was elevated. Why had she pressed Tim so hard about Rena?

Sure, Janelle informed her about what happened, but somehow she wouldn't believe his actions until he told her. If she were honest, she wanted him to say he'd never do anything like that to her. Not only did he tell her what he did to Rena, he demonstrated it by raising his hand to her.

His wide eyes had revealed he surprised himself as much as her with his reaction. Deep in her heart she'd never believe Tim would strike her, yet now she'd ordered him out of her life. She couldn't face him. The reason she and her mom attended another church.

A bothersome concern marched into her mind. Did Tim become irate because he put her in the same category as his adversary Johnny Thompson, since he knew Johnny was her cousin? Surely not. Roxanne panted for breath, and it wasn't because of the elliptical machine's resistance. Though it was no excuse for his reaction, she had pushed Tim too far. Her heart advised her of the blame. Never again would she make that mistake. If she ever had a second chance.

*****

Tim parked his car in front of the sign *Woodlyn Fellowship*. A week now and he hadn't found his church credit card. The finance committee—Pastor, Mr. Thompson, and Jess—knew now. Guess it was Jess who cancelled it. The uncomfortable pang gripping his heart hadn't let go.

How could he have lost it? He opened the long drawer to his desk to get a paperclip to fasten the pages of his Sunday school budget report. He poked his fingers into the little plastic box in the middle of the drawer to find a silver fastener. He gasped as he stared at the card to the right of the box. Had he left his personal credit card there? Was he losing his mind? Since he broke up with Roxanne, his rattled nerves gave him no relief. He fingered the card and turned it over. It couldn't be. *My church credit card.* He looked up as someone knocked. Tim placed the card where he'd found it and rose to answer.

Mr. Thompson stood at the threshold, his face twisted in hard knots. "Garrett, do you own an iPad?" The sarcasm in his voice punctuated the *got cha* look on his face.

Why would he be asking that? "Well, yes, I do."

"Did you get it at Albrights?"

Irritability crept over him. "What's this about?"

Mr. Thompson pushed into Tim's office. "You made a charge for an iPad at Albrights using the church credit card. I'm bringing this up to the finance committee, the elders, and Pastor Downing. What were you thinking, Tim Garrett?"

Chapter Eighteen

Jack Thompson waved a bank statement in Tim's face. "You need to follow me into Pastor Downing's office. He'll want to see this."

Tim's hand quivered. What now? He was innocent of any wrong doing with the credit card other than losing it, but how was he going to prove it to the head of the finance committee? The man's accusations ransacked Tim's emotions. *How much longer can I last in this hostile environment?*

He attempted a breath. "May I please see it?" Mr. Thompson must've heard the way he drew out *please*.

"Here." Johnny's irate father thrust the paper in his face.

Tim perused the itemized report with a section for Pastor Downing, Nancy, and him. His mouth fell open. The charge under his column mocked him—six hundred and fifty dollars at Albright's.

"You didn't provide a receipt so I had Nancy call Albright's, and they told her you purchased an iPad a week ago." He stabbed his finger at the entry. "Albrights looked up the receipt, and a Tim Garrett signed it."

Gall rose in his throat. "That is not true. Do you think I'd be stupid enough to do that? We need to challenge the charge before the church pays it."

"The church will pay for it all right, after you reimburse us for six hundred and fifty dollars. I recommend you be terminated immediately." Thompson squinted and pressed his lips in a tight line.

Tim shoved the statement back at him. "Look. I didn't do what you're accusing me of." He balled his fists as the other man shot him an angry glance. With all the restraint he could muster, he resisted the urge to pound the man in the face. Memories of Pastor's words about Christopher reeled in his brain. "There's got to be a deeper issue than just the bank statement. What have you got against me?"

Johnny's father grabbed the statement and folded the paper in half. "You're crazy. You're weaseling your way out of this. How do you explain the fact that Albright's found the receipt with your signature?"

Guess he isn't going to mention Christopher. "My card has been missing for a week. Didn't Nancy tell you?"

The older man squinted and poked his lips out. "That's not her job."

"Well, today it miraculously appeared again in my desk." He opened his drawer, pulled out the card, and slapped it into Thompson's hand, knocking the pencil holder off in the process. "I'm fed up with your accusations. If you want to know the truth, I've had it with you." He formed a fist with his right hand and shook it in the man's face, invading his space. "Just get off my case." He could almost feel the crack of his knuckles on the man's teeth. But by the grace of God, he relaxed his hand. The finance man just about got a fist in his face this time.

"You'd better not threaten me." Thompson stuck the card in his pocket. "How can you expect me to buy your story?"

The pencils lay on the floor scattered in all directions. Tim picked up one and snapped it in two. "I did not purchase an iPad with the church credit card." Antagonism rose, and he stuffed it back down. How dare the man challenge his integrity?

Glorious Day chimed from his cell phone. He pulled it out looked at the caller ID. "Yes, hello, Janelle."

"Tim, Dad's in the hospital. Can you come to Bayview right away?" She sobbed. "He had a heart attack. I don't know how much longer..."

"I'm on my way." *No time now to deal with this unreasonable man.* He pulled out his keys and thrust his phone in his pocket as he started for the door.

"Uh, hum." Mr. Thompson gave him a cold stare. "How can you take off somewhere when you've got your reckless behavior to answer for?"

"It's my father." His voice caught in his throat. But he wasn't about to show Johnny's father his emotions. "My sister says it's critical. We can continue this interrogation later."

Nothing mattered any more except to get to his dad. He didn't wait for a response but marched past the man.

Mr. Thompson glowered at him. "Humph. If you say so."

He stormed down the hall to the foyer and the outside entrance. *This might be my last chance to make things right with Dad.*

*****

The elevator dinged at the fifth floor. Tim stepped out and followed the sign to the critical coronary care unit. Room 512 appeared on his left. He peeked in the door. His father lay in a bed, his white hospital gown opened on his chest. Three round pads were attached. Each connected to a heart monitor by a wire.

Dad's pale face frightened him. *I've never seen him look so vulnerable.* Janelle and Mom clung to each other on the side of the bed opposite the monitor.

"Excuse me, sir." A nurse pushed past him and stood next to a man in a white lab jacket, probably the on-call doctor. She looked back at Tim. "Are you a member of the family?"

He nodded. "I'm his son." The beeps, the sound of his father's heart, released a jolt of fear to his emotions. *Is he conscious?* With slow steps, he crept to the end of Dad's bed.

Janelle turned from Mom to Tim and whispered, "I'm glad you're here." She laced her fingers and brought them to her chin.

Panic filled him. What if it was too late? "I've got to talk to him. Can he hear me?" he spoke to no one in particular.

She lifted her lips closer to his ear. "He talked to Mom a few minutes before you got here, and he asked for you."

A mix of emotions swirled in his chest. Exhilaration that Dad would want to see him but fear that he could no longer communicate.

The nurse held Dad's wrist as she looked at her watch. Tim moved around to the other side of the bed where the doctor studied the heart monitor. "Excuse me. May I speak to my father?"

The man in the white coat turned toward him and nodded. "He can still hear you." Moving to one side, he motioned for Tim to step forward next to Dad.

Fear, anxiety, and apprehension warred in his stomach. Dad wanted to talk to him. Would it be to rebuke him?

He moved closer, looking at his father's tired, sick form in the bed. "Dad, I'm here."

Dad's eyes fluttered opened and closed again and opened once more. "Tim, the last time... I saw you..." Dad moaned and squeezed his eyes together.

"That's okay. Don't try to talk if you don't feel like it."

Dad opened his eyes and moved his head from side to side on the pillow. "No. I... I'm sorry..." He coughed and cleared his throat then lay still.

If it hadn't been for the beeps of the monitor, Tim might've thought he'd passed away. Would Dad hear if he spoke? "I know you wanted to tell me something, but don't worry. I'll talk for both of us." He blew out a deep breath.

Dad's clammy hand lay in his. Dread then fear spiraled through his stomach. "Things haven't been right between us in the past. I didn't mean it—about hating you. You're my father. I love you." He bowed his head and swiped his cheeks. "Just get well."

Dad squeezed his hand and a thin smile spread on his lips. He opened his mouth, and his words sounded stronger. "I love ... you, too, son." His smiled remained, and he closed his eyes. The beeps on the monitor became more rhythmical. Almost as if Tim's words were what he needed to hear.

A hand fell on Tim's shoulder. "We have him stabilized for the moment, but we need to keep a close eye on him. Could be he'll rally and be able to have the surgery." The on-call doctor picked up Dad's chart and scribbled. "I'll be here another six hours. Ring if you need me." He walked out of the room, the RN following. "Oh, and the nurses will be in and out."

Mom wrung her hands. "I pray he'll be okay."

Tim nodded with a weak smile. "Can we sit with him awhile?"

"Of course, honey." She grasped both his arms and led him to a chair beside the bed then collapsed into the one next to him. "Join us, Janelle."

The steady beeps of the monitor filled the room.

The back of the chair supported his head as he closed his eyes to pray. He stirred and looked around the room. The clock on the wall said an hour later than when he arrived. Until this moment he hadn't realized he'd fallen asleep.

Dad's heart still sounded strong. Tim glanced at Mom and Janelle.

Mom's eyes were closed, and Janelle stood staring out the window.

He glanced toward the door. *Maybe I should ask Jess and Holly to pray.* He slipped out to the waiting area at the end of the hall. With a touch to his speed dial, he called Jess.

His friend's deep, calm voice met his ears. "Hi, Tim. Haven't talked to you in a while."

"Jess, I'm at the hospital." Tim caught his breath.

"Hey, man. Are you okay?"

"Yes, it's my Dad. He had a heart attack before his

scheduled surgery. I believe he's improving, but can I ask you and Holly to pray?"

"Sure, buddy. Do you need some support up there?"

Jess's words soothed his heart. "No, thanks, Jess. I think I'm going home in a little bit because he's doing so much better."

"Holly and I will pray right now. Love you, Brother."

"Same with me. I'll call you in a day or two."

A friend like Jess was more valuable than gold. He slipped his cell back in his pocket. *Dad stood a chance to live.* With a grateful heart, he headed back toward his room.

Swift footsteps sounded behind him. The same doctor who attended Dad rushed past. *Someone must have an emergency.* Tim's heart stood still. They turned into his father's room.

He jogged to catch up, no more than a few feet behind the attending physician. The sound of the monitor recorded a series of rapid, erratic beats then gave a continuous signal. He knew what it meant. He willed it to beep again, but it didn't.

Pressing on Dad's chest, the physician began CPR while he glanced at the flat monitor. After several attempts to restart Dad's heart with a defibrillation shock, he turned to the nurse and shook his head.

Tim rushed toward Mom and Janelle, frozen just inside the door. He looked toward the bed but saw only the nurse and on-call doctor, their backs to him.

Dad had rallied. What happened? He put his arms around his mother and sister, disbelief washing over him. Dad hadn't died.

The doctor turned toward them. "I'm sorry."

Tim could barely restrain his emotions as Mom's sobbing tore at his heartstrings.

*****

The boy's loud mocking laugh infuriated Tim. The kid picked up his Bible and threw it at him. "You know what you can do with your religion and your boring lessons."

Rage rose in Tim's chest. How dare the youth talk to him like that? He rushed to the guy and shoved him. He fell backwards and groaned, his head beside a jagged rock protruding from the grass.

Tim yelled at him. "Get up and fight like a man."

The teen laid still, his face ashen.

"Get up." He stared at the lifeless juvenile. "Get up." He shouted again.

The boy didn't move.

He'd killed him.

Tim bolted up and covered his face with his hands, his forehead dripping. Had he ended Johnny's life? No, he'd only dreamt it. He dragged himself out of the bed in his old room. The bronze plaque with his certificate for memorizing the most Bible verses in fifth grade still hung on the wall from when the neighbors took him to Sunday school. His baseball trophy from high school sat on the dresser.

He slipped down on his knees. What could have caused the bizarre dream? "Lord, every time I become angry, it's because my pride has been wounded. Forgive me for the arrogance separating You and me. Lord, I am helpless to overcome this sin in my life, but I know You are greater than the ruler of this world. I'm weak but you're strong. Help me. In Jesus name."

Seven in the morning, according to the clock on his bedside table. He needed to go home today and back to work tomorrow, since they'd seen Mom through the funeral.

The aroma of coffee coaxed him into the kitchen. He slipped on warm-ups and shook his wet hair trying to rid himself of the dream's effects.

Janelle and Mom sat across from each other at the kitchen table, each with a mug of the steaming drink. His sister offered him a pleasant look. Different than in the past. Can I get you a cup?"

"Please. You both are up early."

Janelle poured him a mug with coffee from the pot on the counter and set it in front of him.

Mom gave him a weary smile. "I couldn't sleep. It's so different not having your father here."

He eased down in the chair next to Janelle and glanced at Mom across the table. "Be honest. How are you doing?"

"Your father and I had our share of problems, as you well know." She studied her fingers. "Some of your childhood memories aren't pleasant."

Tim remembered, but he didn't expect his mother to talk about it. He steeled himself to ask the question he wanted to voice for so long. "Mom, what kept you with Dad all these years?"

"Oh, honey. I guess I got so used to his trying to control me. I wanted to stand up to him but never found the courage. I suppose I loved him in my own way." She stared at the opposite wall, a faraway look in her eye. "But now, the fights and the screaming are over." Her shoulders fell as she exhaled a long breath.

Mom must've found a fragment of relief in his passing. She'd come to the end of her codependent lifestyle. He could only pray for her.

She patted his hand. "Don't worry, Tim. You've always let me know you cared, though your father made life difficult for you. I wished I could've done more about that." She dabbed at her eye with a tissue and straightened. "I'm thinking of taking a job at Carter's Nursery. The owner is a friend of mine. I'm going to be fine." She smiled as she squeezed Tim's hand.

Relief surged through Tim's soul. "I'm so grateful I was able to say good-bye." He swiped the renegade tear from his eye.

"Janelle and I had our chance before you arrived. I'll always be glad you spoke with him."

His sister stared down at her coffee cup. "Tim, I need to tell you something as well. You've been such a help this past week, making the funeral arrangements, being there for Mom." She looked up. Her eyes glistened with tears. "I saw how you said good-bye to Dad and your sincerity. Can you forgive me?"

He never thought he'd hear those words. He turned in his seat and put his arms around her. "You're my sister, and I love you." He looked toward his mom. "We're still a family." He placed his hands on his forehead. "But I'd appreciate any spare prayers you might offer up. I don't deserve your good words. I need freedom from the legacy of anger I've inherited. I've got to go back to my job—if I still have one."

Chapter Nineteen

Tim's breath hitched as he shut his car door. The umbrella, a constant companion, protected him from the pouring rain. His breath hung in the air, then slowly dissipated. So much had changed in one week.

He trudged toward the front door at the church, sidestepping the mud puddles. What would he find when he walked through these doors? Mr. Thompson's anger? Nancy's skepticism? Pastor Downing's passivity?

With an unsteady hand, he pushed the door open and folded up his umbrella. *Guess I better head to the main office first.* They probably would want to resolve the credit card issue immediately.

Nancy sat at her computer keyboard. She glanced up and rose from her desk. "Tim."

He hadn't expected her reaction when she slid her arms around him.

"I want you to know how sorry we are for your loss. Pastor and I prayed for you."

If only Tim could avoid the condolences. The sentiments unearthed the raw emotions on the surface of his soul.

With another quick breath, he nodded. "Thank you." No point in going into the details of Dad's funeral with her. "Guess we better get to the bottom of the credit card issue now."

Nancy's face turned a soft pink. "Yes. As you know, Jess cancelled the card, and Mr. Thompson won't issue you another until we can figure out what happened." She sighed. "I can't imagine you made a personal charge on the church account. Sometimes I wonder..."

What was she going to say? Maybe a word in his favor?

She cleared her throat. "I'm so sorry, but I believe the elders are planning to fire you. I'd rather you hear it from me first than Mr. Thompson."

Her words branded him. Disloyal, dishonest, irresponsible. Fury gushed into his gut. The unfairness of the situation tore at his insides. He'd tried his best. "Okay. Just get it over with." He glared at Nancy. "This job's a dead-end street."

"I'm sorry." She held out her hand and patted his arm.

Though he didn't like his reaction, he slammed out of the main office. He grabbed a breath and blew out hard. Jiggling his key in the lock to his door did no good. Dad's death had been tough. His emotion erupted, no longer restrained. Grasping the key ring in his raised hand, he hurled it at the wall.

The pounding in his chest couldn't be healthy. If he didn't do something about his situation, he'd have a heart attack, like his father.

The key ring lay on the floor near the other side of the hall. He seized it and jabbed it over and over again in the lock, huffing out puffs of air.

A large, warm hand rested on his and took the key.

"Let me, Tim." Pastor Downing's gentle voice radiated peace. He placed the key in the lock and opened Tim's office. His extended hand indicated Tim should go first. The man followed him and shut the door.

Tim flinched. Pastor witnessed his disgusting anger. "I'm... I'm sorry. I've had a rough week." No excuse for acting like a child.

"Sit down." Pastor's kind face urged Tim's emotions to give into the sadness he restrained, something he didn't want to do.

Of the two, he'd rather be angry than cry. Tears were a sign of weakness. Yet when he counseled people, he encouraged them to release their emotions. Maybe he should practice what he preached.

His boss slipped down into the chair opposite his. "First of all, I'd like to offer you my sympathies."

Tim didn't trust his voice. Only stared at Pastor, gulping back the feelings he could barely contain.

A firm hand fell on Tim's shoulder. "I prayed for you the whole week you were gone."

"Thank... thank you." The tear he couldn't control rolled down his cheek, and he whisked it away.

The older man shifted in the chair and peered at him. "Do you want to talk about your father? I know you had problems."

How could he speak to Pastor without showing more emotion? The office already had a bad image of him. "We had a chance to say good-bye." Tim shook his head. "I can't talk about it anymore."

"All right." Pastor gripped Tim's shoulder again. "I'm sorry about Jack's behavior, and the effect it may have on your career. But at this point, the evidence looks damaging—the report of you drinking beer in public..."

"Wait a minute. We talked about that. Harry set me up on that one. I'm sure Jess Colton won't hesitate to confirm my words. Yes, maybe I shouldn't have sat at the bar, but I did nothing wrong."

"I'm sure it will come up at the next elders' meeting. But there are still the other issues—your lack of control with the kids, your sister's report, though she did come in to clear up her misinformation about Roxanne. In addition, there's the confusion with Mandy and Tiffany, and now the credit card problem. I don't believe you're at fault except in how you display your temper. But I'm afraid unless we resolve these issues soon..."

"So, I'm guilty until proven innocent."

"That's the way some of the elders see it. I hate to break it to you, but..."

Though Pastor's eyes held compassion, Tim trembled. He couldn't restrain the words. "I know. I'm getting canned."

"No, I believe the elders are not going to ask you back next year. There's a difference." Pastor Downing fixed his eyes on Tim. "The main issue is the credit card charge. Unless the elders have proof..." He lifted a brow. "I believe someone on the finance committee is going to look into it further."

"I realize the chances could be slim. And I'm sure the elders aren't giving me a recommendation for another job either." He had to face the facts. This whole year had been a failure. But where was he to turn?

The other man stared at his fingers. "You'll finish out this year including the youth camp during spring break next month—the third week in April. Then when school is out for the senior high students, you'll be free to go." Pastor's brow knit into deep grooves. "As you know, I've been praying about the when, where, and how to address the congregation with my past transgressions and Jack Thompson. I'll make that decision soon and am leaning toward retiring and traveling fulltime in our RV with my wife. That may be best."

Tim nodded. "Sounds like a wonderful lifestyle. I guess I'm too young for that, but maybe someday..."

Pastor Downing frowned. "I've failed in this job, not standing up to Jack. But the Lord sees my heart. My only desire was to serve Him. I can say the same for you. Now, I'd like to encourage you to get some counsel."

What a paradox. He was supposed to be a counselor, and he was the needy one. He shook his head. *Glorious Day* sounded from his pocket.

Pastor rose from the chair. "I'll let you get that. Talk to you later." He opened the door and slipped out, giving it gentle push.

Tim reached in his pocket. "Hello."

"Hey, Tim. Jess Colton. I'd like to tell you how sorry I am about your father. I didn't get a chance to speak to you at the funeral."

"Thanks, Jess."

"Look, I'm stuck here at home with the baby. How'd you like to come over for lunch?"

Tim breathed deeply and lifted his gaze to the ceiling. Could Jess possibly be the confidant and friend he needed now?

*****

Tim steered his car into the upscale neighborhood in Northwest Woodlyn. Each dwelling stood on at least a two-acre lot. He parked in front of the sprawling two-story brick home. The first time he saw it after Jess's wedding, he'd been pleased for him and Holly. The sidewalk bordered by a flowerbed of tulips, crocus, and daffodils led to the front door.

The ornate doorbell on the double-door entry was located to the right. A baby's cries met his ears after he punched the round button.

A bedraggled Jess opened the door, his arm around the infant's middle, the baby's feet dangling.

Tim laughed. "Is that how you're supposed to hold a baby?"

Jess grinned. "Hey, I'm a new dad. You know how it is."

No, he didn't know how it was.

Jess slapped him on the shoulder with his spare hand. "Come in. It's great to see you. This is long overdue." Jess raised the child to his chest. "You doing okay, buddy?"

"Yeah, fine."

Jess furrowed his brow as he studied Tim's face. "Okay, man. Holly and I've prayed a lot for you." He looked down at his son. "I want you to meet your namesake, Timmy."

"Hello, Timmy." Tim grinned, stuck out his hand, and shook the baby's tiny fingers. The expansive entry led through a formal living room into a den. A baby carrier sat in the middle of the floor.

Jess pointed to a brown leather couch. "Sit down." With the baby upright against his chest, he plopped down in an easy chair covered in a green and beige woven fabric and patted Timmy's back.

The baby emitted a loud burp.

"Just finished feeding him." Jess chuckled. "Holly left some of her milk in a bottle."

"Hey, man. I'm impressed. How are you on changing diapers?"

Jess smirked. "I try to get out of it most of the time except when Holly's not here. She had a doctor's appointment today."

"You look like you've got things under control. How old is he?" Childcare was about as foreign to Tim as going shopping.

"Let's see, he was born at the end of January. He's almost two months now." Pride radiated on Jess's face. He cupped his free hand beside his mouth. "Don't tell Holly, but I love this job. I still work at home, so it's convenient for me to keep him. Of course, I can't do any work while he's awake. He should be going down for a nap pretty soon."

"So, what's it like to be a father?" He would probably never know firsthand.

Jess glanced at Timmy when he made one of those baby sounds. "There's nothing like it. But the sense of responsibility overwhelms me sometimes. Want to hold him?" Jess stood and moved closer to Tim.

He shook his head. "Uh, I don't know. I've never held a baby before."

"It's easy." Jess placed the baby's head in the crook of Tim's arm. The child's little blue nightshirt pulled up and revealed some kind of white shoes.

How could babies feel so soft—and smell so good? The infant's face was perfect yet so little. Tim shifted on the couch then froze. The corners of Timmy's mouth turned up in a grin. "No way. He smiled at me."

"Hey, buddy. I hate to tell you, but it means he has gas pains."

"Oh." Tim laughed. "Just when I thought I amused the little tyke."

"You'll have one someday, I have no doubt. Speaking of that, how's Roxanne?" Jess gave him a teasing grin.

"Strange you should mention fatherhood and Roxanne all in the same breath. I don't think it's going to happen. We're not seeing each other anymore."

Timmy gave another gas-pain smile along with a peep.

Jess furrowed his brow. "How do you feel about that?"

"I'd hoped for a relationship with her someday." He gazed at the baby in his arms. The infant's eyes were closed. "I think he's out," Tim whispered.

"Next time I need a babysitter, I'm calling you." Jess reached for Timmy, placed him in the baby seat, and buckled him in.

The child made sucking motions with his mouth but didn't open his eyes.

"He'll stay asleep for a while." Jess eased back down in his chair. "Holly and I wanted to talk to you about something. We'd like you to officiate at Timmy's dedication service."

Tim winced. Might as well tell Jess the truth. It would never happen at Woodlyn—not with his termination. "Uh, Jess. I need to talk to you. Perhaps the Lord sent you to help."

Jess peered at him. "I thought so. I'm on the finance committee now, and Mr. Thompson's been filling our ears with information." He ran a hand through his hair. "I'm here for you, buddy."

A river of peace rippled through his soul. Somehow he and Jess would uncover the answers he needed. The baby hadn't stirred when Tim finished his story, Jess's focus never leaving his face.

Jess's Bible lay on the coffee table in front of the couch. He bowed his head. "Father, I commit this time to You. Bless Tim and me with wisdom and healing." He looked up with eyes of empathy. "You had anger modeled to you as a child. No wonder you emulated your father's behavior."

"I know, Jess, but I'm an adult now. The Word tells me to put away childish things. But I don't know how to do it." He paced the den, first on the hardwood floor, then over the tan patterned area rug.

"Tim, relax. Let's look at what your namesake in the Bible says." Jess flipped through the pages. "All scripture is God-breathed. The Word tells you which road to travel, and when you get off that road, it tells you how to get back on and stay there."

He glanced at the sleeping baby. "I envy your little guy—no worries."

Jess sat up straighter in his easy chair. "Brace yourself, Tim. This is the hard part. When a person gives into anger, he's usually thinking only of himself, trying to protect his pride. And he's not a very good witness for the Lord."

How bizarre. Jess was telling him concepts he'd learned in his psychology class. He edged down on the couch. Hearing it from his friend impacted his heart in a personal way. His stomach roiled. "A tough sin to overcome."

"Yup. We all sin but through the power of God, we can find freedom. The Bible has lots to say about anger. I'm not talking about righteous anger, here."

He'd read the scriptures many times. What Jess told him was nothing new, but how well had he applied it to his own life? He hadn't.

"We need to turn away from anger. The Bible says it like this. A fool vents his full fury. You're not a fool."

For the first time in his life the familiar words made impact. He was ready to listen now. Jess's message reached down into his spirit, bringing him hope.

"The Bible says bitterness goes along with rage and anger. I want to ask you the same question you asked me once. Who do you need to forgive? Maybe your father?"

A slow grin stretched across his face. "Who's the counselor around here, you or me?"

"Just put me in the friend category."

Tim lowered his head. "At my father's death bed, I told him I didn't harbor ill feelings. I'm not sure if I really forgave him then."

"All right. Are you ready to forgive your father the way your heavenly Father forgave you?"

*****

Tim parked his car in front of the church. After turning off the ignition, he leaned back in his seat, still full from the delicious lunch of turkey sandwiches and homemade potato chips Jess fed him. Sunshine poked through the gray skies. The rain stopped, and peace calmed his soul. He'd made a start today, however small, getting his life on track.

Lord, Your word is true when it says we reap what we sow. His heart warmed when his friend set up a schedule for them to meet twice a week for fellowship, Bible study, and prayer.

A burden lifted from his shoulders when he prayed with Jess. He meant every word as he confessed his anger and restored his trust in the Lord. But he had a long road to travel.

For a brief moment he closed his eyes. Roxanne's sweet face sprang into his mind. He yearned for her, to be near her, to share his life with her.

His thoughts led to memories of their good times together—Mt. Rainier, the Zoolights, the fundraisers. Her smile so loving, her touch consoling. If he hadn't lost his temper, he'd be in her arms. Was it too late for them?

*****

Roxanne reached for the calculator and set it on the kitchen table. She added the figures for the fifth time. Her credit card debt was unforgiveable. With every prayer or Bible study, she'd begun to realize. She relied on shopping as emotional support instead of the Lord. Yes, it was wrong. And each time she told herself it wouldn't happen again.

She turned to her mother's computer and stared at the screen. SBA—Small Business Administration. Quite a lot of information on the agency. Her dream of owning her own salon sat precariously on the back burner of her life. Yet, she held on to it. Someday... somehow. She could picture it. A tawny brick building with lots of glass. Everyone would gather for the cutting of the red ribbon. Mom, Holly and Jess, maybe even Tim.

She didn't want any other man in her life. When she closed her eyes at night, she saw his face. A day never went by when she wished she'd spent part of it with him. Despite the problems, she'd fallen in love with him. How does one move on from there?

Their relationship ended the night at The Mediterranean. The blame wasn't all his. She'd made so many mistakes—trying to substitute Tim's affection for her own needs and pressing him for answers when it only made him angry.

She peered at the screen. The SBA site gave her links she could explore. One click brought up the Washington State Community, Trade, and Economic Developer. Her hopes escalated. One of the pluses in qualifying for this loan was being a female business owner. The amount of money she could borrow would about cover her startup costs.

Her heart fell. She couldn't qualify for a loan with her debt. Somehow, she'd have to get her balance paid down. Maybe if she worked nights at Albrights and days in a salon. *Hmmm.* She'd look into it. But first she had to find freedom from compulsive shopping, and she knew where to find the answer. She turned off the computer and picked up her Bible. The verses she'd read this morning in Romans eight spoke to her. "The Spirit himself testifies with our spirit that we are God's children. Now if we are children, then we are heirs,— heirs of God and co-heirs with Christ."

Co-heirs with Christ. That sounds pretty important.

If she was an heir of God, she had a vital place in His kingdom. She didn't need to find her identity in her clothes and makeup. Joy bubbled up in her chest. An amazing thought. She lifted her hand in praise to the Lord. The ringing phone brought her back.

She glanced at her caller ID. Evergreen Fellowship. "Hello."

"Hi, Roxanne? This is Tammy, the secretary from Evergreen. We're so pleased you and your mom have made us your church home."

"Oh, thanks, Tammy. We love it there."

"I've got a huge favor to ask you. We're desperate. As you know, our church is involved with Camp Solid Rock. We are in dire need of female counselors. Could you possibly think about serving at camp?"

She tensed. "Oh, Tammy, it would require me to take off work. I don't know if I can afford it. I'll think about it." How was she supposed to save up money to pay off her debt? Skipping work wasn't the way.

Chapter Twenty

Tim followed the road through the trees and under the sign *Camp Solid Rock,* carved on the wooden surface. He parked in the lot adjacent to the building's entrance. A plaque said *The Lodge*. The heavy wooden door opened when he gave it a push.

A middle age woman sitting at a metal table shuffled papers and looked up with a smile. "Welcome."

"Tim Garrett. I'm a counselor."

"Yes." She thumbed through a pile of envelopes. "Please get these registration forms back at your earliest convenience. Your packet of information, including your cabin and schedule are inside. Your quarters are down that way." She pointed past the parking lot.

"Yes, ma'am." He shouldered his duffle bag and ambled along the gravel path through a stand of cedar trees to the boys' cabins. The paper with his assignment said *The Gopher,* his cottage and home for the next six days.

The front door of the A-frame bungalow opened to a one-room lodge that held six beds lining the log walls. A rustic table constructed of hardwood stood in the center of the room with matching chairs. He sniffed.

The room still carried the smell of the last wood fire from the brick fireplace in the corner.

He dropped his backpack and duffle bag on the green army blanket covering the cot nearest the door. Guess he'd claim it before his teenage cabin-mates arrived tomorrow. Maybe his troublemakers, Roger and Johnny, would be assigned to one of the other four cabins in the boys' area, and some guys from other churches would bunk with him.

Outside the window on the wall nearest the fireplace, a spectacular view held his attention. The elevated mountains in the distance were still covered with snow. A forest of evergreens closer to the camp lined the horizon.

He appreciated receiving his assigned duties last month—gave him time to prepare his team games, a couple of hikes, a volleyball tournament, and horseback riding if the weather cooperated. April could be cold and rainy in the Pacific Northwest.

A trail in front of the boys' cabins meandered to the girls' quarters and further on, toward the dining hall. If Roxanne came to camp as a counselor, she'd stay in one of those cottages across the way. But what were the chances of that?

A lump formed in his throat. He disliked the distance between them—no communication since the infamous night at The Mediterranean. But what would happen if he did call her? She'd probably hang up on him or ignore him if he tried to strike up a conversation.

What did his future look like? He prayed it would include Roxanne someday—and a job as a pastoral counselor. He stretched his arms in front of him. The last time he and Jess talked, he encouraged him to apply for the job he found on-line—the opening for a pastoral counselor at Evergreen on the other side of town. His friend was right. Only made sense. Surely it was the Lord's timing. But did he stand a chance of getting the recommendation from Woodlyn? If his name was cleared, what would they say when he told them he was resigning? He shook his head and dismissed the thoughts.

Freshly cut firewood was piled behind the cabin next to *The Gopher*. He strolled out the door and across the grass. When he picked up three pieces, they wobbled in his arms. Grasping them tighter, he hiked back to his cabin.

What an idiot he'd been that night with Roxanne—repeating the same mistake from his past. He pushed the door to the cabin, still ajar, with his foot and set the logs down beside the fireplace.

A surge of peace coursed through him. Thanks to Jess's insight in their twice weekly meetings, he'd confessed his anger, forgave his father, and memorized verses from Proverbs. He chuckled at the mental picture of his mentor as he helped him practice relaxation techniques. In college, he'd learned about trying to see the humor in a situation, but never thought he'd be applying it in his own life.

If he opened two windows, it'd clear the cabin of stale air. *What time was the staff meeting?* He glanced at his watch. Forty-five minutes until he needed to be at the lodge to meet with Bob Martin. The e-mail from the executive director impressed him. Sounded like the man had the kickoff meeting well organized—a time for introductions, then he'd pass out the schedules, give an overview of camp objectives, and conduct a tour.

Maybe he'd explore an alternate trail to the lodge—the one past the stables. Wouldn't hurt to say *hi* to the horses. Something about stroking a horse's mane relieved tension.

He rubbed his corduroy jacket's sleeves. Anything to provide warmth against the chill. The trail lined with Douglas firs and spruce trees took him to the wooden fence surrounding the stables.

A chestnut quarter horse poked his head over.

"Hey, fellow." He bent down and picked a handful of grass. "Here you go."

The horse whinnied and chomped the green treat.

He smiled. "Guess you don't have any filly problems, buddy." He picked up another handful of grass and passed it to the animal. Laughter sounded behind him. Two guys strolled along the path past the stables and waved as they headed to the lodge. Three girls about ten yards behind were occupied in conversation. *Guess it's close to meeting time.*

He turned once more toward the soft neighing as the horse stuck his head across the fence, probably wanting another handout. "Bye, guy." With one last pat on the horse's nose, he turned to follow the others in the direction of the lodge.

The pebbled path wound around a couple of larger rocks. When he looked up, his breath caught in his chest. Roxanne. She stood on the steps at the front of the lodge. So she was here after all.

A boxing match took place in his stomach. Looking at her accelerated his heart rate, but there was no way they could avoid each other. What would he say when he ran into her?

*****

Roxanne swung one of the two heavy doors open and stepped into the lodge. Almost time for the meeting. Her heart had told her she couldn't ignore Tammy's appeal for counselors. She needed to put the Lord first and trust Him. Besides, she loved teens. Working with Tim on his fundraising projects had taught her that.

Her stomach tightened. She'd be attending meetings with him—no avoiding it, but her desire to serve the youth trumped her apprehension of talking to him.

What would happen when she met up with him? She shooed away the uncertainty. Best to face that when the time came. Which could be soon.

She threaded her way through the groups of people and spotted the lady from Evergreen Fellowship. Relieved to find someone she knew besides Tim, she slipped down beside her in the fifth row from the front.

The woman's ponytail flipped to one side as she flashed a wide grin. "Hey girl, I see you're in *The Chipmunk*, almost as woodsy as my cabin, *The Wolverine.* At least none of the cabins are named *The Skunk.*"

"And *The Snake* or *The Frog*," Roxanne said. Her new acquaintance's smile chased away the stiffness from Roxanne's shoulders. She took a breath and closed her eyes. *Thank you, Lord, for the opportunity to help out at Camp Solid Rock.*

She'd thought about it for a while before making the commitment. Because she had to take time off work and she didn't have any sick days, her pay would get docked.

The old temptation still lured her, but she'd read and reread the scripture about seeking first the Kingdom of God. Everything she needed would be added to her life. Why was it so hard to assimilate the meaning of the verse?

She opened her eyes. In the aisle to her right, a nice looking man, graying at the temples, stopped and shook a guy's hand then headed toward a podium in the front. Probably Bob Martin.

Her heart melted when Tim and another man, a blond, drifted down the aisle, never glancing her way. Her gorgeous former friend made her pulse race as he laughed and chatted with the blond guy. They eased down in the first row on the other side. Everything within her told her to wrench her glance from him and look at Mr. Martin. But she gave up trying, her heart transfixed on his presence.

*****

Tim marched his group of ten teens, five girls and five boys, past the camp entrance into the wooded area behind the health center with Jake Casper, the counselor in the cabin next to his. A path led through the Douglas firs, sprawling oaks, and blackberry bushes complete with thorns and spider webs.

The teens' orientation yesterday went better than he expected. Most kids paid close attention to Mr. Martin. Johnny had been assigned to another cabin, bringing a measure of relief, but here the kid was—on the list for his team activity.

He glanced back over his shoulder. The last three kids, Johnny, Tiffany, and Roger shuffled along behind the rest.

Jake shook his head and hollered. "You guys keep up with the group."

An edge of agitation ate at him. How could he lead these people in his team cooperation game if the kids from own his youth group were uncooperative?

He glanced back once more. Johnny and Roger paced a little faster in what looked like a lame attempt to catch up, arriving in line behind Tiffany.

Little clumps of red, purple, and yellow wildflowers grew in a grassy spot near the elm trees. A spark of hope filled his heart. Most of the teens waited with wide eyes for him to speak, as if anxious for his instruction.

He rubbed his hands. A welcome change to find kids who wanted to work with each other. "Okay, listen up. We're doing an activity called Team Radar encouraging trust and cooperation." He pointed to the path ahead. "The beginning and end of this winding course is marked with red flags, the last one about a hundred yards through the woods."

Johnny leaned over to another guy and whispered something. The boy turned a shoulder to him.

"I'm going to give you time to set up a series of landmarks on the course. Your job later on is to get through the woods blindfolded holding onto a rope. You'll help each other by calling out the things you find beside the trail, helping you to know which way to go."

A few puzzled faces stared at him.

A short girl with dark brown hair waved. "What do you suggest we use to mark the area?"

"Good question. You can pile a number of rocks up on the side of the path, place a downed branch pointing in the right direction. Someone could leave a backpack, a hat, a belt beside the path—something like that. Get creative and work together. But please don't destroy any plants. And no peeking after you're blindfolded."

He set his backpack on the ground. "You'll have twenty minutes to mark your route."

The kids scurried toward the course he'd mapped out earlier this morning. Their eager laughs and lively conversation buzzed in the air.

He pulled the thirty-foot rope from his shoulder, uncoiled it, and dug in his backpack for the red and white bandanas. Teens piled up rocks and placed belts, a water bottle, and a baseball cap along the path. Two guys picked up a couple of evergreen branches and stuck them into the soft soil side by side. What a difference. Most of the kids worked well together.

Tiffany, Roger, and Johnny stood at a distance, only entering into the group activity to whisper to others. These kids, not used to Johnny's antics, shrugged him away. Maybe at Woodlyn, the kids found it easier to go along with Johnny since they'd always known him.

Or maybe, like Johnny's father, he held sway over some of them by the information he possessed. The boy had a knack for knowing things—like when to take a picture that could be misconstrued as something very ugly.

He shook his head as the rowdy boy peered back at him. Other kids needed his attention—kids who wanted to be a part of this exercise. *I've allowed Johnny Thompson to interfere with my ministry for too long—a ministry that God gave me to teach and counsel young charges.*

"Now, get in line." He passed a bandana to each.

"Blindfold yourselves. I'll hand you the rope when everyone is ready. The first person will lead off." The teens placed the cloths over their eyes and secured the knot in the back. "Oh, yes. And one more thing. If I see anyone walking into an obstacle or place of danger, I'll say *stop* and for your safety, you should do it."

The short dark haired girl led the unsteady group as they inched forward holding onto the rope. "Here's someone's backpack. We're on the right track."

A tall boy third in line held the rope and waved his hand."Yeah, here are the leaves I piled up."

The fifth girl called out. "I remember this. Go a little to the left."

Another girl patted the trail with her toe. When she encountered a girl's plastic head band, she yelled. "Curve about one foot to the right."

Pacing a few steps in that direction, the leader hollered. "Here's the marker I set up—sticks in the shape of a teepee."

Tim sucked in a breath. The last person, Johnny, curved too far off the path and headed toward a bush he suspected to be poison oak.

"Stop," he commanded.

The leader, down to the person in front of Johnny, froze in place.

The teen must've decided he didn't need to follow directions and continued toward the bush catching his foot on an exposed root. He tripped and fell into the leafy plant, the rope no longer in his hand.

Roger attempted to pull the limp end of the rope toward him as if to draw Johnny back from danger.

Johnny wrenched off his blindfold and struggled to get to his feet. "Ouch." He picked bits of leaves and stems off his jacket as he stumbled back toward the path.

Tim stifled the urge to laugh. "Okay, guys. Take off your blindfolds. We've got a mishap."

The others stared at him. No snickers or laughs. Only determined faces appeared to want to try again.

Why should the rest of the kids miss out on finishing the activity because of Johnny's foolishness? "Go back to the start and try again with your blindfolds on. Johnny, come over here and let me see what damage you've done."

Mr. Thompson's son hung his head and kicked a rock as he trudged to him. The rest of the group started down the route again.

"Ow. Ow." He scratched his hand and his face. "My skin is stinging."

"Jake, I need you to watch the group while I take this guy to the nurse. Come on, Johnny." He glanced at the kids maneuvering through the course and turned to the boy. "At the risk of sounding preachy, I'll remind you Hebrews says to obey your leaders. Might have been a good idea today."

He stared at the kid wiggling around and rubbing his face. Would Johnny absorb the scripture, or would he scoff at his attempt to counsel him? Tim's mouth dropped open when Johnny looked at him with soulful eyes and nodded his head.

*****

The mountain air produced an appetite. One thing about Camp Solid Rock—the food was superb. Fried chicken, mashed potatoes and gravy, green beans, tossed salad, and apple pie and plenty of it tonight.

From the dining hall past the stables, Tim took the path to the Fire Ring and the evening devotional. He craved time with the Lord after the stress of Johnny's accident this morning. But the distance between he and Roxanne only added to his tension.

An amphitheater with a series of seven levels of circular steps surrounded a concrete stage at the bottom. A wood burning fire pit sent sparks into the cool night air as the aroma of smoldering wood chips drew him closer.

Most of the teens crowded down in front nearer the fire. He took a seat on the top row level with the ground—needed an hour or so to himself.

The crisp evening breeze penetrated his jacket. He pulled the zipper to the top, rubbed his arms, and inhaled a long breath of fresh, mountain air perfumed by the cedars, shrubs, mosses, and early blooming wildflowers.

Bob's guitar accompanied his rich voice in song proclaiming how great our God is. Tim's heart soared as his voice blended with the worshipers—other counselors, the teens, and Bob. His lifted hand in praise to God, the Giver of life, expressed his joy.

The singing ebbed as Bob prayed facing the crowd flocking together on one side of the amphitheater.

Tim closed his eyes, allowing the peace and quiet of the evening to wash over him.

"And Lord, I pray You will touch every heart at this camp. Draw us nearer by Your Holy Spirit." The flames radiated a spray of brilliant sparks illuminating Bob's features.

The camp director rose from his stool to face the

group. "Now people, I want to tell you about a teenager named Rick Hoyt and a father who gave so much to his son because of his great love for his child."

Bob's words faded as Tim glanced toward the person on his right not more than eight feet from him.

Roxanne shivered, rubbing her hands over the arms of her green sweater. Her shoulders slumped, and she pressed her knees together. He had to encounter her sometime at camp. This must be it.

Compassion and his protective inclination toward her flooded his heart. He couldn't stand to see her cold. What would she do if he got up to sit by her? At worse, she'd move away. He sidestepped between the rows and eased down next to her. "Mind if I sit here?"

She probably hadn't seen him until then as she jerked her head up, her eyes wide. Her expression held expectancy, not at all angry as he'd thought. She nodded but scooted away an inch or two.

"At age fifteen, Rick told his father he wanted to participate in a five-mile run. Only problem was, Rick was a quadriplegic." A few *oh's* and *wow's* ascended into the air, the teens apparently spell bound by Bob's story.

She trembled again.

Though he was cold, he'd rather Roxanne be warm. He slipped his arms out of his jacket and placed it around her shoulders, expecting her to give it back and move farther away.

With a half-smile on her lips, she nodded and pulled the coat tighter around her. "Thank you."

His heart thudded. Did she experience even half what he did—the desire to reconnect?

Until he sat next to her, he hadn't realized how empty

he felt these last weeks without her.

"Up until now, Rick's father had never done any long distance running, but out of love for his son, he agreed to push his wheelchair in a race."

The teens sat motionless.

Bob's deep voice, the only sound in the still night air, murmured the story of the courageous father who loved his son enough to allow him this experience. It thrilled Tim's heart. How like his heavenly Father. A Father who could free him from anger and allow him to love the woman by his side.

The breeze picked up and more sparks shot into the air. "After four years of marathons, Rick and his father accomplished the amazing feat of attempting a triathlon. Today they've run more than two hundred of these races. The story of Rick Hoyt is a powerful reminder of God's love for us. Never doubt it."

Tim slid his hand over Roxanne's cold one at Bob's last prayer, glad she didn't pull away.

"See you tomorrow morning at seven in the dining hall. Good night, people."

Teens filed out in twos and threes heading back in the direction of the cabins. Tim stood. What would Roxanne say if he asked her to go for a walk? Maybe she'd given up on him. Maybe she'd never trust him again. He tried to clear his husky voice paying no attention to the cold air surrounding him. "Would you like... do you want... to walk to the lake? I... I thought maybe we could use a few minutes to talk."

She looked up at him with a puzzled expression. With a nod of her head, she took a step from the top row of seats onto the grass. He held her hand as she brought her other jean-clad leg over the concrete bleachers.

Without a word, they strolled to the lake in the opposite direction from the stables and dining hall. A path led through a stand of poplar trees and passed a big leaf maple to an opening. Ripples of moonlight danced on the water as a Whippoorwill twittered.

"Do you want to sit down?" He pointed to a flat rock near the bank.

When she nodded, he picked up a downed branch with pine needles still attached, looking like a miniature broom, and swept debris off the top of the rock.

She slanted a sideways glance at him and sat, drawing her knees up under her arms. A silent Roxanne—unusual for her.

"I was glad you volunteered for camp." He gazed toward the lake, the moonlight illuminating the evergreens lining the opposite shore. He dared a glimpse at her.

She trained her face toward the lake.

"I've missed seeing you," he whispered.

"Have you, Tim?" She breathed her quiet question in a small, feminine voice.

He'd said those words to her before but for the first time, he spoke them with security, knowing he could be the friend and maybe the husband God designed him to be. "If you could look into my heart, you'd see how sorry I am for what happened the last time we were together. I would never hurt you. You've got to believe me."

"Somehow I do."

Her answer accelerated his pulse. Was there hope for them? He'd been so sure earlier at the campfire after Bob told his story. "Some things are changing. Jess and

I have spent a lot of time together. Roxy, I'm moving forward each day, trying to become the man God wants me to be. I want to please Him."

"That's fine, but how can I be sure?" She wrapped her arms over her chest, pulling the jacket closer around her.

He didn't blame her. After all the months of witnessing his angry behavior, how could he expect her to believe him? "I have no guarantees other than by the grace of God I'm getting better day by day."

She faced him. "I wish I could be certain."

"What will it take to convince you?"

"Time, I guess."

"I want to prove it to you."

"How?"

"After I treat you like you're the most important woman in my life, maybe you'll trust me. And that won't be hard, because it's true."

"I've prayed for you, Tim." Her hand glided over to touch his.

She must've found a small place in her heart for him. He breathed a sigh. "Roxy, can you ever forgive me? I don't want to spend another lonely month without you. I... I love you."

"You once said you wanted to take things slow. That's how I feel now." She pulled a string off his jacket. "I want to believe in you." She pushed off the rock and strolled nearer the water.

"Can we try this again? Can you give me another chance?" He spoke to the back of his jacket as she faced the lake.

She swiveled around and stared at him.

He rose from the rock and grasped her hands. "It's

chilly tonight." His heart attempted to leap into his throat. He drew her close and breathed in the scent of her silky hair. "Hmm. You smell like a woman."

Roxanne moved away and laughed. "Like a woman? Is that good or bad?"

He pulled her close again and nuzzled her cheek. "Very good."

"What does a woman smell like?" Roxy whispered in his ear.

"Flowers, or something," he mumbled, his eyes closed, his heart caught in the moment. She belonged in his embrace.

The swishing of the breeze through the trees soothed his soul. How long had he held her? Tomorrow would come early. It took a measure of willpower to lower his arms and move away. "Thank you for not turning from me."

She ran a finger under her eye. "You weren't the only one at fault. I added to the problems."

He cupped her chin. Her lips invited his affection. Within inches of her face, he stopped, feasting on her loveliness. Desire told him to journey the rest of the way, but his breath caught. Would any of his charges see him if he kissed her? For now he'd be content to hold her hand as they strolled to her cabin. "I'll see you tomorrow." He raised her fingers to his lips. "Good night, Roxy."

"Oh Tim. Thank you for your jacket."

He smiled as she held out his coat to him. When he slipped it on, the scent of her perfume swirled around his nose. Could he disguise the wide grin he knew plastered his face? No point in providing the teens a chance to give him a hard time.

The warmth of the room embraced him as the soft feminine presence of Roxanne had before. For once in his life, would he get a relationship right?

He shivered, but it wasn't from the cold. For the rest of his time at camp, he'd put the upcoming elders' meeting out of his mind—couldn't entertain thoughts of the ordeal and his impending termination.

*****

Roxanne turned toward the door of *The Chipmunk* and reached her hand for the wooden handle.

"Roxanne."

She whirled around to the whispered sound of her name.

Tiffany, in a pink down jacket, stood at the side of the cabin.

"Oh, hi, Tiffany. Is everything okay?" She must've walked over from *The Wolverine* next door.

She inched closer to Roxanne. "Yeah. I just needed to talk to you for a minute." Lines creased her forehead. "I'm kind of worried about Johnny."

"Oh, what's the matter?"

She grasped an object with both hands.

Roxanne peered at the expensive-looking iPad with a keyboard. "It's just kind of odd. He came up to me this afternoon and said he wanted me to have this."

Roxanne gave her a chuckle. "Well, you are a very attractive girl. Maybe he likes you."

Tiffany moved her head side to side. "We kind of had a crush on each other at the first of the year, but we're just friends now."

"Maybe he wants to ask you to be his girlfriend

again."

"No, I don't think so." She bit her lip. "I've known him a long time. He's not himself lately. I've got the idea Johnny's planning something crazy again."

"Like what?"

"I don't know. He sounded so serious."

Roxanne scratched her head. Tiffany was probably just overreacting—getting worked up over nothing like Roxanne used to do when she was a teen. "Guys." She laughed. "I don't think we'll ever be able to figure them out. Don't worry about it."

She waved good night to the girl and walked in to her cabin. Did she brush off Tiffany's concern too readily? Should she tell Tim about what she said? *Maybe not.* He had enough on his mind.

She slipped on her pajamas, folded her clothes, and packed them in her case under the bed. Snuggling between the smooth sheets, she allowed the memory of Tim's warm lips on her cheek to embraced her. With all her heart she wanted to believe in him, that he was finding victory over anger. But would he lapse back into his old habits? *Lord, be God over Tim's heart and make him whole.*

She pulled her spare pillow from under the bed and held it to her chest. She wanted a life with him, but would it ever happen?

Chapter Twenty-One

Tim lifted his backpack onto his shoulders. He juggled the clipboard with one hand and checked off names of his hikers with the other. Where were the last two? He glanced up toward the archery range. Two husky guys made their way past the circular straw target bases and up the grassy knoll near the forest where he herded the other eighteen.

Relief had swept over him this morning when Roxanne found she wasn't needed in crafts and could help. Now if he could keep his mind on the hike and off his beautiful assistant.

Tiffany, Roger, and Johnny looked bored as they huddled together, appearing to ignore the others. Of all the kids in his youth group, why did these three have to get assigned to the hike today?

So far Johnny hadn't acted out. Maybe he didn't feel well. Looked like he wasn't paying attention to the nurse's advice not to scratch his face and hands.

The two stragglers climbed the last few feet of the sloping grassy hill. "Sorry, Pastor Tim. We got stuck with KP duty in the dining hall." The huskier of the two panted then gave an embarrassed grin.

"That's fine." He chuckled to himself. *More like they got stuck eating extra servings of breakfast.* "Okay, guys. Listen up. This will be a three-hour, four-mile circular hike. The route is a succession of gradual ups and downs crossing low ridges. The pathway is level, but stay on the trail. The drop-offs at certain points could be dangerous. You'll be fine if you keep up. Don't worry. We'll be back in time for lunch."

The teens surrounded him in groups of twos and threes with the recommended backpack and water canteen attached to their belts.

"I'm glad to see you all wore some type of raingear just in case. You never know." He flipped the hood of his rain jacket over his head. "We'll pass two bodies of water, Lake Ohana and Bench Lake. You'll have a chance to take pictures and hopefully catch a glimpse of Mt. Rainier and observe some wild life. If you're into journaling, jot down any thoughts you may have on God's creation. Keep your eyes and ears open. Any questions?" Most shook their heads.

The short, dark-haired girl from Team Radar raised her hand. "Are there any bears on the trail?"

A round of masculine chuckles met his ears, and the girls' eyes grew larger. "We haven't received any reports about bears in this area." He stuck a hand in his pocket and drew out a canister of pepper spray. "The chances are slim, but if we do, avoid eye contact and walk slowly away. If necessary, I can use this." A snicker escaped his lips. "Oh, yeah. And pray."

He lifted his grin to Roxanne next to Tiffany. "I'm appointing Roxanne to bring up the rear and make sure no one lags behind. And she'll fight off all bears if necessary." He offered her a teasing glint.

"Yeah, right, Pastor Tim." She winked as a sly smile sat on her lips.

The teens probably heard his pounding heart. "Whistle or holler at me if you see any problems." Could she hear him when his eyes said he loved her? "One last thing before we go. Bow your heads." He looked to the forest floor. "Father, in Jesus name, I ask for Your protection on every person today as we investigate the beautiful world You have created. Amen." He glanced up. "Okay, let's go."

Twenty teens and one lovely lady followed him to the trail's entrance at the group of trees ahead. They walked along a timbered platform transporting them over a wetland for about four hundred yards into the forest. The route tapered off to a hard, moss-covered path cleared of trees and bushes.

He swiveled around to glance at his group. They all followed him—no one lagged behind—not even Johnny.

The woods provided a canopy over their heads, shafts of light streaming through breaks in the towering trees. He inhaled a deep breath of the fragrant woodland air as a gentle breeze flicked across his cheeks.

The route led them on a steady upward climb. A glance at his watch said they'd hiked for over an hour—time for a water break. "Five minutes, people." He plopped down on a log and took a swig from his canteen. At the other end, Roxanne chatted with Tiffany.

Memories of last night when he held her jolted his pulse. What journeyed through her mind when he told her he loved her? He knew he'd spoken the truth. He did love her. God willing, they could make a life together.

Every time he awoke in the night, he remembered her pretty face and the feel of her warm arms around him. Did he dare ask her to marry him when the time was right? His heart plummeted. He couldn't make any decisions until his career fell into place.

He took another swig of cool water from his canteen, refreshing his dry mouth and stood. "Okay. Let's go."

The drop-offs on the trail became steeper farther down the path. His main concern today was Johnny—based on the past with the kid. He prayed the troubled boy would follow directions and not continue to disobey in an effort to punish him for taking Christopher's job.

Bushy elderberry plants, broad-leaf vines, and lacey ferns grew among the birch and maples that dominated the forest floor. Happy chatter and laughs punctuated the air. His heart warmed. For once, a group of kids seemed to enjoy an activity he'd planned.

"Hey, Johnny, hurry up." Tiffany's voice yelled behind him. "Pastor Tim said to stay on the trail."

"Tim." Roxanne's voice held an edge of urgency. "Johnny isn't keeping up, and he's on the side of the path next to a drop off."

Tim's blood pressure rose. Couldn't the kid just listen for once? He twisted around to peer toward the end of the line.

A split in a huge rock on the side of the trail nearest the drop-off to the canyon formed an eight-foot wide crevice. Johnny perched on the side of the boulder nearest him, his arms out like he could fly. "Hey, who thinks I can make it over to the other side?" His bragging laugh echoed across the valley to the mountain beyond.

He gave Tiffany a smirk. "Hey, Tif. What do ya think? Plenty of action-stars do it. Why not me?"

"Johnny, get over here!" Roxanne screamed.

Fear vaulted through Tim's nerves, but he needed to remain calm. "Johnny." He willed his voice to stay low and composed. "Get back on the trail."

Tim dropped his backpack and inched closer to the errant boy glaring at him. "Remember what we talked about. Obeying your leaders. I'm telling you to back away from the rocks."

"Just try and make me," he yelled.

The kid's disobedience must spring from something deeper than his resentment of me. If the boy didn't back away from his foolish act, Tim feared he could hurt himself. "Johnny. Come. Back. Over. Here. Now. We've got a lot to talk about." His pulsed pounded in his throat. "Please."

Tim held out his hand and crept in front of the other hikers standing in clusters as they gaped at the wayward teen.

Johnny took a few steps away from the rock.

Tim exhaled a sigh of relief, then gasped.

The boy stopped on the trail and propelled himself forward. Tim dove for him, trying to grasp his legs, but before he could reach him, the errant kid raced to the rock and heaved himself up to scale the opening of the crevice, his arms straight up in the air. When he flew to the other side, he thrust his foot out. The sole of his tennis shoe slipped on the edge, and his body caught on the jagged pieces of granite. He slid down out of sight. "Aww."

Tim reached for his cell. No signals. He didn't have

any other means to notify camp headquarters.

The other hikers stood transfixed then ran to the gap in the rock.

Roxanne clutched her throat. "Oh, dear Lord."

He pushed through the crowd. "Move back." The space between the split was wide. Leafy bushes grew on the floor between the two massive parts of the boulder. A tall tree with a slender trunk and sturdy branches protruded from the ground hugging the face of the rock. Johnny dangled on a limb moaning.

Feeling desperate, Tim surveyed the area around the crevice. A steep slope wound down to the bottom behind the tree. Pieces of rock jutted out, and bushes dotted the vertical slant.

He had to risk scaling the landscape. "Roxanne, stay with the kids."

"You've got it. We'll be praying."

Could she see the fear in his eyes?

Nineteen teens gawked at him, their mouths wide.

"When I get back closer to the top, some of you guys give me a hand." *Lord, please protect Johnny and help me get him out.* He scrambled around the surface of the boulder to the other side where the slope curved down to the bottom. With a careful step, he lowered himself from a rock outcropping and placed his foot on the branches of a bush abundant in foliage. His tennis shoe wobbled, but the bush held.

To scoot in a sitting position would be the best option. He inched down the side of the terrain about eight feet. His arm caught on a thorn bush, and he cringed when his skin ripped, but he didn't have time to attend to it.

With one leg forward, he slid a few more feet along

the path, grasping exposed roots and arrived at Johnny's precarious location.

His first aid training told him not to move him, yet he had to get the boy back to safety. He slid close enough to touch him.

"Oh," Johnny moaned. "My leg hurts, bad."

"What were you trying to prove?" His heart thudded.

The teen shook his head and stared past Tim. "Nothing." His breath caught in a sob. "I didn't slip by accident."

Tim's mouth tumbled open. A cold finger of apprehension knifed his stomach. "What?"

"I meant to fall." The boy panted. "I don't want to go on." He wiped his eyes with the back of his hand.

"Johnny, you're not telling me you were trying to -"

"Yeah. What's the use? My life isn't worth living. You won't tell anyone what I said?"

"Not for now, but we need to talk." He squeezed the sadness back as he caught Johnny's drift. He didn't want to believe the words.

"Dad doesn't care about me, not like he does Chris. My brother's perfect. I'm just a..." Johnny sobbed, tears running down his cheeks onto his neck. He yanked his head toward Tim. "Dad used me this year to get to you."

His chosen moment to make this concession didn't surprise Tim. The matter was probably tied to the rest of Johnny's poor relationship with his father. "Listen to me. No matter what, nothing is worth taking your own life."

The kid moaned. "I know. I'm seeing it was a pretty foolish idea." He squeezed his eyes shut. "I'm sorry, God."

The precarious slant of Johnny's leg between the rock and the tree trunk disturbed Tim. "We've got to get you out of here now." Though he had to take care of the immediate need, what could he do for Johnny later?

The injured boy nodded and closed his eyes.

If I'm not careful, we'll both fall the last twenty feet. "Can you move at all?"

Johnny whimpered and twisted toward him.

"Let me slip my arm around your side." If he could ease him away from the tree, maybe the teen could hold on to his shoulders.

The boy reached for Tim moving toward him using his knees. "Ow. Something's wrong with my leg. It might be broken."

"Okay, buddy. I'm getting you help." Thank God for Johnny's slender build and shorter stature. Not like the husky boys in the group. "Put your arms around my shoulders when I turn around. And hold on as tight as you can."

He shifted toward the steep rock path.

Johnny grasped him around his neck, in a strangling hold. "Ow, this hurts."

"Whatever you do, don't let go. Try not to move your leg." He heaved himself up a few inches on the same path, a lot harder than coming down. "Uggh." Shallow gulps of air sustained him. "Lord, please help us out of here and ease Johnny's pain. In Jesus name."

Johnny sniffed a few times.

Tim caught his chest and stomach on the sharp rocks. Johnny's weight bore down on him with every inch. At least the guy held on.

"Lord, give me the strength." He grabbed a root and dragged himself a bit farther and dared a look up. *Four feet from the surface now.*

At the top, bright faces beamed. Roger squatted down near the edge of the decline, gritted his teeth, and thrust out two hands. He held Tim's wrists in a tight grip as Tim steadily moved upward, thanks to Roger's amazing strength, more than Tim could imagine one teen would possess. When his head reached the crest, he couldn't believe his eyes.

The husky boy knelt down behind Roger with his arm around his stomach. Behind him, the remainder of the kids formed a line, holding onto the middle of the person in front of them—a team effort.

With one last heave, Roger pulled Tim up as Johnny rolled off his shoulders. The injured boy curved onto his back in a clump of grass. With a groan, he grasped his shin.

Tim fought his emotions as he perched at the edge of the crevice. "I... thank you, guys." He glanced at Johnny. He had to move him away from the rock's edge.

The injured boy still moaned, his hand on his leg. "Hold on, Johnny." Slipping his arm under his shoulders, Tim picked him up and repositioned him under a tree about twenty feet away then turned to the rest of the kids. "We've got to get help. I need for some of you to hike back with me to get a rescue squad up here. Roxanne, can you stay with Johnny?"

"Sure. Let's try to elevate his leg to decrease the swelling and keep it immobile."

Tiffany took off her backpack. "Would this work?"

Tim's heart warmed. "Thanks, Tiffany." He slipped it under the injured leg. "And I need some of you to stay with Roxanne."

"I'll volunteer to take care of Roxanne and Johnny." The second husky guy grinned at Tim.

The boy's twinkling brown eyes wrapped Tim in joy. The kid showed him the love of Christ. His own youth group hadn't quite lived up to that standard.

Pain shot through his chest and up his arms, but he had to ignore it. "Who wants to come with me?"

About half the kids raised their hands, including Roger. "Okay, the rest of you stay here."

He raised his backpack on his shoulder. "I'll return with help as soon as I can. An ambulance can't get up here, so we may be back with a stretcher." He hoped his look told Roxanne how much he appreciated her. "And I want everybody praying." He started out down the trail.

"Hey, Pastor. Your arm is bleeding." The short, dark haired girl followed him. "Let me carry your backpack."

The girl's concern blessed him. He slipped it off and passed it to her. "Thank you."

Tim's whole body ached. He glanced down at his tee shirt, stained with blood. The gashes on his arms and chest stung, but he couldn't stop now. A wave of dizziness washed over him, and he grabbed onto a tree to keep from falling.

"Hey, Pastor Tim." Roger wound Tim's arm over his shoulder. "We'll make it down the mountain. Together."

*****

Roxanne settled under the tree next to Johnny and took off her jacket, rolling it up. The makeshift pillow cradled her cousins head where he lay on the grass. She gritted her teeth. Tiffany had warned her something was up. Now she regretted not mentioning it to Tim. But she never dreamed the boy would do something like this.

Tim and his group disappeared behind a Douglas fir around a bend in the trail, Roger supporting him.

She glanced up at the teens who remained. Tiffany, one of the heavyset boys, three girls she didn't know, two more boys, and Johnny. She peeked at his pale face. "How ya doing?"

He blinked his eyes and shook his head. "I was pretty stupid, wasn't I?"

"Well, your cousin has done a few stupid things in her life, too." She ran a gentle hand through his hair. "Tim's going for help now. Don't worry. We'll get you back to camp."

Tiffany and the other three girls strolled to a log about fifteen feet away and huddled together.

The larger guy who'd volunteered to stay behind glanced at Roxanne and grinned. "I think I'll rinse out my bandana in the spring over there for a makeshift ice pack."

The other three boys joined the girls on the log.

Roxanne nodded and drew her attention back to Johnny. "You know, Tim saved your life today."

He winced. "I can't blame anyone besides myself for this." He held his palm out toward his leg and gulped with a moan.

"You and Pastor Tim have clashed from the beginning. Is it because... because of Chris?" Should she have asked the question? Maybe the kid didn't feel like talking. On the other hand, the conversation would get his mind off his leg.

Johnny closed his eyes and slowly opened them.

"You know, Tim's not so bad. Sometimes I feel guilty about..." He touched his thigh. "Ow."

"It's okay if you don't want to talk about it."

A grimace painted his face. "Your dad and my mother—they're brother and sister. Mom says she misses him. I think she wants to try and contact him. Where did he go?"

"I don't know." Her words sounded hollow to her own ears. She ran a finger down her temple. Didn't the Thompsons know where he was?

Johnny moved as if to shift his leg on the backpack.

"Keep your leg still. We're not sure if it's broken." She couldn't tell him she suspected it was.

"Sometimes I wonder if my life would be easier if my dad wasn't around." He gasped as if in pain and rubbed his forehead. "I shouldn't have said that."

Did she hear a catch in his voice?

"It's just that he's resented Pastor Tim from the start—ever since he found out someone besides Chris got the job. Dad would've hated anyone in the position besides his son." Her cousin gulped. "He told me to give Tim a hard time—to try to get the other kids involved. His goal was to run him off."

She sipped in a gulp of air—couldn't believe his words.

"At first it was easy. A lot of the kids went along with it. But after a while..." He stared out at the forest. "It got old, even childish. I felt like an immature fool." Her cousin swiped a tear from his eye.

"Why did you pull that trick today?" Surely the stunt wasn't to give Tim a hard time.

"I... I don't know." He closed his eyes and squeezed them.

How could he not know? He held something back. "It was stupid. You could've lost your life."

He blew a stream of air drawing his lips in an *O*. "I know." He spit the words out and rose up on an elbow. "Dad always loved Chris more than me." He sank back with a cough and turned his head from her.

She touched his shoulder. "Shh. It's okay. I know what it's like to feel rejection from a parent. It works on your insides, tears you up. But I had to learn to give the pain to the Lord." She patted his hand. "It's not so easy."

Johnny curved back to her, not bothering to disguise his tears now. Was his display of emotion from the pain of his leg or the pain inside? "I... I love the Lord but haven't lived like it. I need to tell Tim I'm sorry about messing with him this year."

She pulled a tissue from her waist pack, dabbed the tears from Johnny's eyes, and slipped him another. "I'm sure you'll have that chance."

Johnny nodded and closed his eyes.

Roxanne leaned back against the tree next to him. The clouds from earlier this morning had cleared, and rays of sunlight flickered down through the evergreens. A squirrel's chatter from a nearby maple scolded her. She closed her eyes and took a deep breath. Her prayer included Tim, the rescue squad, the teens, and Johnny's healing. And finally for reconciliation between Tim, Johnny, and Mr. Thompson—a big, bold request, but she had a God with whom all things were possible.

Chapter Twenty-Two

Tim panted for breath and stumbled a few steps behind Johnny and the camp volunteers manning the stretcher. Though he'd lost his footing the first time he and the teens started down the mountain, Roger had tightened his grip, supporting him. At the camp, after he'd reported the accident to Bob Martin and the nurse, Tim and two strong teens along with two staff members started back up to Johnny's location. Faster than waiting for Woodlyn Rescue Service. His heart went out to Johnny as they lifted him, moaning in pain, onto the emergency pallet.

Several yards ahead next to the clinic, the ambulance's red and white lights flashed. The paramedics opened the back door and took out the rolling table. Johnny pushed up, looked around, and fell back with a groan as the stretcher neared the emergency vehicle.

The staff nurse pulled one of the medics aside. "Looks like a fracture, probably the tibia."

Tim never realized the extent of Johnny's problems. Yet he could only do one thing. Report Johnny's confession to the Thompson family. The law compelled him.

The paramedics lifted the teen from the stretcher onto the rolling table. Before they moved him into the ambulance, Tim edged closer. The boy's face was ashen. Despite their differences, Johnny's circumstances touched his heart. "Hey, buddy. I'm praying for you."

The kids features squeezed into a grimace, and he nodded. "Thanks." He closed his eyes, shook his head, and opened them again. "I'm... I'm sorry, Tim."

Johnny's expression held a look he'd never seen before. Maturity? Contrition? He patted the guy's shoulder. "It's okay. We're going to get you help."

Gasping, the boy's eyes widened. "Do you have to tell Dad?"

"Yes, I do. But don't worry. God is in control. He'll see you through this. I promise."

The technicians lifted him up into the back of the ambulance. Tim waved before the driver closed the van's back doors.

The vehicle sped down the main road out of camp, the siren wailing. Tim sunk down on the log in front of the health clinic. *Lord, you are able to use all things for our good. Bring John healing, and comfort him in his fear and pain. And help me when I have to talk to Mr. Thompson.*

"Hey, Tim." The well-toned, muscular nurse who accompanied the group back up the mountain strolled toward him. "Let me take a look at those cuts. In all the confusion, we haven't tended to your injuries."

He lifted his stiff body off the log with dread. The antiseptic would undoubtedly burn, but he couldn't avoid it. "I suppose you're right."

Tripping on his own feet, he followed her through

the log door into the second room. She motioned to a chair. "Sit down. I'd suggest you take off your bloody t-shirt."

When the fabric stuck to the gashes in the process of peeling off his jacket and shirt, he winced.

The nurse gathered first-aid supplies on a cart. She rolled the table closer and grasped his arm. "This may sting, but I've got to sterilize these wounds."

Tim sipped in three short breaths as the woman ran a cleansing cloth over a cut on his shoulder. Maybe he could distract himself from the discomfort by conversation. "Did someone notify Johnny's parents?"

"Yes, I phoned them right after we called 9-1-1 when you first returned from the mountain." She used a cotton swab to dab liquid on him. "The Thompsons were meeting the ambulance at the hospital."

"I'm sure they were concerned." He clenched his jaw.

"Yes, they had a few questions about what happened." She focused on the sterile wipe in her hand. "At that point I wasn't sure of all the details. I'm so sorry, but Mr. Thompson asked who was in charge of the hike. I told him it was you. I guess now is as good a time as any to relay the message." She swabbed the scrape on his arm.

"What message?" He jerked as she applied a white cream.

"You should be prepared. Mr. Thompson was furious. He said he blamed you for the accident, and he intended to look into a law suit."

*****

Roxanne rolled her head from side to side and massaged her stiff shoulders. Embers in *The Chipmunk's* fireplace still glowed. Most of her teens had crawled into their cots, pulled the covers up to their shoulders, and closed their eyes.

The dab of cleanser smoothed over her skin as she applied it with her fingers. With a tissue, she whisked off her makeup. When she closed her eyes, a vision of the rescue squad materialized. She'd brought up the rear as Tim, with Roger by his side, and the four other guys, carried Johnny down the trail. One prayer after another had flowed from her lips. *God, why do we wait for a crisis to pray?*

She smoothed moisturizer on her face, pulled her hair into a ponytail, and rubbed her hand over the tension in her stomach. *Only two more days of camp.* The time had flown and she'd be back to her old routine—working at Albright's and trying to pay off her credit card debt.

A sigh escaped. *A ridiculous dream owning my own salon.* It took somebody with more business savvy, not a recovering shopaholic. Still, she'd kept the information she'd found on the Small Business Administration web site.

A good paying job became mandatory now, especially if she didn't have a husband to share expenses. Her insecurities about Tim and a future with him screamed at her. Last night when he said he loved her, had he spoken under the spell of the moonlight shining on the lake—caught up in the romance of the evening, and had he changed his mind by now? He couldn't really be in love with her.

She yanked on her tennis shoes. No way could she

fall asleep. The frustrations built. Her coat hung from a hook on the wall. Slipping her jacket on, she closed the door softly behind her.

Maybe a walk to the lake would help allay the doubts tramping through her heart. A salon, a relationship with Tim. She drew her coat tighter around her shivering body, not sure if she trembled from the cold or her anxiety.

She took the trail to the lake and made her way through the trees again easing down on the same rock where she'd sat last night.

"Hi, Roxanne."

She froze. Tim's voice. Why did she have a feeling this would happen? Her worst fears realized. Was it dark enough so he couldn't see her face and lack of makeup? No, though the sun had set, the moonlight would expose her.

"Oh, T...Tim. I didn't expect to see anyone." She rubbed her temple. Could she hide herself?

"I'm sorry, did I startle you?" He edged down beside her on the rock.

"No. I... I..." Maybe she should run for it.

He stretched his arms out in front of him.

Her breath snagged as she stared at his wrist. "You're wearing the bracelet I gave you," she whispered. Somehow it connected him to her

He turned his hand to look at it. "The Lord is our refuge. The verse has helped me more than once." In slow motion he shifted toward her and moaned.

Either the guy was aching, or he'd caught sight of her face minus the foundation and mascara. She chided herself—hadn't even asked about him. "You were brave today. I hope you know that. How are your injuries?"

"I'm okay. I'll admit to acting like a baby when the nurse cleaned and treated the scratches. There's one on my shoulder that's pretty deep, but mainly I'm just sore."

Pain ripped through her heart. She could barely think about how he'd taken so many scrapes and cuts when he slid down the crevice. "I'm sorry." She caressed his arm.

He laughed. "Hey, I'm tough."

"Even if you are a big tough guy, I'm still proud of you. Have you heard anything about Johnny?"

He stared at the grass. "Yes, an orthopedic doctor in the ER at Bayview treated him. I understand after X-rays, they found a fractured shinbone. He'll have surgery and be in the cast for a couple of months. He was fortunate it wasn't worse."

"I had a talk with Johnny after you left to get help. He was sorry for what he did. Not just today, but since you took the job as youth pastor."

"Yeah, I had a second to speak to him before he left in the ambulance." He drew his face closer to hers as his features grew serious.

Though the evening was cool, heat flamed her cheeks. "What's the matter? Why are you looking at me like that?"

"You look so pretty. So fresh. I don't know what's different."

Her heart raced. She knew the difference. No makeup and he thought she looked good? Her face must've turned bright red. She gave him a half grin. "Maybe it's because... I took off my eye shadow tonight and hadn't planned on running into anyone." There, she'd said it.

"I've never seen you so attractive." He traced her chin with a feather light touch.

His fingers sent heat from her stomach to her spine. "I don't know. But if you think so..." She ran a hand through her ponytail.

"I've never seen you without it until now. Do you always wear makeup?"

His question was bold. "I suppose."

His scan moved from her forehead to her chin. "You're so beautiful without it. Why?"

"If you want to know the truth, I've always believed I had to look perfect to be successful—or to attract someone." She folded her arms over her chest.

"Is that why you buy so many clothes?" His words pierced her.

Why was he asking these things? *Tim, the counselor.* She squirmed. She couldn't bare much more of this scrutiny. "People won't like me if I don't wear a new outfit. It empowers me."

He scratched his head. "You know, Roxanne. God sees the inside of people and not the outside. He loves you just as you are, with or without makeup. And if He feels like that, others should, too." His eyes twinkled with the moonlight. "I do. You're even more attractive without makeup, and you look cute in sloppy clothes, too."

Face it. Tim was analyzing her. Anger built up in her chest. Was it any of his business what she wore and didn't wear? She let out a sigh. His heart was in the right place. No doubt. She put her face in her hands. "It's not easy to talk about, but ever since Dad left, I've had this need—to be picture-perfect."

"He hurt you, let you down. The little ten-year-old

thought her dad left because she wasn't good enough. You compensated for it by adorning the outward Roxanne. But look at the inner person. She's a beautiful child of God whom Jesus died for on the cross." He turned his head toward the lake as if to hide emotion.

Though he was dissecting her, tears of joy and relief rushed down her cheeks at the significance of his words. "Women do have the tendency to primp more than you guys."

"Yeah, thanks for the reminder." He laid his hand over hers. "But in my mind you're beautiful like you are, and I'm in love with the little girl who's all grown up now."

In love with her. He said it again. "How does the grown woman get over the pain her father caused?"

"Keep reading the Word and pray. God is faithful. He'll put the understanding in your heart and life." He slid his arm around her shoulders. "Something else I learned is forgiveness. I had to forgive my father before he died, and then I confessed it again afterwards." His fingers tightened on her shoulders. "You should do the same concerning your father."

"I know you're right. But it's so hard." She folded her arms around her middle as if to contain the feelings welling up inside. "Maybe I'm not able to, not yet."

"Then when? When there's no more time?" Tim brushed his hand over hers. "One more thing I learned, when I hadn't forgiven my Dad, I was filled with bitterness and resentment. It manifested into anger, uncontrollable rage."

"Maybe that's another reason I got addicted to shopping. I missed my Dad so much. Shopping filled the empty place where I craved his attention." Speaking the words set her heart free. "Will you pray for me and with me?"

He bowed his head as he caressed her hand. "Lord I pray for my Christian sister and the woman I love."

Her heart soared at his words, and she gripped his fingers tighter.

"Help her to know how wonderful she is in Your sight. Let her be aware that no tangible possession on this earth brings her worth, but your declaration of 'not guilty' through Your Son. I ask You to guide her in forgiveness of her earthly father and oversee our future together. Bless it according to your perfect will."

She squeezed his hand. "Lord, I choose to forgive. Not because I feel like it, but because I know You first forgave me." She opened her eyes and looked at the man she loved, the man who knew the real Roxanne, flaws and all, and thought she was beautiful. "I pray God will lead you to the counselor's job. So many people could benefit from your gift."

"First, I know one guy who could benefit from holding a beautiful woman in his arms." He laughed and pulled her close.

Chapter Twenty-Three

Tim marched toward the teen Sunday school room, his nerves screaming *help*. He stopped in the hall and bowed his head. *Only You, Lord, can see me through this ordeal with the elders.*

Mr. Thompson hadn't waited long to call the meeting. Tim knew it was coming, but the next day after camp? He'd only arrived home last night and found the message on his voicemail at the house.

Telling the Thompsons about the incident at camp weighed on his mind, his top priority. When he returned the man's call, he only got his machine. He'd prayed Johnny's father would respond to his message confirming his attendance at the meeting and his request to speak to him as soon as possible. Since Mr. Thompson hadn't called back, he'd have to delay their conversation until after the meeting. He took a deep breath, grasped the knob, and pulled the door open.

Facing a firing squad couldn't be worse. The elders, Pastor Downing, three of the four teens he'd requested to attend, and Jess sat around the large circular table where his young people usually assembled. Now if the witnesses to the event would only tell the truth.

"Hello, Tim." Mr. Jones, Mandy's father, stood and smiled. "We asked you to come later than the others. The elders needed a little time."

He stiffened. *Time for what?* How long does it take to fire someone?

"Sit down." Mr. Jones pointed to a chair between Mr. Baker and Roger.

"Let's pray first, please." Pastor Downing raised the corners of his mouth to Tim in a smile and bowed his head. "Lord, we ask Your blessing, Your wisdom, and Your direction today as we must accomplish this difficult task. In Jesus name."

Difficult? They'd already made up their minds to terminate him. He plopped into the chair and raised his head to face the group. Across the table Mr. Thompson glared under scrunched-up eyebrows.

Roger shifted in his chair and jerked his head toward Tim then looked away again.

Tiffany and Mandy stared at him.

Mr. Jones tapped his pen on the notebook in front of him. "As you know, we've had some problems. The elders need to make a decision about the youth pastor position for next year. I understand you would like to resign but need a recommendation for a job in another church as a pastoral counselor."

"Yes, sir. That's correct." He cleared his throat. "There have been concerns, but that's not the reason I've decided to resign. You see, sir, I've trained primarily in Christian counseling, and my heart's desire is to serve the Lord by helping people overcome difficulties in their lives."

"Humph." Mr. Thompson cleared his throat. "What, are you going to slap them around and yell at them?"

Heat rose in Tim's face. The man was a constant challenge to his new skills. A drop of perspiration ran down his cheek and onto his neck before he wiped it away.

Mr. Jones hurled a frown at Mr. Thompson. "Jack, you'll have your turn. Please. Let me finish. As you were saying, you'd like to ask the elders for a recommendation. That's our goal this morning. In the light of this last year's events, can we, in all fairness to another church, give you our endorsement? That's the question we're considering."

An involuntary swallow vaulted into Tim's throat. *Dear God. Let Your will be done.* "Yes, sir. And I pray truth and honesty prevail."

Mr. Thompson leaped to his feet. "Was that some kind of accusation?"

Tim stared at the table and squeezed his eyes shut. "No." Why did the man hate him so? He curled his fingers into fists and released them. In the past, the remark would've angered him. Right now he slipped into a corner of silence—better than losing his temper.

"While I'm standing, I may as well point out the offenses this man has been responsible for this year." He held up a clipboard. "As you can see, I've got a long list."

"All right, Jack. Go ahead." Mr. Jones's scrutiny traveled from Mr. Thompson to Tim.

"Let me start with the latest which has impacted my family personally." The disgruntled man's face became scarlet. "With no care or preplanning, he led a group of teens on a mountain hike at camp last week and with poor or no supervision, he allowed my son to fall off a cliff and break his leg."

Tim held his breath. He wasn't to blame. Johnny's admission had proved that, and the teens had been properly supervised. "Sir, you need to hear me out." He would defend himself when he had the chance, but he couldn't reveal what he knew about Johnny until he and Mr. Thompson were alone.

Mr. Jones looked at him with kind eyes. "Tim, if you'll wait until Jack is finished with his complaints, we'll take each issue one at a time."

He shook his head and scooted farther down in his chair.

Johnny's father scowled at him. "And for your information, I'm considering legal action as well."

"Yes, I got the word." Now he couldn't restrain the sarcasm in his voice.

"Well, shall I continue?" The man with the clipboard raised it a few inches below eyelevel. "Next we have the matter of Garrett's iPad purchase on his church credit card. Which, by the way, we cancelled and won't be issuing him another."

Tim pinched his lips together in an attempt to prevent the words, but they barreled out unsolicited. "Yes, as you know I've been paying for all my supplies out of my own pocket and getting reimbursed from Nancy after she compares the purchases with the receipt." How much longer could he hold his frustration inside? *Lord, give me victory.*

"Don't complain to me. We need to use the wisdom God gave us. As head of the finance committee, I have to be accountable. I'm sure Mr. Colton would agree."

Jess rolled his eyes and raised his hand to his mouth, probably covering a smirk. "Uh... yes, sir. We need wisdom and truth in making any decision in this life."

"Well, if I don't continue, we'll be here all day. I've still got quite a list." Mr. Thompson cleared his throat. "Next we had the issue of a Mr. Dixon reporting he saw Garrett in a bar drinking. These initials incidents have never been resolved."

"But..." Tim gasped and forced himself to remain in his seat.

The elder held up a restraining hand. "The next two items on the list involve Tim's own sister and her accusations. They are too risqué to even mention in front of these young people, but if you'll recall, it has to do with Garrett's former fiancée and a second charge concerning Roxanne Ratner." He lifted his face and cast a half grin toward Tim. "One reason we didn't see fit to invite her to this meeting."

Tim glanced at the table and moved his head from side to side. Even squeezing his fists into balls again didn't help. The old temptation to burst out in anger overwhelmed him. The hardest thing he'd ever done weighed on him, to listen to the lies and not defend himself or Roxanne.

"The next incident I doubted whether it actually happened at first. You can imagine Mandy's embarrassment over the occurrence. Originally, she, Tiffany, and Johnny denied it, but later she wanted the truth to come out." He placed a fist to his mouth and coughed. "Garrett seems to be quite the ladies' man. Though I believe it was unsolicited, he allowed Mandy..." Mr. Thompson curved a glance at the girl, "to embrace him. Johnny's speedy timing caught the event on camera." He rubbed his forehead. "My son has made several copies now."

Mr. Jones coughed. "Jack, this issue needs further

discussion."

Tim raised his hand to slam his fist on the table but caught himself before he did. This meeting tested his composure beyond measure. He dug his nails deeper into his palms.

Mandy and Tiffany stared straight ahead, each with pinched lips forming a straight white line. What would they say about the incident when they had the opportunity? Would they tell the truth?

"Further discussion? I don't know what more proof we need than these pictures." He patted his pocket. "And if all that wasn't enough, we can't ignore Tim's recurrent anger problems, like walking out on the youth group." Mr. Thompson laid his clipboard down on the table and surveyed the group. Finally, he stopped at Tim. "I could understand if there had been one or two issues, but they couldn't all be coincidence. These questions demand an explanation and action. Gentlemen, I suggest to this group Tim Garrett be dismissed immediately but not before he pays the $650 for the iPad. Afterwards he should leave without a letter of recommendation."

*****

Tim buried his head in his hands. Mr. Thompson made a good point—if the accusations were true. Yet, he wouldn't admit to any of it except the ramifications of his anger issues and maybe being in the wrong place at the wrong time. He should've used more wisdom the day at The Grape Vine. But unless something unforeseen turned up today, he'd likely be terminated. He supposed Pastor Downing didn't want to embarrass himself by revealing his problems with Mr. Thompson. Though Tim wished Pastor would make the situation public, he'd understand if he didn't.

"Tim, as much as my family and I love you, I'm afraid the situation looks condemning." Mr. Jones's quiet voice brought him no measure of hope. "But let's take each issue one by one. If anyone has any information, please share it when we address the concern. I'm aware many of you have something you'd like to present to the group. At the end of the discussion, you'll be free to comment, Tim. If we haven't adequately uncovered all the facts, we'll call for a delay in our decision."

Mr. Baker stood and picked up his clipboard. "I'll be conducting this portion of the meeting." He pulled his glasses out of his pocket and hooked them over his ears. "Let's work with the copy you provided everyone, Jack." He pushed his glasses farther on his nose and perused the clipboard. "First is the issue from camp—Tim's supervision of the hikers. Does anyone have anything to say?"

Silence screamed at Tim. He ached to give his side of the story, how the kids were well supervised and how Johnny disobeyed him, but how much weight would his words hold? He held his breath.

A hand next to him shot up. "Sir," Roger cleared his throat. "I saw the whole thing. Pastor Tim did a good job of leading the hike, gave instructions, even prayed before we started. Roxanne supervised the end of the line, but Johnny ignored them, maybe trying to prove something to himself or someone else. It wasn't Pastor Tim's fault. In fact, if it hadn't been for Tim rescuing him, Johnny might not be alive." Roger turned to Mr.

Thompson. "Didn't Johnny tell you?"

Tim pressed his lips together. The boy had no idea about Johnny's motivation for jumping.

Mr. Thompson scowled. "No, the poor boy hasn't been able to talk about the incident yet. It's too painful for him. But based on Garrett's past record and my knowledge of my son, there's no other answer. It had to be Garrett's fault."

Tiffany raised her hand. "Mr. Baker, I was there, too. It was like Roger said." She looked at Tim. "Show them the gashes and cuts you got scaling down the rock."

He gave her a half smile and shrugged. "Yeah. They're still here." He rolled up his sleeve and exposed one of the wounds.

"I believe we need to speak to Johnny on this matter as soon as he feels better." Mr. Baker pushed his glasses up on his nose. "But let's go on. The next incident involves the iPad charge at Albrights with Tim's church credit card."

Jess broke his silence. "Sherwood, I can speak about the charges." He stood up at his place with a pen and piece of blank paper. "If I may?" He stepped toward Tim. "Would you please sign your normal signature on this paper?"

Tim bit his lower lip and reached for the pen. What did Jess have on his mind? "Sure." Though he spoke the word, he couldn't raise the volume of his voice. He scribbled his name on the bottom half.

"Thank you." Jess returned to his chair and picked up a copy of the senior high Sunday school workbook and another piece of paper. "Since I now serve on the finance committee, I took the liberty, with Pastor Downing's permission, to get to the bottom of this issue—something that should've been taken care of before now. I went to the business office at Albrights, and they were able to supply me with a copy of the original charge when the iPad was purchased."

"Why wasn't I informed of this?" Mr. Thompson fumed.

"I'm informing you now." Jess held up the paper with the Albrights logo on the front. "This is a copy of the $650 charge with the signature Tim Garrett."

Jess pointed to the paper Tim had signed. "Here's the signature you saw me get from Tim."

Jess held up the Sunday school book. "This is Johnny Thompson's book with his signature on the front. Pastor Garrett had each student write his name. I got that information from Mandy."

She smiled and nodded her head.

"If you'll compare the three signatures, you'll see the one on the charge card is not Tim Garrett's but probably Johnny's."

Tiffany gasped. "Oh, no." She drew her hand to her throat.

"Did you need to say something?" Mr. Baker turned his attention to Tiffany.

"N...no." Her face turned pale. "Well, maybe." She squeezed her eyes shut then opened them. "I think I have the iPad. Johnny gave me one at camp."

Mr. Thompson pounded his fist on the table. "That's ridiculous. Why would he give you his iPad?"

Jess continued. "I'm not sure, but let me go on. Notice the T in Thompson on his book. It's identical to the one on the charge slip and completely different from the T in Tim's signature." Jess passed the three items to his left.

"What? That's crazy. Johnny wouldn't do anything like that. How would he get the card in the first place?" Mr. Thompson cracked his knuckles.

Tim squared his shoulders. "If you'll recall, I told you my church credit card was missing for about a week. On occasion, I leave my office door unlocked. Someone could've taken it at one of those times." Now Tim saw the mistake he'd made. He should've kept the card in his wallet.

Mr. Thompson growled and narrowed his eyes.

"So, in any case, I've made my point. Tim didn't make the charge." Jess sat back in his seat. "And Pastor Tim already had an iPad—one of the less expensive kind, if my memory serves me correctly." Jess chuckled.

Tim rubbed the tension at the base of his neck. He'd befriended Jess once. Now he reaped the benefit of the favor many times over.

Mr. Baker scratched his head. He grasped the clipboard once more. "All right. I'll continue as the rest of you examine the three signatures. The next item has to do with Tim drinking beer at the Grapevine."

Jess stood. "Sherwood, I can vouch for Tim on this one, too. I was having lunch with him. His drink of choice was root beer in an amber-colored bottle. From what I understand, Harry Dixon had a grudge against him, which explains his motives for trying to get him in trouble."

Mr. Thompson stood to his feet. "Maybe we should hear about this grudge."

"Jack, that's probably a personal issue. Let's stick to the agenda," Mr. Baker said. He glanced at the elder and back at his paper. "All right. Next item. Tim's sister's report."

Pastor Downing coughed. "I have information on this." He stood. "For the sake of the young people in the room, we won't mention the specifics. Jack's right about that. They don't need to hear the gory details."

Tim cowered. Pastor Downing was behind Mr. Thompson and his agenda. His boss was caving in to the blackmail. He chanced a glance at Johnny's father. His arms folded over his chest, and his face held a smirk.

The lines on Pastor Downing's face smoothed. "From what I understand, Tim dealt with anger issues in the past and accepts the responsibility for the concerns with his former fiancée. But since I know him to be a God-fearing man who's sought the Lord about this issue more than once, I believe he's come a long way in finding freedom."

Jess raised his hand. "Ladies and gentlemen, I can vouch for this as well. Tim and I have been in concentrated prayer and Bible study. Pastor Tim's gaining the liberty he's sought for so long."

Mr. Baker nodded his head and scanned the group. "Well, the second issue we can't speak of directly concerns Roxanne Ratner."

Pastor Downing remained on his feet in front of his chair. "Tim's sister returned to my office recently and confessed she'd made the story up. She wanted to do something to spite her brother but now deeply regrets it. There is no truth whatsoever in the story concerning Ms. Ratner. I have Janelle's signed statement." He held up a piece of paper. "I acquired it just in case I needed proof."

Mr. Thompson's eyes rounded. He pressed his lips

together and glared at Pastor Downing.

The preacher glanced at his fingers and cleared his throat. "There's another issue I wish to bring up at the end of this meeting." All heads angled toward him.

Tim blew out a breath. Pastor might be using this opportunity to reveal the blackmail he'd allowed himself to endure all these months. Or to resign.

Mr. Baker wiped his forehead with a handkerchief. "All right. Let's finish this last item—the incident with Mandy. I understand her parents denied any knowledge of the issue at first." He looked toward Mr. Jones. "They said Tim made it up. But Jack gave us a different story."

Mandy raised her hand. "Sir, I have something to say."

Tiffany gave a shy nod. "I do, too."

Tim swallowed. In spite of the fact that he'd been cleared of most of the issues, this could spell trouble if the girls didn't tell the truth. To have the elders think he behaved in an improper manner toward Mandy could mean the end.

"All right, girls. Mandy, you go first." Mr. Baker locked his fingers. "Just tell us what you know."

The teen played with the button on her sweater. She raised her face to Mr. Baker. "This is hard... but I need to tell the truth." She drew a finger under her eye. "I had a crush on Pastor Tim, and messed everything up."

She glanced at Tim and looked back at Mr. Baker. "I told Tiffany about it, then cornered Tim in the sanctuary one night after youth group." She wiped her tears with her palms now. "I just wanted him to notice me."

The sound of her sobs dominated the silence. "When

Johnny took the picture and Tiffany laughed, I knew it would be a problem." She raised her gaze to her father. "I'm sorry, Daddy."

Mr. Jones nodded to her, the lines on his face deepening.

Tim's pulse throbbed. He hadn't seen this coming even though at the time he thought she was making trouble. Now compassion filled his heart. Teenage infatuation. Poor girl. He raised his hand. "I'd like to thank Mandy for telling the truth and being brave enough to talk about it to the group."

"Sir, may I speak?" Tiffany raised her hand. "It was like she said. Johnny and I were trying to make trouble for Pastor Tim after Mandy told us she had a crush on him. We both knew of her plans to talk to him."

Mr. Thompson stood to his feet. "She's lying. Garrett's got them on his side somehow."

"Jack, please watch your words," Mr. Jones said.

Tiffany raised her open palm. "No, sir. It's the truth. If Johnny were here, he'd verify it."

"Okay, Jack. Let's go on. May we see a copy of the photo?"

Glee filled Mr. Thompson's face, and he dug in his pocket. "Yes, right here." He handed it to the moderator.

Mr. Baker held it up and appeared to examine it. "I'm going to pass this around, but in my opinion, Tim is clearly uncomfortable. Though his face is obscured, the way he's holding his arms out and his palms up facing Mandy as if he wants her to back off is proof enough for me he was set up."

"Mr. Baker, may I say something else?" Roger held up his hand.

"Yes, please."

"Johnny and I have been good friends since seventh grade. We talk. A lot. I think you all know how disappointed the Thompson family was when Christopher, Johnny's older brother, didn't get the job of youth pastor." Roger swallowed hard and glanced toward Mr. Thompson.

Johnny's father scooted down in his chair as if he wanted to disappear, a scowl on his face.

"Mr. Thompson ordered Johnny to give Tim a hard..."

The booming voice filled the room. "Look. Johnny knew the injustice, the suffering his brother endured. Chris worked hard to get his degree, and this church couldn't even let him have the job. Chris said Tim ripped the opportunity from him." Now the resentful elder could barely catch his breath, and his hands shook.

Tim lowered his head. *I thought I'd been the angry person.* He stared at the man, sympathy flooding his heart. Johnny's father was losing control.

"Please, let Roger finish." Mr. Baker intervened.

"The night at the youth group Johnny and I pretended I was bleeding." Roger looked at Tim with sad eyes. "Mr. Thompson remembered a stunt he'd pulled when he was a kid and thought it'd be fun for us to try it." Roger turned in his seat and looked at Tim. "I'm sorry about it, now, Pastor Tim. Forgive us."

Tim couldn't restrain the emotion in his throat. Even a quick breath didn't hold back the moisture forming in his eyes. "It's okay, Roger. Thanks for telling the truth."

Roger's eyes brightened. "And Pastor Tim, I'll always remember your bravery in rescuing Johnny. You didn't pay any attention to your cuts and gashes. Just wanted to help my friend. Please stay and be our youth pastor again next year."

Roger's words tore through him. He never expected to hear one of the teens who gave him such a hard time say something like that.

Tim shuffled his feet under the table. "Thank you for asking, Roger, but I need to listen to what God is telling me to do." Memories of pulling Johnny out of the crevice brought a chill to Tim's bones, but he had to talk to Mr. Thompson privately about the real circumstances of Johnny's accident as soon as possible.

Mr. Baker nodded." All right. If no one has anything else to say, I'd like to ask Tim to speak."

Tim stood to his feet. "Thanks, everyone, for standing up in this meeting with the truth. It's been a rough year, but God had his reasons." He threw his palms in the air and laughed. "I have no idea what they are." He paused and looked across the table. "Thanks to my friends Jess and Pastor Downing, and the Lord, I'm finding freedom." He sat down. "I don't need to say any more, thank you."

Mr. Baker smiled. "All right then, we'll ask you to wait outside, Tim, and—"

"Excuse me, Sherwood." Pastor Downing stood. "Kids, thank you for being a part of the meeting. You may go now."

Mr. Thompson's glare darted from Mr. Baker to Pastor Downing as the teens shuffled from the room.

Pastor cleared his throat. "I've left something unsaid for too long. I've been a coward." He stared at his feet.

"What are you talking about?" Mr. Jones looked at him with a frown.

Tim closed his eyes and covered his face then looked up again.

Pastor Downing's gaze traveled around the table. "Tim Garrett knows this story, and though it would've helped his case, he kept it in confidence at my request."

Compassion for the man welled up in Tim. "Sir, are you sure this is the right time?"

"Yes, Tim." He studied his hands and looked back to the group. "For a time in my life, I gave into an addiction to gambling. Almost lost everything, but by the grace of our Lord, I'm free of it. Unfortunately, I didn't reveal it to the hiring board, and later Jack Thompson found me out quite by accident. He's threatened me all this time. If I didn't go along with his agenda, he'd get me fired. Well, I'm beating him to the punch. I'm retiring in May. I'd like to make the announcement next Sunday if I may."

Every mouth in the room with the exception of Tim, Pastor, and Mr. Thompson fell open.

Mr. Baker stared at Mr. Thompson who wrote furiously on a notepad in front of him. "If this is true, and I don't believe Pastor would lie about something like this, we have a serious matter on our hands." Mr. Baker turned to the troubled elder. "Is what Pastor Downing says accurate?"

Johnny's father shrugged. "No comment."

Jess rose to his feet. "I'd suggest we call another meeting to discuss this matter further."

Pastor Downing trudged around the table and put his hand on Tim's shoulder. "As far as I'm concerned, there's no need. In any case, my cowardly behavior impacted you more than anyone. I'm sorry. Please forgive me." Pastor didn't try to disguise the emotion in his voice.

Tim stood and gave Pastor a bear hug.

Mr. Jones rose and marched toward Tim and Pastor. "You'll have my support. Whatever you decide. You've been one of the best ministers I've ever served under."

Mr. Baker joined the group. "You have my backing as well." He cleared his throat. "I believe if no one else has anything to say, Tim, will you please wait outside?"

He surveyed every face in the room. All held a smile, except for Johnny's father who stared at his fingers. "I'll be in the hall."

He paced the length of the corridor a couple of times. A glance at his watch told him he'd endured ten minutes. Jess stuck his head out the door. "You can come in now." A quick decision. What did that mean?

He wandered back in the room and stood facing Mr. Baker. The smiling man opened his mouth. "Tim, the elders have voted to give you the recommendation for your job at Evergreen Fellowship. We hate to say goodbye and would love for you to stay on another year as youth pastor, but we understand you must obey the Lord."

Joy rose from his heart and caught in his chest. "Thank you." The tension in his shoulders dissolved. His name was cleared, and the doors opened for him and Roxanne.

Mr. Baker held up a finger. "By the way, Tim. Just to let you know, Mr. Thompson feels it's in his best interest to move his church membership elsewhere. And I can guarantee it won't be at Evergreen."

His heart soared when each person in the room with the exception of Mr. Thompson stood and shook hands with him. Thank God truth had prevailed. But on his bright sunny horizon, one small dark cloud hovered. Johnny Thompson. Could the teen escape the unhappy influence of his father?

*****

Tim jogged to catch up to Mr. Thompson as the man stormed out of the room and down the long hall. "Please, wait a minute. I need to talk to you."

The angry father looked back over his shoulder and growled. "What?"

Tim raised his hand indicating the Sunday school room on the right. "Please step in here a minute. I've got something urgent to tell you."

Johnny's parent glared but followed him into the room.

He swallowed hard, closed the door, and forced the words out. "At camp, when Johnny fell, it wasn't like everyone thought."

"What are you talking about? My son broke his leg because of your neglect."

"No, Mr. Thompson. Because of your neglect to nurture your son, to make him feel important..." He curved to face the man. Maintaining eye contact was impossible when Johnny's father looked away. "You need to know, your son tried to commit suicide."

Mr. Thompson pressed his lips together and raised his eyebrows. "Look, Garrett. That is a serious accusation. Even you wouldn't be stupid enough to lie about that."

"No, I wish I were. Johnny confessed to me when I climbed down to him. He feels he's walked in Chris's shadow all his life, that Chris can do no wrong, and you don't love him."

For once, the man didn't have a smart remark. When he finally looked up, his eyes were rimmed red.

Tim's attempts to capture Mr. Thompson's focus were fruitless. "Look, I had issues with my father as well—one of the reasons I've struggled with anger. But by the grace of God, His word, and my supportive friend Jess, I'm going to make it."

The distressed father nodded and looked toward the window.

"It's not too late for you and Johnny."

The man finally raised his face to Tim. The sadness in his eyes reminded him so much of his own father's as he lay dying in a hospital bed. "Johnny never took an interest or excelled in school like Chris..."

"But the boy is your son, your flesh and blood. You can still show him how important he is to you. There'll never be another John Thompson." He cleared his raspy voice. "Let the kid know you respect him as an individual. Take him on a father-son trip, spend time listening to him and affirming him. My father and I didn't make amends until there was no time left. Don't do that, Mr. Thompson. John is crying out for a true relationship with you. Don't disappoint him."

The disheartened man rubbed his eyes. "I hate to admit it, but you're right."

Tim's mouth fell open at his statement. "I learned from my own experience how important a healthy father-son relationship can be. I want the best for John. He shouldn't be made to suffer another day, not knowing that you love him—that in his own way, John's made you proud. I don't want either of you filled with regret."

The other man nodded again, perhaps not trusting his voice. "I need to go now. To the hospital to visit my son. To tell him how much he means to me." He stuck his hand out to Tim but dropped it to his side. He slunk out of the room.

Tim took a deep breath. Would Mr. Thompson lay aside the past and do the right thing?

*****

Roxanne gave a yelp and stuck her cell in her pocket. "Mom, you will not believe it." She gasped for breath. "That was Tim. The elders cleared him of any wrongdoing and of all those ridiculous charges, and they're recommending him to Evergreen."

"Oh, Roxy. That's wonderful news." A smile spread over Mom's face. She placed the last plate in the dishwasher and took off her apron. "Sit down and tell me about it."

Roxanne restrained the urge to jump up and down in the middle of the kitchen floor and pulled out the chair. "I prayed for him all morning, and he called me first after the meeting." She giggled. God had heard her prayer, but more than that, He allowed the truth to come out.

Mom patted Roxanne's shoulder. "I'm sorry Johnny broke his leg, but I pray he's matured from this experience. Hopefully Tim's doing better after his encounter with those bushes and trees."

"Yeah. Poor guy." She reached for Mom's hand. "If he's offered the job at Evergreen, I'll keep attending." She couldn't restrain a chuckle.

Mom patted her fingers. "How are things with you

two?"

She beamed then held her hand to the side of her mouth and whispered. "Now that he's been cleared... I'm hoping for a proposal."

Mom shrieked. "Oh, Roxy. I'm so excited. The sooner it happens, the sooner I can have grandbabies."

She rolled her eyes. "Mom, he hasn't even asked me to marry him yet."

Mom grinned. "I know, honey. Just doing a bit of premature celebrating."

"Honestly, I'd like to concentrate on buying a shop first, but it seems hopeless." She shook her head. "Why am I talking like that? It doesn't hurt anything to try."

"What do you have in mind?"

She switched on her computer sitting on the kitchen table. "I've been looking over the information on a government web site. To get an SBA loan, I have to find a lender in Washington State and make a proposal for a business. Some of these institutions would let me know in a matter of days."

"Wonderful. But what about your credit card debt?" Mom folded her hands under her chin.

Roxanne clicked on the Internet and retrieved the website. "I'm working out a payment plan with my creditors. I need to come up with a portion of the money for my budget." Smoothing her hand along her cashmere sweater, a new thought came to mind, one more painful than giving up shopping. "What if I sold...?" She swallowed the lump in her throat.

"Sold what, dear?"

"Coach purses, or even some of my sweaters on eBay. They are practically new."

"That's a great idea."

"I've learned my lesson. No more overspending. Someone else can enjoy my foolishness as I earn a little money."

Mom's eyes twinkled. "A good plan."

"Okay. I want you to sit right there and pray." She lifted her hand to the keyboard.

Chapter Twenty-Four

Tim followed the winding road up to the waterfall—every bit as impressive as last year when he and Roxanne visited Mt. Rainier. *Finally, a beautiful day.* He could always count on the month of May. The sunrays dancing on the bushes emitting sparkles of light brought him almost as much exhilaration as his purpose today.

Glimpsing the woman in the passenger seat beside him, he pinched his arm. His slender blond girlfriend wasn't an illusion.

With a quick breath, he trained his gaze to the road. Exhilaration bubbled up in him when he thought of the reception the congregation gave him last Sunday—a send-off with plenty of time to talk to church members. Time to once and for all put to rest any of the false rumors. Thank God he'd left on positive terms.

Since he'd received a *yes* from Evergreen Fellowship and his contract began in the fall, he had a whole two months until starting his job. The thought of walking through the doors as a married man sent his head spinning. Maybe he ought to pinch himself again.

Steering the car off the road, he parked. The whoosh

of rushing water only twenty feet away at the roadside stop, the regal evergreens, and the silent, mountaintop wilderness at Mt. Rainier provided the most romantic spot he could think of.

Cool breeze brushed against his face. Roxanne's angelic smile sent his heart thudding in his chest when he opened the door, and she stepped out.

"Let me help carry some of the picnic supplies you packed." She pointed to the sacks and cooler in the backseat. "I don't think we're going to be able to eat all that."

Tim chuckled. Not everything was for the meal. He prayed the afternoon would turn out as planned so Roxanne would always remember the day he proposed.

He opened the rear door and handed her the blanket and the sack with the towel, washcloth, and the plastic bin.

She put her free hand on her hip. "That cooler looks brand new. Did you buy it especially for today?"

"Borrowed it from Jess." He leaned down and kissed her cheek. "Your lectures about being frugal have hit home, and I don't want to be on your bad list."

"Silly, I just want to remind us to spend money wisely."

What a woman. She'd morphed from a shopaholic to a thrifty spender. He lifted the heavy metal cooler and half gallon of water down the short boardwalk to the grassy meadow across from the road and set it down under a hemlock tree. "How's this?"

"It's lovely." A giddy sigh left her lips. "This mountain air is giving me an appetite."

"You, Roxy? I thought you never got hungry." He grabbed the blanket, and together they spread it out under the tree.

"Well, today I am." She opened the lid on the cooler and peered in. "Look at this feast." She lowered her eyes and brushed away a stray leaf from the blanket, her voice barely a whisper. "This must be a special occasion."

"It is. You'll see." He pulled out two bottles of lemonade, the plastic plates, napkins, two plastic forks, the platter of sandwiches, and the macaroni salad he'd labored over earlier this morning.

"Did you make all this?" She sat cross-legged and set a plate on the blanket.

"Of course." His amusement brought a smile when he thought of the last time he cooked for her and how far they'd come in their relationship.

"This looks almost as good as the meal you fixed New Years Eve." When her smile faded, he suspected she remembered as well.

He touched her hand. "We're in a different place, a better one. Let me pray." He paused allowing the fragrant forest air, the intermittent sprinkle of the waterfall, and the sunshine to feed his spirit. When he was ready, the words flowed. "The peace of God that passes all understanding will keep our hearts and minds in Christ Jesus." He squeezed her hand intertwined with his. "Roxy, that word was for us." He bowed his head. "Lord, thank you for this food. Amen."

She laughed, lifting a hand to shield her eyes from the sun. "I've never felt like this before in my life. The Lord is more precious to me now than ever. We love each other, Tim. But we're more in love with the Lord. Praise God."

"You're right." He traced her ring finger and looked

up to her with a grin before he took his hand away.

The last of the turkey and ham subs on whole-wheat bread disappeared. He dug down to the sack of chocolate cookies in the bottom of the cooler.

"Now you're really pampering me." She bit a piece off the crispy morsel. "I'm going to gain a few pounds if I keep eating like this." She laughed.

I hope she gains more than a few pounds someday, but for another reason. His heart sprinted with the thought. Ever since the day he held Timmy, a longing had formed in his heart—a child of his own, their own.

They gathered the trash and placed it in a spare plastic bag. "What do they say? Pack it in and pack it out." He tossed the bag next to the cooler.

She gave him a lazy smile and leaned back against the hemlock's wide trunk.

A chipmunk, his tail waving in the air, scampered off toward the tree line on the other side of the road.

With the cooler in the back seat, he shut the door and strolled to the little meadow, glad they were alone today. No summer tourists yet.

Sunbeams played with the wisps of Roxanne's blond hair swept into a ponytail. The corners of her mouth turned up, and her eyelashes rested on her cheeks.

Tim folded his legs and sat down next to her. How could a man be happier?

Her slender curves in the fitted pink sweater sent his pulse out of control. The light dab of makeup made her beautiful.

On New Year's Eve, he'd wanted her, but the time wasn't right, not until they were married. He thanked God they'd waited. Now they had the chance to do things the right way if she'd agree to marry him. Would she accept him and be a pastoral counselor's wife?

He slipped his arm around her shoulder. *Courage, man.* On impulse he blew a whisper of air into her ear. Then his lips touched the delicate skin behind it.

Her warm fingers inched their way to his neck sending chills down his spine. "Tim," she whispered.

He trailed his mouth from her ear to her chin, and then to her lips. His heart joggled when her embrace tightened.

Her nearness sent hot blood coursing through his veins. He pulled back, away from her. One day soon, God willing, he wouldn't have to pull away.

The time had come. The box was still in his jacket pocket. He rose to his knees in front of her. "You probably guessed why I brought you here today."

"What? This is so sudden." Her sly smile played with his serious words.

He chuckled. "The first day I met you, I thought you were a teenager. I'm so glad you weren't," he gulped. "But if you had been, I'd have waited for you to grow up." He cleared his throat. "I love you, Roxanne, and want to spend the rest of my life with you."

Her eyes glistened as she smoothed her hand over his.

The sound of rushing water seemed to still. Was it because he only heard his beating heart? "Roxanne Ratner, you mean more to me than any other woman I've ever known."

A twinge of pain marked her face. "More than...?"

"More than anyone. You are the person I want to turn to for encouragement. The person I want to share my successes and failures with." He grasped both her hands.

A tear trailed down her face. "It's so incredible to believe that you love me, for me."

A mockingbird whistled a call as if to say *hurry up, ask her*. "Yes. I love you, the fashionable Roxanne, the hardworking Roxanne, the soft-hearted Roxanne, and even now the frugal Roxanne, more than any other woman in the world. Will you marry me?" He opened the blue velvet box and showed her the solitaire diamond with its white gold setting.

"Oh, Tim," she shrieked. "The ring's stunning."

"Well, will you be my wife?" He winked at her.

"Yes, Tim. My answer is yes."

With steady fingers and a purpose in his heart, he took the diamond out of the box and slipped it onto her finger.

She gazed at the ring and glanced back at him, her lips parted. Her arm slid around his neck. "I love you, Tim Garrett."

"There's one more thing." He grinned and looked toward the one remaining bag on the ground. "I was reading in the Bible where Jesus humbled himself and washed the disciples' feet because he wanted to show them how to be a servant."

"Hmm, I've always been fascinated by that story."

He rose and retrieved the plastic tub from the sack, then picked up the gallon of water, poured it in the container, and set the towel and cloth on the blanket.

"Tim, what are you doing?"

"Take off your shoe and put a foot in here." He kneeled back down in front of the bin of water.

She laughed as she sat up straighter. "Are you serious?"

"Yes, very." He drew his brows together.

"Okay." She rolled up her jeans cuff and placed a shoeless foot in the water.

He dabbed the cloth over her toes. "This is a symbol of my love for you. I want to serve you as your husband, care for you, cherish you, and love you as Jesus loved His church. Now the other foot."

"I... I don't know what to say."

Heat filled Tim's face. Now he was feeling shy. "I've never done this before. Hope you don't think I'm demented." He washed her other foot then toweled off both.

"No, I don't." She laughed, put her socks on, and fastened the Velcro on her tennis shoes. "That's the most amazing thing that's ever happened to me." She leaned close to him and placed her arms around his neck. "I love you with all my heart. I want to be a helper to you, to cherish and love you all the days of my life as your wife."

Love for Roxanne swelled in his heart. "The words we're saying to each other. It almost sounds like wedding vows. Are we married? When can we start the honeymoon?" He laughed.

She gave him a friendly tap on his shoulder. "Not until the pastor makes it official." She studied her fingertips. "Speaking of the honeymoon." Her cheeks turned pink. "I... I'm not a ..."

He'd suspected it and was glad she told him. "It doesn't matter. We'll be starting this marriage as God ordained, because *we* waited."

With a stream of waterworks, she threw herself in his arms. "Now I know you love me for me."

He kissed a tear away. "We need to make those wedding plans quick before I lead us into temptation and have to ask God to deliver us." Sitting back against the trunk of the tree, he pulled her to his chest. "Jess and Holly want me to conduct the dedication service for little Timmy next Sunday at Woodlyn. Would my fiancée go with me?"

"Yes, I'd love to." She stared over his shoulder at the waterfall, her chest rising with a deep breath. "Maybe we'll have a little baby to dedicate one day."

A thrill ran through his stomach. She wanted a child with him, too. His heart could barely contain the joy.

*****

Tim attached the microphone to the lapel of his suit coat. His chest filled with pride. A wide-eyed Holly and Jess Colton stood in front of him, the four-month-old baby in Holly's arms. He smiled down at them from his perch on the first step to the stage.

Earlier this morning after he walked through the front doors, he'd received a warm greeting from the elders and at least a dozen congregational members, including Pastor Downing. It warmed his heart they'd welcomed him after all the tension and conflict of this past year.

"Holly and Jess. Before we know it, Timmy will be in grade school, then junior high, and high school, sitting in the pews, God willing, listening to the gospel. Proverbs 22 says to train up a child in the way he should go and when he's old, he won't turn from it. As Timmy's parents, do you pledge to train your son in the knowledge of God's word?"

They looked at each other and smiled. "We do."

"Though Timmy's name appears in the Bible as one

of the major Biblical characters, I happen to know you named him after a present-day person as well." He grinned when the chuckles of the congregation filled the sanctuary.

"This is for Timmy, to be opened on his twelfth birthday." He pulled the letter out of his pocket. "I've written instructions about a personal relationship with Jesus and Timmy's walk with the Lord. Please see that he reads it." He handed the letter to Jess. "Deuteronomy six admonishes you as parents to love the Lord with all your hearts, your souls and your strength. You have a duty to train Timmy in your faith teaching him the Word of God and explaining to him your trust in the Savior."

He reached his hands out for the baby, this time with confidence. The memory of little Timmy when he gave him the gas-pain smile popped into his head. He cradled the child to his chest and bowed his head. "In the name of the Father, the Son, and the Holy Spirit, we dedicate you to the Lord, Timmy Colton."

Tim cleared his throat. He couldn't allow the emotion to tell in his voice. The baby was indeed a miracle of the Lord. And God had given him a miracle as well. His beautiful fiancée Roxanne Ratner, who would be his wife in a matter of weeks.

The sleeping baby hadn't peeped when Tim eased him back into Jess's embrace. His friend leaned toward him and whispered. "Take this opportunity to announce your news." Jess stepped back by Holly's side.

Tim beamed and nodded. "Jess and Holly want me to announce an upcoming event. I'd like to offer an invitation as well. Though there is a corporate invitation on the church bulletin board, I'd like to reemphasize the message and ask the Woodlyn church body to attend my wedding to Roxanne Ratner on June 25 at the home of Holly and Jess Colton." He glanced at Roxanne in the first row. "Stand up, Roxy."

When she rose from her seat and waved, his knees wobbled. For a moment he caught a vision of her in her long white dress—standing under the flower-laden arch in the Colton backyard repeating her vows as she gazed into his eyes. He counted each day now.

*****

Roxanne tried to still her anxious breathing. Aunt Marty Thompson had called her, something she never thought would happen. Roxanne's father wanted to pay her a visit. Her heart gave an uneasy spin in her chest. Good thing Mom had gone to work. James Ratner, the last person Mom would want to meet up with, would be here any minute.

When the doorbell rang, she wiped her wet palms on her jeans. Would she remember what her father looked like? She took a faltering step toward the door and with a shaking hand, opened it.

A trim middle-aged man clasped his hands in front of him. He gasped when he raised his eyes to her as she opened the door wider. "Roxy." He shook his head. "Why did I think you'd look like a ten-year-old girl? You've grown into a beautiful young woman."

Surreal. The clean-shaven, handsome man, her father, shifted from one foot to the other on the porch. How should she respond?

"Odd ringing the doorbell of the home where I used to live, but I'm a stranger to this place and to you and your mother."

She stepped back, allowing him to enter and pointed to the couch. "I guess things haven't changed too much. Sit down." What could she say to the man she hadn't seen for fifteen years? She certainly hadn't felt the need to embrace him.

Her father looked around the room, then lowered himself down to the sofa. "You're probably wondering why I'm here."

"Aunt Marty said all this time she knew where you were—in San Francisco." She twiddled her fingers in her lap. "She said when you heard about the wedding, you decided it was time to make a visit to Woodlyn."

He ran a hand through his light blond hair. "It should've been sooner. Roxanne, when we're young, we do stupid things sometimes. The older I get, the more I realize how important family is—how important you are to me."

She couldn't believe his words. He admitted he'd been foolish and all those years she thought she'd been the problem until Mom tried to convince her otherwise. She'd made mistakes, too, but she knew what it meant to forgive—herself and now perhaps her father.

"Dad, I'd like to tell you..." She swallowed trying to vie for time to regain her composure. "I forgive you for leaving me, and I will take your recommendation you gave me in your letter to respect Tim and consider him the head of our household. But as far as walking me down the aisle on my wedding day, Mom has earned that right."

"Your mom..." Dad looked around the room again. "I pray your mom will forgive me as well. I'd like to earn her trust again someday, too, and build a relationship with you both."

Roxanne never thought she'd hear these words from him. A relationship with her own father. Could it be possible some day?

Chapter Twenty-Five

Roxanne peered across the pebble walkway to the poplar trees strung with twinkling silver lights. Her fingers traced the outline of her silver cross necklace, the single piece of jewelry she'd chosen to complement her strapless, satin A-lined gown with the beaded bodice. Her wedding band sat snugly next to her diamond. Mrs. Roxanne Garrett. *I can't believe it.*

Her husband, in a summer tuxedo, took her breath away. He and Jess, his best friend, huddled in conversation. God had blessed her with a man who offered understanding without judgment. He'd designed a spouse who had protected her against temptation and when she fell short, hadn't looked down on her.

Smoothing her white dress, a small cloud lifted from her heart. God had forgiven her for her poor choices and kept her from ruining something precious and special. "Thank you, God. Keep this marriage in Your hands. Bless our path."

Wiping the lone tear of joy from her cheek, she soaked up the gorgeous sun. A perfect garden wedding. Jess and Holly's backyard provided a lush, green landscape with lilac, rhododendron, and rose bushes lining the tall wooden fence surrounding their property. She ran her hand down the edge of the white gazebo decorated with gardenias and Calla Lilies, their fragrance filling the air. Only an hour ago she and Tim stood under the arch in front of Pastor Downing as they exchanged their vows.

"Hi, honey. Where's that handsome husband of yours?" Mom squeezed her waist.

She glanced toward the round tables with white cloths and pink flower arrangements. "He's talking to Jess and some of the elders. Did you see who else showed up? Johnny."

"I'm so pleased. And Chris came with him." Mom dabbed her eye with a tissue. "I could hardly contain my tears—walking you down the grassy path in this beautiful backyard."

"Hey, married lady." Holly floated toward her in her pale pink organdy. "Did you see your cake?" She pointed to the table on the deck. The bride and groom's cakes sat next to the hors d' oeuvre under a lace tablecloth.

Roxanne signaled her mom. "Come on. Let's go see." She glanced around the backyard at the multitude of guests who'd attended the wedding, some seated at the round tables, others filling their plates.

"This way, ladies." Holly stepped up onto the deck and walked toward the cake table. A banner on the wall with pink and silver hearts said *Tim and Roxanne*.

The miniature bride and groom stood guard over the three-tiered pink cake. "My friend, I still can't believe you and Jess did this for us. How can I thank you?"

Mom waved her hand. "I can think of a way. Invite Holly to be your very first customer. Did you tell her your news?"

"In all the excitement, I forgot. My SBA loan came through, and I'm soon to be a shop owner." Every mention of her new venture sent a thrill through her.

"I'm so excited." Holly fluffed her hair. "It's almost time for a new hairdo and Roxanne's the best. What does Tim think?"

"He's very supportive. He helped me crunch the numbers and thinks my business plan is spot on."

"Oh, Roxy, you can be sure I'll be your first customer. Along with your Mom. And since the Lord is God over this business, it can't help but prosper."

*****

Tim clasped his hands behind his back as he stood near the poplar trees and the winding path. He rested his fingers in the pocket of his dress slacks he'd wear on the trip. So many people showed up from Woodlyn Fellowship. Nancy and her husband, the elders, and the kids from the youth group and their parents. Even Mr. and Mrs. Thompson attended. It warmed Tim's heart that the man was trying harder now to do better by his son.

Tim's mouth had remained open for ten minutes after Roxy told him about another guest who would be attending—her father. At first he worried it would upset her, but when she assured him she was fine, he relaxed. Even Mom Ratner didn't seem to object.

Jess and Johnny stared at him. Hadn't they ever seen a married man before? He held up his left ring finger and twisted the silver band. "Hey guys, can you believe this? I'm married. I'm still trying to get used to the idea."

Jess laughed. "Trust me, you'll get used to it. Especially the first time Roxanne gives you a *honey-do* list."

Johnny lifted his eyebrows and smirked. "Is that what all wives do?"

Tim snickered. "I don't know, but Roxanne confessed to me she isn't much of a cook. I think she's been practicing though." He puffed out his chest. "Anyway, with her working at the shop, I may be doing most of the cooking."

"Well, a wife is a long way off in my life." Johnny took a bite of wedding cake that Tim and Roxanne cut a few moments before.

Tim stared at the boy's face who'd caused him so many problems. Johnny had changed, matured. "What are your plans after next year when you graduate?"

"I'm going to college out of state—to study veterinarian medicine."

"That's great." He stared at the grass. "I really appreciate you coming out to our wedding."

"Anytime, dude." The teen gave a shy smile. "Did you notice Chris over there?" He pointed in the direction of the deck. "He wants to meet you. He's got a job in a church in Idaho next fall as a youth pastor. He's pretty stoked. And he met a girl." Johnny's eyes twinkled.

"I'm happy for him." Tim studied the grass and looked back to John. "How are things now? I mean with your father?"

"Not perfect. But better. We're both trying." John set his plate on the nearby round table. "Tim, I wanted to ask your forgiveness for all I put you through. Not just at camp but the whole year."

"Hey, buddy, it's okay. I was a teenager once. You know I forgive you." He laughed.

"I'm sorry, dude, that I took your card. It was totally illegal." The boy buttoned and unbuttoned his suit jacket. "I'm lucky the church didn't press charges. I'm working to earn the $650 Dad paid Woodlyn. My job at McCluskies flipping hamburgers helps."

"You're learning what it means to accept responsibility—a big part of growing up."

"Yeah." John glanced toward the trees and ran a hand through his hair. "That stupid stunt I pulled at camp—it made me realize how valuable life really is. I'll always regret what I did."

"You're a stronger man for it. The Lord used it for your good. But I wish it'd never happened as well." He reached toward John with a man-hug and slapped his back. "With God on your side, you can't lose."

John looked up at him with a grin, thrust his hand forward, and shook Tim's.

Jess nudged him. "Hey guy, I think it's about time for you to make your exit with your bride."

Most of the guests left the backyard and roamed around to the side of the house.

Roxanne waved at Tim as Holly passed out little bundles of birdseed wrapped in netting. His pulse tripped at the sight of his wife in her fitted pink and black floral dress.

Jess gave him a high-five. "Hope you enjoy your trip to the San Juan Islands, and we'll see you in a couple of weeks."

"It took a lot of convincing to show her it wasn't too expensive of a trip, but I told her I'd make it worth every penny." He snickered.

Jess waved a hand at him shooing him away.

When he strolled up to the most ravishing woman in the world, he put his arm around her small waist. "Ready, Mrs. Garrett?"

She fixed her eyes on him with a dazzling smile. "I am so ready. The San Juan's are calling." She grasped his hand.

They followed the pebble path to the front driveway. A spray of birdseed bombarded them as they dashed to the sidewalk and slipped into his car, *Just Married* on the back window and cans tied to the bumper.

"I love you, Tim." Her sweet voice brought him joy. She was his for as many days as God gave them on this earth.

He looked at her and winked. "I love you, Roxanne."

The End

Keep reading for a sample of Flawless, Book one

Chapter One

The overweight guy leaning against the mirror in the corner of the elevator caught Holly Harrison's attention, not because of his girth, but because of the kindness on his chubby face. Embarrassed she'd stared too long, she turned toward the closing doors and pushed *five*. The motor whirred with a quiet hum as the floor beneath her lifted for a second or two, then ground to a halt. She punched her apartment floor number again but nothing happened.

A chill crawled up Holly's spine. She'd never liked confined places. Was she trapped?

The man moved to the panel and poked a few numbers before he lifted his chin and glanced at the ceiling. "Hmm. Not sure what's going on."

Holly tried to breathe but only took in shallow gulps of air. Things like this happened on television -- not in the real world. A knot formed in her stomach. "Are we stuck?" She fought to control the rising tone of her voice.

The man's eyes sparkled as he gazed at her, then he looked about the small space. "Could be. Don't worry. We'll get out."

His assurances brought no relief. Holly's heart

pounded harder.

He fingered the panel, pushing the *Door Open,* and the *Door Closed* buttons a couple of times. Still nothing. "I think we better ring the alarm."

An alarm sounded in her head.

The three mirrors around the perimeter of her prison scoffed at her. She hadn't suffered from claustrophobia for a long time, not since the gruesome afternoon she lay bound to a gurney in the back of an ambulance.

"Oh dear God, I need to get out of here." She sank to the floor and drew her knees as close to her chest as she could. Her rocking motion did little to soothe her jangled nerves.

"Look." The big guy opened a metal compartment. "Here's the emergency call button. Relax. I'll get help."

She wrenched away from his kind eyes and hugged her knees tighter. The walls threatened to squeeze the life out of her. Gulping for air didn't help.

"Hello, hello. Can anyone hear me?"

The sound of clicking buttons drifted toward her.

The other occupant placed his mouth close to the panel. "Help! We're stuck in the elevator."

He settled back against the mirror appearing calm. His lips moved without a sound.

Holly pressed into the corner. Her reflection blurred.

"Hey, are you okay? Let me try something else." He punched another button and a shrill sound grated against her eardrums. The emergency alarm. Still nothing. The elevator was a dead thing suspended in space. She slumped against the wall as everything spun.

With a groan, the broad man bent down beside her and patted her arm. "I'm going to keep trying. But first, let me pray for us. It'll help." His warm hand caressed her shoulder. "Dear Lord, I trust You for our safety today. Please provide us with the way out of here. Until help arrives, I ask You to bring this lady peace. In Jesus name."

Her breath came easier, and she rubbed the pain in her leg. After standing all day, she'd only wanted to get home and rest.

Her companion hoisted himself up and poked his fingers into a small crack where the doors met. The gap widened two inches.

Some kind of metal tubes were visible beyond the double doors. The car was between floors. Panic struck again. "Oh no, what if this thing falls? How many floors did we go up?"

"It couldn't be more than a couple. This is a newer elevator. I doubt it would go into a fall." The man pried at the door again. It opened another inch. "Hello. Can anyone hear me? We're stuck in here."

Holly tried to steady her intake of air, remembering his soothing prayer.

"Hello." A voice sounded from below.

Thank you, God. She stopped digging her nails into her good leg.

The man put his mouth to the opening. "Yes, hello. Can you hear me? We're stuck in the elevator."

"Craig Schackelford, the general manager here. I've notified the fire department. We'll get you out. Shouldn't be more than a few minutes."

"You can stop worrying now." The heavyset man looked down at her and smiled. "For a second, I was concerned about you. Are you okay?"

She gulped. "I... I think so."

He ran his hand along the opening between the two

doors. "I'd suggest you look out, but all you're going to see are the hydraulic cylinders. Just breathe."

"Hey there. This is Craig again. The good news is they've begun working. It may be a while. Try to relax. I'm terribly sorry about this."

Holly drew in a breath and looked up at her fellow inmate still poking at the space between the doors. For the first time, she allowed herself to take in his appearance to discover what she'd found so intriguing at first glance. With golden brown hair and soft blue eyes, he had one of the most handsome faces she'd ever laid eyes on even with a roll of flesh framing his chin and a large stomach protruding from his tee shirt and warm-ups.

"Looks like we're going to be out of here in a bit, Holly." The man knelt beside her, then plopped down on the floor.

"How... how did you know my name?" Her eyes widened.

"It says Holly right there on your nametag, just below *The Happy Smile Center*." He grinned, a twinkle in his eye again. "I'm Jess Colton. Seventh floor."

His face expressed compassion, like he really cared. She slapped a hand over her mouth as a giggle escaped, a release from tension. A neighbor? If his clothing was any indication, like her, he probably had to stretch his budget to live at Rainier Regency. "Holly Harrison from the fifth floor."

"Nice to meet you, Holly, even under these circumstances. Hope you wouldn't pull all my teeth if I come down to the Happy Smile Center?"

"No." She laughed, part of the stress melting away. "I'm a dental hygienist with Dr. Murphy. How about you? Where do you work?" He certainly wasn't dressed for his job in those sloppy clothes.

Sweat poured down his face. "I'm a systems analyst for Evergreen Technologies. We're based in downtown Seattle."

Wow, that sounded like an important job. "A systems analyst? I have no idea what that is." Holly glanced at their reflection in the mirror. She looked a wreck, but her leg sat in the right position.

"I don't think you want a full explanation now, but I plan, configure, and install computer applications for various companies."

"Are you off today?" While she may have misjudged him based on his clothing, he sure wasn't dressed to go downtown.

"No, I work at home. Just started about a month ago. Beats fighting the Seattle traffic."

"Not as nerve wracking, I'm sure. Oh, and thank you for reminding me to stay calm. The prayer helped."

He nodded as if he knew a secret. "You're welcome. If I didn't have the Lord to rely on, I'm not sure what I'd do."

"I agree, but sometimes I think..." She wouldn't go there. God saved her from her sins, and she prayed to the Lord, but deep down, she doubted it did any good. After all, her sister Diana said the past would always have a bearing on Holly's life.

Yet how could she have known? Those months during college changed everything.

She wrung her hands. Maybe getting stuck and dying in this elevator would be her final payment on those sins. *Oh, God. I'm so sorry.*

He patted her fingers, stilling them.

"Just so you know. I don't go to church anymore." Having Diana remind her of her wretchedness was enough. She didn't need to hear it from other people.

The elevator groaned and shifted with a jerk. Her heart slammed into her stomach. "Are we going to fall?" She grabbed Jess's arm and hid her face against his shoulder. "Dear Lord, please get us out of here safely." She tightened her grip on the stranger as the elevator jerked again. Maybe Jess could convince God to save them. "Look, if we get out of here, I'll attend church once. Tell God for me."

Jess chuckled. "Will do." He lifted his gaze to the ceiling. "Lord, Holly says she'll go to church if You'll see us out of here." He held her at arm's length. "Okay, I think He heard that. We're fine."

"I'm being childish." Warmth climbed up her neck and into her face.

"I don't think so," he whispered.

The elevator wrenched, and Holly shrieked.

Jess put a finger to his ear and shook his head, but the knowing smile never left his handsome face.

Oh, finally. The cab moved downward, and the doors slid open. Never had she been so glad to see Mr. Schackelford.

Jess struggled to his feet, wheezing for breath as he held out his hand to her.

She clasped it and managed to stand. He was her hero -- he and the repairman. She straightened her slacks and stepped out into the lobby.

Mr. Schackelford bit his lip. "Ma'am, I'm so sorry. Please accept my apology for the delay." He ran a hand through his hair. "If I may, I'd like to offer you both dinner on the Rainier Regency at any restaurant of your choice."

Holly waved him off and headed down the hall. "Thank you, but another day. Right now I'm going to my apartment. I just need to relax."

Jess probably couldn't follow her up five floors at his size, but then, it wouldn't be easy for her either.

He chatted with Mr. Schackelford but looked up and smiled at her as she opened the door to the stairwell. If she could get away, maybe he'd forget about her promise to attend church.

~

Work was a nice distraction from the claustrophobic thoughts crowding Holly's memory since yesterday's incident in the elevator. Still, she welcomed Friday afternoon, the end of her week.

"I'm almost finished with the last step, Mrs. Blaine. Your teeth will be sparkling after I polish them." She dipped the brush into the cup of cinnamon paste and applied the powder as she glided the instrument along the front surface of the woman's enamel. "You can rinse in a moment."

What would she do this weekend? Maybe she'd call Diana and see what she and Red had planned, but knowing her sister and husband, they were probably either balancing the books at Sound Fitness or devising some new weightlifting class. They never took a break.

"There. You're done." Holly gave the woman a cup of water and pushed the receptacle of whirling water in front of her mouth so she could rinse.

Mrs. Blaine patted her lips with the green paper bib. "Thank you. As usual, you did a wonderful job."

"I'm afraid not everyone is as devoted to keeping up their dental home care. You're my star patient." Holly unhooked the chain attached to the bib.

The receptionist stuck her head into the cubicle. "Are you free, *hija*? You've got a phone call." Marcela always called her "daughter" in her Spanish tongue.

"Yes, thanks, Marcela. Be there in just a minute." Probably a dental products salesman.

Holly waved good-bye to her patient and replaced her polishing tool. Then she tossed the disposable brush, quickly sanitized the equipment, and followed Marcela to the front.

"Here you go." Her friend pointed to the phone at the empty desk near the wall.

She picked up the receiver and punched the button with the blinking light. "This is Holly Harrison."

"Holly, Jess Colton. I apologize for calling you at work, but I didn't get your number yesterday. I wanted to know if you'd like to go to church with me Sunday."

She stiffened -- never dreamed he'd follow up with her. "Oh... maybe I'll pass this time."

Silence stretched between them for a moment, then he snickered. " Remember? You made a promise to God."

"I did?" She cleared her throat. Of course, and Jess hadn't forgotten as she'd hoped he would. "Yes, I did."

What choice did she have? She couldn't add a broken promise to her list of things God could hold against her. "Okay."

"Great. You want to meet in the lobby?"

"Oh, all right." How did she let this guy talk her into going to church? Jess seemed nice enough, but why was he so insistent?

She rubbed her forehead. Learning to forgive herself was first on her list. Learning to trust people again was the next.

~

Even in his dreams, Jess Colton never imagined he'd have a woman as pretty as Holly Harrison sitting beside him in his car. Her green eyes and light brown hair caught his attention the first time he saw her, the day she stepped into the elevator. The sprinkling of freckles over her nose gave her a childlike look, but he guessed she was close to his age, early thirties.

"I'm glad you decided to go today. Woodlyn Fellowship is a small, friendly church. I promise the people don't bite."

Holly hadn't stopped fiddling with the tissue in her hands the entire way from the apartment complex. Was she nervous around him, or ill at ease about attending church?

"Yeah, well, I suppose a promise is a promise."

"You said you used to go to church?"

She turned the tissue over in her hands then stuffed it into her opened purse. "Yeah." She swallowed hard. "It's not easy for me to talk about."

"Okay, but I'm a good listener when you get ready." The tense look on the woman's face tugged at his heart. What could have happened to keep her from church?

She opened and closed the clasp on her purse. "I don't think I'll ever be ready."

He gave her a wide grin. "The offer stands, just in case."

Holly cleared her throat as she chewed on the nail of

her little finger. "Thanks."

Jess parked the car in the lot nearest Lake Wycot. The crystal waters next to a stand of Douglas firs always blessed him through the picture window over the altar.

He lumbered around and opened the door for his reluctant companion. The cool rainy season of Western Washington had given way to the more sunny days of late June.

She swung her legs out, tugged down on her pants leg before standing, and gazed straight ahead. Did the little building with its white vinyl siding and gray roof threaten her? He grasped her elbow and nudged her toward the door.

Joe and Connie Tyler stood on the threshold.

Jess leaned close to her ear. "Watch out. Here comes the attack of the friendly greeters."

"Good morning and welcome to Woodlyn Fellowship." Joe passed a bulletin to Holly, then one to him.

Connie spread her arms and engulfed them in a hug. Not an easy task.

Jess backed away and tugged his blazer to cover his big stomach. "Joe and Connie, this is Holly Harrison."

She held out her hand to the Tylers and smiled. He had to give them credit. They got her to loosen up when he couldn't.

His usual seat with more room waited at the end of the aisle toward the back. The feeling of being trapped between two people didn't appeal to him.

A hush came over the congregation when Pastor Downing's wife began the organ prelude.

The choir director announced, "What a Friend We

Have in Jesus," and he stole a look at Holly. Her lips moved part of the time. But when they sang, "Oh what needless pain we bear," she slumped forward and twirled a strand of hair.

Pastor Downing rose from his chair and stood at the pulpit, the lake visible behind his thin frame. Jess couldn't remember a Sunday when he wasn't blessed by the man's power-packed message. "My beloved, I want you to understand who you are in Christ."

Holly fingered a tissue again.

"Satan would have you believe you are of no value, but the Lord says you were bought with a price, and you belong to God."

Jess's new acquaintance crossed and uncrossed her legs. She rummaged through her purse before setting it down on the pew.

"God is patient and slow to anger. You have been chosen by Him. Your relationship with Him is not based on yourself or anything you've done, but the work He did for you on the cross."

Now she picked up a hymnal and flipped through the pages.

"Believe me when I say you are free from condemnation. God loves you that much, my beloved."

Finally she grew still, her gaze glued on Pastor Downing. His words must've struck a chord. Her hands lay quietly in her lap as she stared at the preacher.

"You may approach God with freedom and confidence. Hope is only found in the Lord. Our regret or grief should turn us toward Him, not away from His presence."

She glanced at Jess then looked toward the front, a furrow on her forehead. Did the pastor say something that touched her?

With a punishing thought, Jess froze. Maybe her unease wasn't about church after all. Maybe it was about sitting next to him. The fattest man in the building.

www.ingramcontent.com/pod-product-compliance
Lightning Source LLC
LaVergne TN
LVHW011946060526
838201LV00061B/4223